ONCE AGAIN

THE REWINDING TIME SERIES

Inspirational Novels of History, Mystery & Romance

book 1

DEBORAH HEAL

ISBN: 1503014827
ISBN-13: 978-1503014824

This is historical fiction. While every effort was made to be historically accurate about the real people and events of the past, they were fictionalized to one degree or another. As for the contemporary characters, any resemblance to actual living persons is purely coincidental.

"According to This Map" and "In Answer to the Sun's Prayers" are original poems by Laura Merleau-McGrady and are used with permission.

"Scrapyard Nightingale," an original poem by Ruth E. Bell, is used with permission.

Other Novels by Deborah Heal
Available in audiobook, e-book, and paperback.
The History Mystery Trilogy:
Time and Again (book 1)
Unclaimed Legacy (book 2)
Every Hill and Mountain (book 3)

DEDICATED

To my sister Susan Steingrubey, who not only provided invaluable editorial feedback for this book, but is also indispensable to me in every other way... and my best friend.

ACKNOWLEDGMENTS

My heartfelt thanks goes to my editor Michelle Babb, whose insight and eagle eyes helped me shape *Once Again* into a much better story than it otherwise would have been. And thank you, Susan Steingrubey, Terri Woods, and Beth Bicklein, for your valuable suggestions for steering the course of *Once Again* when I was too delirious from writing to see what needed to be done.

CHAPTER 1

"We have to remember that in 1811, the Illinois Territory was the wild, wild West." Merrideth Randall realized she was leaning on her podium and straightened her spine. At five-foot-two it was difficult enough to look like a mature professional without slouching. At twenty-six, she was the youngest professor at McKendree College and only a few years older than her students, which was why she always dressed in suits and high heels. At times, she had a feeling it only made her look like a child playing dress-up.

She had started the day feeling confident in her new black gabardine suit. The label had bragged about the comfortableness of the three-season fabric. But even though it was a cool October afternoon, she was already sweating like a pig.

Furthermore, the fabric was a magnet for her hair. She picked two long blond strands from her sleeve and turned her eyes back to her students.

"And as amusing as it seems today, the governor's job description then included riding into battle, leading the soldiers at his command."

Apparently, they didn't find that historical tidbit as amusing as she did. The class continued to look apathetic. She mentally sighed. At least they were awake, to a degree. And most were even taking notes, in a desultory fashion. But the gleam of curiosity she had hoped to see in their eyes was absent. As usual.

McKendree College was small, the current enrollment only about 2,000. But it didn't aspire to be a large institution. Class sizes were intentionally kept small and intimate, and the professors and instructors were encouraged to get to know their students, to interact with them outside of class. All that had weighed heavily when Merrideth was deciding which of the three job offers she would accept. But sometimes she wondered if she should have chosen the large school in Chicago where she could remain anonymous and not be expected to remember the students' names, at which she was an epic failure. In the end she decided that a big school would be too intimidating. No, it was much better to be in a small pond where there was a better chance of becoming a big fish one day.

She had thought, naively it turned out, that after a couple of weeks at McKendree she would be nicely settled in, and her history classes would be well on the way to becoming campus favorites. Instead, after over a month, her students remained aloof and only mildly interested in what she had to say. She found their nonverbal feedback incredibly dampening, to say the least. It was a vicious cycle, of course. The more she worried about being boring, the more difficult it was not to be.

Marla White, a seasoned pro from the French Department had advised her to act confident even if she didn't feel so. "And whatever you do, don't ever let 'em see you bleed, or they'll be on you like wolves."

But that was easier said than done, wasn't it? Taking a deep breath, she shuffled her notes and soldiered on.

"Tecumseh was off trying to organize a coordinated Indian resistance that November day in 1811. If he had been successful…"

A student in the third row—Allison? Alyssa?—raised her hand. She was a beautiful girl and always looked cool and collected, as if *she* weren't familiar with the human phenomenon of perspiration. And as far as Merrideth could tell *her* blond highlights had not come out of a bottle. She was one of the few students who ever asked a question or offered a comment. Unfortunately, they were usually so tinged with sarcasm that Merrideth had begun to dread calling on her. But now as always, hope rose that at last she was about to experience a lively interaction with a student.

Merrideth pointed to the raised hand. "Yes?"

"The proper term is *Native American*. Besides, they aren't really Indian anyway."

Merrideth was sure the smile she had drummed up looked fake, but it was the best she could do when her teaching competence was under direct attack. "I'm glad you brought that up. I recently learned that most Native Americans actually prefer to be called Indians."

The girl looked decidedly skeptical.

"I was surprised myself." Merrideth glanced down and shuffled her notes again. "Anyway, if Tecumseh had been successful, who knows what the map of America would look like today? While he was gone, Harrison and a force of 1,000 soldiers defeated the Shawnee at Prophetstown.

"At the time it was considered a huge victory for Harrison. He picked up the nickname *Tippecanoe* from the river of that name near the battlefield. Twenty-nine years later in 1840, a Whig campaign song called *Tippecanoe and Tyler Too* helped Harrison win the presidency."

The girl raised her hand again. "Yes?" Merrideth said as pleasantly as she could.

"Will that be on the final exam? The nicknames and songs, things like that?"

"Maybe. Probably."

A disdainful expression flittered over the student's face, and then she lowered her eyes and resumed writing. Just as Merrideth looked back at her own notes, the girl muttered, "I registered for Illinois History, not Trivial Pursuit." It was said loudly enough that it was clearly intended for Merrideth to hear.

She stifled the urge to smack her. To reward herself for her restraint, she decided to wrap up class three minutes early. "But historians know," she said tersely, "that the victory at Prophetstown only ratcheted up the violence between the whites and Indians. Six months later when the War of 1812 began, the Indians naturally sided with the British. We'll talk more about that next time. Be sure to keep up with your readings."

The students began gathering their things with an eagerness that was a further insult to Merrideth's confidence. Then she remembered her announcement and called out, "Don't forget, if you want to be a volunteer at the Fort Piggot archaeological dig Saturday, there's still time, but you'll have to be a member of History Club. Just let me know if you need a sign-up form."

No one responded. No one even looked interested, much less

3

stayed behind to get the details. She felt her face heating and turned away to gather her own things. Her embarrassment grew ten-fold when she realized Dr. Garrison was watching her from the door. With a mind of its own, her hand started to rise, intent on checking her hair. But she forced it back down to her side. She would not allow Brett Garrison to trigger any fluttery female instincts she might have.

The thought that the most popular professor on campus had witnessed her debacle just added icing to the cake. She had heard that gushing groupies congregated outside his classroom like he was Indiana Jones, and they were there to catch him before he cast off the trappings of academia and went off on an action-packed adventure.

But Brett dressed more stylishly than Indy had—never in tweed jackets with leather patches on the elbows, for sure. And he was much better looking than Harrison Ford. His black hair was thick, and his eyes were so green that Merrideth once asked Marla White if she thought he wore colored contacts. Marla had smiled knowingly and said, "No, ma'am! They're the real deal. It's the Irish in him."

The moment he was introduced to her at the faculty icebreaker at President Peterson's residence, he had set her nerves on edge. Sure, he was pretty to look at, but his vanity ruined it. Twice she had caught him admiring himself in Peterson's hall mirror. She had avoided him ever since.

But now she smiled and said, "Hi. Don't you math types do your thing in Voigt Hall?" It hadn't come out in the friendly manner she'd intended, and she mentally kicked herself for letting her rattled nerves show. He sure didn't need anything more to stoke his ego.

But he didn't seem to take offense, just grinned. It did not help her nerves one little bit.

"I was just taking a short cut to 1828."

"It was a very good year, from all I've heard."

The witticism was a mistake. He laughed, and her pulse skipped. It was confirmation that Brett Garrison was a man she should continue to steer clear of.

A therapist had once chided her for being a reverse snob when it came to good-looking men. She had reminded Merrideth that they couldn't help the way they looked any more than anyone else could. If she were here now she would tell her to give Brett Garrison a chance, for crying out loud.

"I meant the 1828 Cafe, not the year," he said. "I heard the last part of your lecture."

"Really?"

"It was very interesting."

"What?" she said.

"Your lecture on William Henry Harrison."

"Oh. Well, tell that to my students."

"They looked interested to me."

"Not Allison...Alyssa...what's-her-name."

"Ah, yes, Alyssa Holderman. I have her in Calculus. She has an attitude problem. You know Holderman Library is named for her great-grandfather?"

"That explains a lot."

"Don't let her get to you. The other kids are cool."

"I'll try not to. Thanks."

"Would you like to join me at the cafe? The have good coffee."

The offer put her hackles up. "No thanks. I need to get home." She started down the hall, hoping to put distance between them, but he fell in beside her.

"So, Dr. Randall, what do you do when you're not lecturing about the past?"

"Prepare more lectures. It takes a while to get them polished into the scintillating gems that they are."

"Don't be hard on yourself. You'll hit your stride soon enough."

He held the door for her and she went out ahead of him onto the quad. Brilliant orange maple leaves, carrying the scent of autumn, fluttered by against a deep blue sky. Nearby, Alyssa Holderman and four other girls, busily texting on their phones, paused and looked up with interest.

Brett doled out one of his smiles. "Hello, ladies. Nice day, isn't it?"

The girls preened and twittered like pretty birds in designer jeans. "Yes, Dr. Garrison," one said. "It sure is."

The girls' heads swiveled in unison as they watched their idol pass by. Merrideth was pretty sure she heard a sigh. Surprisingly, Brett Garrison didn't seem to notice their worshipful adoration.

"So what about family?" he said.

"Oh, I'm all in favor of them," Merrideth said. "How about you?"

He chuckled. "I'll go first so you'll know how to answer that question. I have a brother in Texas and a sister in North Carolina. My parents are deceased, but I do have an Aunt Nelda."

She smiled. "You do not have an Aunt Nelda."

"I do, in fact, have an Aunt Nelda. A very nice Aunt Nelda."

"Oh, sorry. I didn't mean to be rude."

"And you being a history expert would like Aunt Nelda, for her old house if nothing else."

"Really? How old?"

"Aunt Nelda or her house?"

"The house," she said, smiling in spite of herself.

"I'm not sure of the exact date. The family has owned the property for generations."

"I love old houses."

"Then you should take the Haunted Lebanon tour in town. I know someone who could get you a ticket, if you're interested."

"No, I'm good. I did the Haunted Alton tour a couple of years ago, and once was quite enough for me. Life is scary enough as it is. Besides, I'm tied up with the dig."

"See, you do other things besides preparing lectures. Where is it?"

"We're looking for a fort that was once down in the American Bottom."

He laughed uproariously. "I know I'm reverting to my junior high self, but a fort in the bottom? Really?"

Merrideth rolled her eyes. "The American Bottom is the southern Illinois floodplain of the Mississippi River. After the Revolutionary War it was the western frontier of the brand new United States, hence the name American. The French who had lived there for more than a century, migrated across the river to the French city of St. Louis, and the Americans began to arrive. The early settlers built several blockhouse forts there."

"And you think you know where one was."

"We hope so. Fort Piggot was the largest of them, but ironically, historians didn't even know of its existence until relatively recently when the so-called Piggot Papers were discovered. Just by coincidence, someone found them concealed inside a framed river pilot's license that had been hanging on a wall in the Green County Museum since forever. It's really fascinating and…I'm boring you to death. Sorry. I get carried away talking about this stuff."

"I'm not bored at all."

"Really?" And she realized that he wasn't. Either that, or he was a good actor.

"Sure. I don't even particularly enjoy history, but you've made me curious to know where this fort was."

"Near Columbia. About thirty minutes from here. James Piggot built it in—."

He laughed. "You're kidding, right?"

"I never kid about history."

"My Aunt Nelda's farm is not far from Columbia, above the famous American Bottom, although I had no idea that historians had given the area such a charming name. Come have coffee and tell me more."

Inexplicably, Merrideth found herself standing at the sidewalk that led up to the 1828 Cafe. Somehow while she was yammering on about the fort, she had forgotten to make the turn that would take her to Hunter Street where her apartment was. Somehow, she had just followed where Brett Garrison led like a mindless twit. Worse, students were staring at them from the cafe's windows. Marla White had warned her that rumors spread faster than the speed of light in a small town, faster still in a small college. There was no way would she let false rumors about her and Brett Garrison prevent her from achieving her career goals.

"Sorry," she said. "I have to get home. Enjoy your coffee."

"Then I'll say goodbye. And, Merrideth? You should get *carried away* in your classroom like you did just now. Enthusiasm is contagious. Your students will sit up and take notice."

"Thanks for the advice. See you."

He made it sound so simple. As if being enthusiastic was all it took to be a successful instructor. It went counter to her own personality, and besides, her friend Abby, who was an excellent elementary teacher, had told her that the old "Don't Smile Until Christmas" guideline that worked for her fifth grade classes would work equally well for her college students, especially the freshmen. "If you're too friendly," she'd said, "they'll think you're soft and take advantage of you."

Maybe she'd ask some of the faculty friendlies, like Marla White and Jillian Burch, their opinion of the subject. But for now, her first line of defense was to be prepared with the best lecture in the world, tomorrow and every day thereafter. Sure, that didn't allow much time for a life, but what did that matter to an introvert anyway?

Today, as she did on most days, she had left her old Subaru parked behind her apartment and walked to work. The ghost of her obese pre-teen self still haunted her sometimes, even though mentally she recognized that she was now at a good weight for her height. But even if she didn't need the exercise, it was a glorious walk on a bright fall day.

It was ironic that she had ended up living in another small southern Illinois town, when for years she had longed to leave her mother's home in Miles Station and get back to Chicago where they had lived before her parents' divorce. But Merrideth had come to appreciate small towns. And Lebanon was a pretty little town of just under 6,000 souls, with quiet streets and beautiful old homes. Everyone at McKendree had assured her it was virtually crime-free and safe enough for her to walk about alone. She had already explored quite a bit of the historic district.

Charles Dickens had put Lebanon on the map when he mentioned his stay at the Mermaid Inn in his 1842 travelogue *American Notes*. The inn still stood and was open to the public, although Merrideth had not yet taken the tour.

But McKendree College was Lebanon's greatest achievement. It was the oldest college in Illinois, established in 1828 by pioneer Methodists. It was rich in tradition and proud of its history. Several of the oldest buildings on campus were rumored to be haunted. There had been much talk of it as Halloween approached.

Her friends Abby and John, who loved old buildings as much as she did, had come one weekend to tour the school and town. Abby had gone a little nuts shopping in the antique stores on St. Louis Street. Their own Victorian home was filled to the brim with beautiful old things, but Abby had an insatiable need for more antiques. When she wasn't buying for herself, she was looking for little things to spruce up Merrideth's apartment.

Hunter Street was quiet and lined with mature trees that were slowly releasing their leaves onto the sidewalk. She lived on the second floor of a huge old house that had been subdivided into four apartments. Her landlord Mr. O'Conner looked as old as the house and wasn't able to keep up with repairs as well as she might like. But Merrideth didn't mind. The house had character, the rent was cheap, and the other tenants were quiet. It would do until she had the money for a down payment on a house of her own.

She trotted up onto the porch and checked her mailbox. There wasn't anything in it, nor had she expected there to be. The utilities weren't due yet, and the credit card company hadn't gotten her change of address yet. Her mother had never been a letter writer even back in the day when most people were. But when November rolled around she'd have at least one letter in her mailbox. The return address would read, Bradley Randall, #1254387, Route 53 Joliet, IL 60403. She wasn't certain he'd ever be "rehabilitated," but fifteen years of the state's hospitality had turned her father into a faithful letter writer. She'd give him that much.

She reminded herself to tread quietly on the stairs. Mr. Haskell worked nights and slept during the day. That's all she'd been able to discover about him since she'd been living above his apartment. He gave her suspicious looks whenever they met. She still hadn't decided whether it was his natural temperament or only sleep-deprivation. In any case, the poor man had even less of a life outside work than she did.

Once inside, she laid her keys on the mantel. The fireplace was no longer operational, and the mantel was only faux marble, but she displayed some of her most valued possessions there. In the center was a framed family photo, taken during a brief moment of calm before her parents split. It was a terribly unflattering picture for all three of them, especially her. She was overweight and under-groomed, her dishwater blond hair hanging in her brown eyes. But everyone was smiling in the photo, so she kept it on display because it gave the appearance of a happy family.

To each side of the photo were the silver candlesticks she'd bought for herself to celebrate finishing her doctoral thesis. And then there were the treasures from Abby and John's girls Lauren and Natalie for whom she was an honorary aunt: a homemade birthday card, a "fairy house" made from a tissue box, and a garland of construction paper fall leaves. All were heavily glittered, as were nearly all the crafts she and the girls made together whenever she babysat them.

Merrideth smiled and went to see what was in the fridge for dinner.

CHAPTER 2

When Merrideth asked Marla's opinion about classroom management, she told her that she would have to find her own voice and style in the classroom. But Jillian said she leaned more toward Brett's philosophy than Abby's, so Merrideth had made the conscious effort to loosen up and be enthusiastic. So far it hadn't inspired her students to dizzying heights of interest and involvement, but neither had it led to a breakdown in classroom order. Merrideth wasn't sure that her lectures had met Alyssa Holderman's exacting standards, but at least she hadn't made any more smart aleck comments, at least not loudly enough for her to hear. And once, she had actually laughed along with the class at one of Merrideth's little jokes.

So things were looking up, although she'd never win a popularity contest with Brett Garrison, even if she wanted to. Other than his vanity, he seemed to be a nice enough guy, thoughtful, actually. She saw him across the quad taking time to talk and laugh with students, ordinary students of the non-groupie type. Another time she happened to overhear him asking a freshman about her mother's Parkinson's disease.

The unseasonably warm fall continued, and Saturday dawned clear with no chance of rain in the forecast. It was perfect weather for the dig. She and the other volunteers had met two times previously to get the history of Fort Piggot and to be taught the procedures necessary for a productive and scientifically verifiable dig. Their center of operations was at Sand Bank School, a beautifully restored one-room schoolhouse dating from the mid-1800s. It had been built on the site of an even earlier log cabin school that early pioneers had erected for their children.

It seemed fitting to use Sand Bank School to teach amateur archaeologists how to conduct an exploration of the area's past. And it was the practical choice, too, because the school was located only 200 yards from their dig site.

The discovery of the so-called Piggot Papers had led to other to various other obscure documents in numerous libraries and collections. It had all eventually led to Mr. Schneider's soybean field in Monroe County, where today, if they were lucky, they would find James Piggot's fort. One of the documents described the fort's location as "west of the Kaskaskia Trail where the *Grand Ruisseau* comes down from of the bluffs." There was no creek of that name on modern maps, but Glenn Parton, the organizer of the dig, was certain that the present-day Carr Creek was the one described.

Merrideth was a few minutes late getting to the school. When she walked inside she was struck anew with the sense that something of the students and teachers who had worked there down through the years still lingered. She pictured barefoot children sitting in the desks writing on their slates under the watchful eye of their teacher.

But today the schoolhouse was filled with chattering adults. It looked like most of the twenty or so volunteers were already there. She spotted her assigned team members near the front of the room. Donna Bradley made Merrideth smile every time she saw her. She was an octogenarian who made up for her lack of youth and strength with an enthusiasm for all things historical. She was Merrideth's height, but her humped back indicated that she had once been a much taller woman. Today she was decked out in an Aussie outback hat and denim trousers with an elastic waistband, into which she'd tucked a neon orange T-shirt.

Frank Griffin, a burly middle-aged car salesman, was listening attentively to something Donna was explaining in her warbly voice. He was a thoroughly nice man, and Merrideth had liked him instantly. Today he'd probably spend less time digging holes than he would making sure Donna didn't fall into one of them.

"Oh, I didn't see you there, Merrideth," Donna said, adjusting her glasses. "Isn't this a perfect day for our adventure?"

"It sure is."

"I brought my shovel," Donna said. "But I may need someone

11

to help me get it out of the trunk."

"I'll get it for you," Frank said with a sidelong grin for Merrideth.

Glenn Parton whistled at the front of the room. "I think we're all here, so let's get started. Remember, we only have a narrow window of opportunity in which to find Fort Piggot. Mr. Schneider finally harvested his soybeans on Wednesday, which gave us the chance to stake out the grid. But he's anxious to till his field. He's willing to give us one week to find something that shows the fort is where we think it is. That's seven days, people—if the weather holds. If rain shows up in the forecast, Mr. Schneider will start plowing, and that'll be it for us until next year. Needless to say, we need to work hard today."

He turned the meeting over to Eugene Parks, a retired high school biology teacher who was something of an amateur archaeologist. Over the past twenty years, he had participated in digs all over the state. For the next twenty minutes, he rehashed the procedures required for the shovel test pits they'd be digging. It seemed like an inordinate amount of time to spend when that precious commodity was in such short supply. But finally, when Merrideth thought she'd expire from impatience, he dismissed them, and at last everyone gathered their equipment and walked down to the site.

Each ten-foot square in the grid was numbered on a chart Eugene had on his clipboard. The holes were to be about eighteen inches in diameter. They would dig down about three feet looking for anomalies in soil color and texture, which could indicate things like the location of the fort's midden and latrine. Either of those would be great, but what they were really hoping to find was a pattern of soil staining to show where the stockade's posts had been sunk, thus allowing them to see the fort's footprint, that is, its size and exact location. All the soil they removed would be carefully sifted through for artifacts left behind by the settlers. Eugene and Dennis would photograph and catalogue anything they found and take detailed notes describing the soil.

By the time Frank got to the site with Donna on one arm and two shovels in his other hand, Merrideth had already removed eight inches of topsoil from the first hole in their assigned square. She had found a bolt that had probably fallen off one of Mr. Schneider's farm implements and a small white button that had probably fallen off one of his shirts. Eugene carefully noted them, and she went back to digging. She was feeling pretty happy with herself until she got to the clay subsoil and discovered that the digging was much, much harder.

Frank put his substantial muscles to work, and together they moved and sifted a lot of dirt. Donna cheered them on but seemed to be everywhere Merrideth intended to put her shovel. In spite of Donna's eagerness to be in on the adventure, after a short time her strength waned, and Frank talked her into going back to the schoolhouse to rest. Soon after she left on wobbling legs, Frank uncovered a flat stone that he thought was an Indian hatchet. But when they showed it to Eugene, he quickly nixed the idea. Another team did find an arrow head, and their excitement spread through all the volunteers. It wasn't what they were hunting for, but it was a genuine artifact from the past, keeping everyone's hopes up that they'd find the fort.

By noon they were ready for lunch, which they ate up at the schoolhouse, courtesy of volunteers from the Monroe County Historical Society. While they ate, Glenn filled them in on the group's progress so far. He tried to put a positive spin on it, but the bottom line was that not one significant soil anomaly had been found to suggest that they were even working at the right location. But he reminded them there were still lots of squares in the grid to be worked.

Everyone went back to the site feeling hopeful, except for Donna, whom Frank convinced to go home. "The best way for you to help, Miss Donna," he told her, "is by praying for all of us." When put that way, she was satisfied to leave the digging for younger people.

The afternoon seemed to go by much slower than the morning had. There was a rush of excitement when the group working next to theirs found a skeleton. After a half hour carefully brushing the dirt away from it, Eugene told them it was either a dog or fox.

That morning she had thought the weather would be perfect for the dig, but as the hours passed, the day became uncomfortably warm for the strenuous work they were doing. As the sun waxed hotter, their hopes of finding something pertinent waned. At six o'clock Eugene told them to go home and rest up. Many of them would be back the next day, but Merrideth had only committed to working next Saturday, assuming Mr. Schneider allowed them to.

She was trying to drum up the strength for one last shovelful of soil before she left for the day, when a shadow fell over her.

"Boo!"

She looked up to find Brett Garrison, daisy-fresh in khakis and a brilliant white shirt, smiling down at her.

He looked like he was trying not to laugh at her pitiful condition. "Happy Halloween."

"It sure doesn't feel like Halloween weather." She thought about wiping her face with the bandana on her head, but she knew that under it, her hair was a flat, sweaty mess. Too bad she hadn't thought to borrow Donna's Aussie hat.

"How's the excavation going?" he said.

"What are you doing here?" Hopefully, it hadn't sounded as cranky as she felt.

"I'm on my way to Aunt Nelda's for dinner."

"That's nice." Merrideth went back to digging the hole. With enough effort, it might grow big enough to swallow her.

"Speaking of Aunt Nelda, I just heard about another hobby of yours."

"Oh?"

"Marla White was going on about it the other day in the faculty lounge. Said you'd been an amazing help with her genealogy."

Merrideth leaned on her shovel. Maybe her brain had had more sun than she realized. "I'm still waiting to hear what this has to do with your Aunt Nelda."

"It has to do with Aunt Nelda because Aunt Nelda's been hounding me to help her track down ancestors for the old Garrison family tree. But I'm clueless about that sort of thing. So when I heard that you did genealogies—"

"Sorry, but I'm already working on three other projects as it is—besides my actual job. You know, the one I get paid to do. At the moment I'm helping Jillian Burch find out more about her ancestor who came over from Switzerland, and after that—"

"You're doing it for free? On the beggar's wage they pay non-tenured people, I would think you could use a little extra dough."

"Oh, I definitely could. It's just that I hate to ask colleagues to pay for something I enjoy doing. Like you said, it's a hobby."

"That's crazy talk. You deserve to be paid for your work and time. I fully expect to pay for your services. Oh, that came out so wrong."

Merrideth laughed. "I knew what you meant." A little extra money would really come in handy. And genealogical research did take a lot of time, at least it did when you researched it the old-fashioned way. During Marla's project she had found herself longing for the software she and Abby and John had used back in the day. Sometimes she wondered if she had imagined that fantastical summer fifteen years before. The *Beautiful Houses* program had come already installed on the computer her dad had sent her as a sop to his conscience. On the surface, it looked like nothing more than a slideshow of noteworthy houses from around the world. But it had turned out to be much, much more, because with it they had been able to virtually rewind time. And research—both genealogical and historical—had been a snap.

Brett was watching her curiously, and she realized that she had been quiet too long. "I'll think about it."

"You should come with me to Aunt Nelda's. Hold still. You've got a smudge." He ran a finger down her cheek and then wiped it on his shorts.

She nearly shuddered at his touch, but managed to pull herself together to say in a normal voice, "You've got to be kidding. Look at me. I'm filthy."

"I am far too much of a gentleman to agree with you, but if *you* think you're filthy, you could get a shower at Aunt Nelda's before you hit the road. And she would be glad to feed you, too."

"Maybe some other time."

Like maybe never, she thought as she watched him walk away. So he thought she was that easily manipulated, did he? Okay, apparently she was. It was just one more reason to keep her distance.

He was probably right about charging for her research services. Maybe she would do that down the line. But no way would she take Brett Garrison on as a genealogy client. Being in his company that much was bound to turn her into another sophomoric groupie, miserably pining after a man completely out of her league. And even if she were in his league, she would never date a colleague on the faculty anyway. It was career suicide. Everyone knew that. Then she laughed at herself. The man had merely asked for her advice on a subject in which she was something of an expert, and she had mentally turned it into a date. As if that would ever happen.

CHAPTER 3

Naturally, on Monday she ran into Brett Garrison everywhere she went on campus, even in places she had never noticed him before. And not all the meetings were coincidental. He dropped by her classroom to chat twice, and as far as she could tell, he wasn't even on his way somewhere else.

On Tuesday morning he brought two coffees from 1828 to her office and sat on the edge of her desk, chatting about their respective classes. It was unnerving. She was beginning to wonder how he had time to teach his own classes. He seemed genuinely interested in helping her adjust to her job at McKendree and offered lots of tips for handling her students. It was all good stuff, but she found it difficult to follow what he was saying, because she was concentrating on not blurting out, "Why are you talking to me?"

Could he actually be interested in her? Of course not. She was just blowing his attention all out of proportion. That the great Brett Garrison, idol of McKendree College co-eds, was actually pursuing her, plain old Merrideth Randall, was just laughable. He was just being nice to the new kid on the block.

And then it hit her: he was mentoring her! And probably getting a stipend to do it. President Peterson had mentioned something about a mentoring program early on, but when nothing further had been said, she'd forgotten all about it. All the friendly chats, complete with those killer smiles of his, had been nothing more than Brett's professional courtesy. What if she had responded to one of his smiles with her version of an alluring, come-hither smile? It was too humiliating to think about. She nearly fainted with relief that she hadn't made a fool of herself.

To keep herself from thinking about him, she focused on the progress of the Fort Piggot dig. The rain Glenn Parton had feared bypassed Monroe County, and the weather remained warm and dry, allowing the volunteers to continue their work. Glenn emailed to say that they had finally found an interesting patch of stained soil, and Eugene was running tests on it. They hoped to have the results soon.

And when she wasn't thinking about the fort or grading papers and preparing for classes, she continued to work on Jillian's genealogy. With only a little more time she'd be ready to print out a nice chart for her. She was thinking about it on Wednesday when she left Carnegie Hall after her last class and ran into Brett just outside the door. He smiled as if had been waiting for her.

"Hey, how was your day?" he said.

"Great. How about yours?"

"It was awesome. I just came from a stimulating class discussion about quantum objects and cell memory."

"Sounds like you really enjoy your classes."

"I do. I love it when students get revved about my favorite topic, especially when they start thinking outside the box. Today I threw in the concept of Intelligent Design. You should have seen Alyssa Holderman's face," he said, chuckling at the memory. "You know how she gets that superior smirk right before she says something sarcastic?"

"You get that, too? I figured it was just me."

"Oh, no. Alyssa is an equal-opportunity know-it-all smart aleck."

When they reached the sidewalk she expected their paths to diverge. He'd go to the faculty parking lot, and she'd walk home in peace, free of his unsettling presence. But he continued walking with her, talking about quantum objects, wave function, and other things she had no real understanding of. He was certainly passionate about his subject. His first piece of advice for her had been to be enthusiastic in the classroom. She wondered if his intent now was to model that for her.

Suddenly he stopped walking and said, "Sorry. I must be boring you."

"Not at all. But I'm still thinking about something you said. Could you rewind to the part about Intelligent Design? You don't believe that, right? You were just getting the kids to think."

"Don't you believe in a Creator?"

"Yes, but you're a physicist. I figured you didn't."

He laughed. "That's what Alyssa said, only with a disparaging sneer. As I told her, there are plenty of scientists and mathematicians who believe in Intelligent Design. Albert Einstein and Erwin Schrodinger, two of the most famous physicists ever, believed in God. Actually, quantum physics provides a strong logical argument against the atheist philosophy of Materialism, the idea that the universe is a closed system of cause and effect and we are mere 'machines made of meat.' In my opinion, the evidence is overwhelmingly in favor of creation. As Psalm 19:1 says, 'The heavens declare the glory of God; the skies proclaim the work of his hands.'"

"You know the Bible?"

He smiled. "Yep. Aunt Nelda saw to that."

Hopefully, Brett Garrison would not turn out to be one of those people who had a Bible verse for every occasion. One of her freshman roommates had been like that. Emily had started in spouting verses the first day and hadn't let up until another roommate told her to stop already with the proselytizing. By their sophomore year, Emily had gotten metaphorically slapped down enough times that she stopped quoting Bible verses altogether. Merrideth always felt a little guilty when she thought about that. Maybe she should have stuck up for Emily, but hadn't she needed to learn not to be so pushy with her beliefs?

She blinked away the memory and noticed that they had walked farther than she realized. She smiled, thinking how embarrassed Brett would be when he realized he had missed his turn. "Isn't your car back that way?"

"I didn't drive today. I've been inspired by your pedestrian ways. Thinking of the fossil fuel I could save finally guilted me into walking. I live near you."

She laughed, but then wondered how he knew she walked to work. More importantly, how did he know where she lived? A minute ticked by.

"Egad, you think I'm a stalker. I can see it on your face. Sorry, I saw your address in your office yesterday. I didn't mean to, but there it was on your desk."

She laughed uneasily. "So where do *you* live?"

"Over that way," he said waving vaguely to the west.

The whole package of blue skies, autumn leaves, and Brett Garrison at her side suddenly seemed overwhelmingly romantic. She tripped over a broken chunk of sidewalk, and he grabbed her elbow to keep her from falling.

"Are you all right?" His concerned expression was funny considering the maple leaf in his hair.

She smiled in spite of herself. "Of course. I'm no hothouse daisy, that's for sure."

"I could see that at the dig Saturday. I was impressed."

They had reached her apartment house, and Merrideth stopped at the sidewalk. "Well, here I am."

"It's a stately old house."

"I wouldn't call it stately. More like crumbling wreck, but I like it. It will do until I figure out what I want to buy. Well, thanks for the lecture on physics."

"I'm sorry. I guess it *was* more of a lecture than a two-way conversation. I do know how to do that, you know. Go to the Halloween dance with me next Saturday, and I'll prove it."

She had convinced herself that his interest was only professional. But, in the unlikely event that she was wrong about that, she had also spent time imagining what she would say to him if he ever asked her out. But all the cool and measured responses she'd practiced in the mirror flew out of her head, and she stood there gaping at him like an idiot.

When she didn't answer he added, "You could think of it as a good way to get to know your students. We try to show up at these things as much as possible."

Finally, she blurted out, "Sorry, I don't date. I mean I do, but not professors. Not at McKendree, anyway. It's not wise. I mean career-wise, it's not wise, you know?"

"You don't?"

"No, I don't. Besides, I'll be at the dig all day." Why on earth had she added that disclaimer? Why hadn't she left it at, sorry, *I do not date colleagues?*

"I thought that was a bust."

"No, they're starting to find things."

"Then I'll come help you. If I just happen to be working in your general vicinity that won't be a date, will it?"

"No, I guess not."

"Great. What time should I pick you up?"

"Six, I guess."

"Okay, six it is."

"But it's not a date."

He grinned. "Not a date."

She felt a little dazed. How had that just happened? And what was wrong with her? Even if it wouldn't be an actual date, she had just agreed to spend the day with Brett Garrison. And that was the first stop on the slippery slope to a romantic entanglement. But why had he asked her? He seemed like a nice guy, not the type who thought he had to seduce every new addition to the faculty. Maybe he was genuinely interested in the archaeology dig. But even if his motives were innocent, she knew full well that it was a career trap. And she had just fallen into it. Now she would just have to climb out of it to safer ground.

.

CHAPTER 4

"I know," Merrideth said. "But it's not a date, Marla. Really, it's not."

Marla White shook her head disbelievingly. Merrideth had stopped by her classroom to visit and found her sitting cross-legged on her desk, calling out in French to her departing students.She was a short, fire plug of a woman who tended to wear long tunics over pants in an attempt to disguise her figure. She got down from her desk and went to erase her white board. "Of course it's a date."

"He probably only asked to go along because he's my mentor. He's just taking a friendly interest, that's all. And it's not like he's ever going to ask me out on a real date. I mean, look at me."

Marla put the eraser down and faced her. "What do you mean, look at you?"

"I mean I'm hardly in his league, now am I?"

"Are you kidding me?" Frowning, Marla put her hands on her sturdy waist and stared at her. "You really don't know, do you? Merrideth Randall, you are beautiful and intelligent. And witty, too. Of course you're in Brett's *league*."

Her therapist used give her similar compliments during their sessions, but Merrideth had never taken them too seriously. After all, she got paid to say stuff like that.

"Thanks, Marla. That's sweet of you to say."

"And as for the part about him being your mentor, well he's not."

"I'm pretty sure he's my—"

"I happen to know he's not your mentor, because I am."

"You are?" So Marla was getting paid to say nice things, too. She probably figured it was morale-building for the department.

"Didn't Peterson tell you? Figures. Well, I am, so listen to my words of wisdom. I want you to picture this, Merrideth. It's six months from now. You and Brett have been dating, to the prurient interest of all your students. Then you have a fight. One of you breaks things off. It doesn't matter which one of you does it, because either way, you'll be the one coming to class with red eyes."

"That's ridiculous."

"I'm not finished. You try to patch things up, but find to your surprise that Brett's dating someone else. You're furious and lose control in front of your students or worse, in front of other faculty. We all find ourselves sucked into the drama. Some of us support poor Brett. Some poor Merrideth. Peterson hears about it and calls you into his office. You, not Brett. You were the one who made the scene. You were the one who cried and wailed. Besides, Peterson is gender-biased. He thinks he's not, but he is. You promise Peterson it won't happen again. Then Peterson reminds you that he's hoping to see that you've published something awesome real soon. You leave, vowing to get right on that. But you keep pining for Brett. I mean who wouldn't? You're not eating or sleeping right. You can't concentrate on your classes, much less find time to publish a paper. Then Brett starts flaunting his little floozy in front of you, and you fly into a rage. Peterson calls you into his office again, only this time it's to tell you McKendree will no longer need your services next semester. And don't imagine for a minute that Brett would be the one they let go. He's tenured. You aren't. So, if I were you, I would think very carefully about dating our charming Brett."

"Wow, Marla, that was quite a story. You should write a novel," Merrideth said stiffly. "Thanks for the advice, but you needn't concern yourself with my social life. As I said, it's not a date."

Merrideth left, taking care to close the door softly. She couldn't remember the last time she had been so angry—and so insulted! Marla obviously didn't know her at all, or she would never think she would endanger her career by doing anything as imprudent as dating Brett Garrison. And even if she were dating him, she would never be so weak, shallow, overly emotional, or...or...stupid over a man! Merrideth didn't claim to know Brett well, but she could tell he was no shallow fool either. He would be just as insulted to know Marla thought he was the type to take up with a "floozy."

Of course Merrideth would never tell him, but that didn't stop her from thinking about it the rest of the week. Since he wasn't her mentor after all, the question running in a continuous loop through her brain was why was he being so darned nice to her?

In spite of what she had told Marla, Merrideth would not have let Brett come with her to the dig if she had remembered the sweat. At least her hair would stay halfway decent, because Donna had lent her the Aussie hat that morning, after admitting sheepishly that she was too old to dig in the dirt any longer. As for Brett, he had worn a baseball cap to keep the sun off his head and a black McKendree Bearcat T-shirt, which had distracted her all morning. His bulging biceps proved he didn't spend all his time behind a classroom podium. Lots of it must have been spent at one of the local gyms.

"So why are we digging in this particular bean field?" Brett asked.

She took a moment to answer because she didn't want to sound all huffy and out of breath. "Because of the Piggot Papers."

"Tell me more."

She stopped digging and leaned on her shovel. "It's an awesome story. Someone ought to make a movie about it."

"Starring our hero Captain James Piggot, I presume."

"Actually, it ought to be about a Mississippi riverboat pilot named Howard Lame. If he hadn't hidden the Piggot Papers in the frame behind his pilot's license, we probably would never have known our hero even existed.

"The papers were almost destroyed in 1880. Lame was piloting a riverboat called the Golden Eagle down the Mississippi when a fire broke out in the cargo hold. He and the boat captain got the burning boat to shore and then helped the sixty passengers to safety. The last one off was Howard Lame, carrying his pilot license.

"In the 1950s his granddaughter donated it to the Greene

County Historical Society, and it hung on their walls for twenty-four years before someone discovered the interesting papers tucked behind Howard Lame's pilot license."

Brett threw the dirt in his shovel onto the discard pile and then grinned at her. "Including a treasure map that said, *Go west forty paces. Then dig holes in Farmer Schneider's bean field?*"

"Not exactly. It was the papers themselves that were the treasure. Among other things there were James Piggot's commission papers as a captain in the Pennsylvania Army and a letter from General George Washington in 1777 granting his request to be relieved of his command."

"How did those lead you to here?"

"It was the other papers, family letters, diary sheets, thirty-two in all. There were only bits and pieces of pertinent information—names, dates, and places. But it was enough that a St. Louis newspaperman named Carl Baldwin was able to piece it all together. And voila! Here we are!"

"But why *here* specifically?" Brett said, thrusting his shovel into the hole. "Why not there or there?" he said pointing randomly.

"That's where the dowsers came into play. They narrowed it to this portion of the field. Of course it's not a precise science, but..."

Brett dropped his shovel and scowled at her. "Do you mean to tell me I'm spending the day digging holes *here* because some quack's dowsing stick started quivering?"

"You don't have to sound so patronizing. Dowsing has been used successfully to find things all over the world for centuries. Not just water either. Look it up, Mr. Science. Besides, no one forced you to come."

"Look, I'm sorry. I do try to keep an open mind. And anyway, I came today because I wanted—"

He was cut off by Glenn's booming voice telling everyone lunch was ready at the schoolhouse. She was dying to know how he had intended to finish his sentence, but he didn't say anything more.

Once they got to the schoolhouse, Merrideth picked up a box lunch for herself and one for Brett, while he got cold sodas from the cooler. Some of the volunteers were small enough to sit in the school's antique desks. But Brett was too large, so they sat on the floor and leaned against the wall.

Glenn whistled for their attention, and when everyone stopped talking, he turned it over to Eugene. "I can't begin to tell you how grateful we are for all your hard work this week. I drove you hard, especially today, our last day, but you didn't complain, just kept on doing everything I asked of you. I was going to send you out after lunch to work until dark. But Glenn and I have decided to call it quits."

Disappointed muttering filled the room.

"We have nothing to be ashamed of," Eugene continued. "We did the research, we followed protocols, we worked hard, but we came up empty-handed."

"Don't worry," Glenn added. "We haven't given up. It could be that we just weren't out far enough. Or maybe Baldwin had it wrong, and they built the fort north of the creek—just a typo or something. We'll keep researching, and we're thinking about hiring a different dowser."

Next to her Brett whispered, "You think?"

"Do not say anything, Brett. I mean it."

"Sorry."

Eugene smiled encouragingly. "So plan on another dig next year. We'll find Fort Piggot eventually, by hook or crook."

"What about the testing, Eugene? On the soil staining we found," Frank said. "You never told us."

"I didn't want to discourage you all when you were working so valiantly. Unfortunately, the test was inconclusive. They think it is wood, but since there are no other stains in the whole grid, we have nothing else to go on. It may be only a log that got buried during a flood."

"So enjoy your lunch," Glenn said. "Then go home and relax the rest of your weekend."

"I'm sorry, Merrideth," Brett said softly. "You must be disappointed."

"I am, but we all knew from the beginning that it was a long shot."

They finished their sandwiches, and then Brett put his face in front of hers and bared his teeth. "Do I have any lettuce stuck anywhere?"

Merrideth laughed. "You have caps."

"It's not funny. They're a blasted nuisance. Food's always getting stuck on them."

"I guess that's the price of vanity."

"Tell that to Aunt Nelda. When I fell on the ice and broke my front teeth, I thought my new snagglies made me look like a fierce pirate. But she said she was rather fond of my normal teeth and insisted I get caps."

Merrideth's laugh came out as a snort. "Oh. Sorry. I assumed that—" She laughed again. "So the reason you're always looking in mirrors is lettuce?"

"I do not always look in mirrors."

She smiled noncommittally, and then they went to say goodbye to the other volunteers. When they got in Brett's car, he started it, but didn't put it into gear. "We've got extra time, and Aunt Nelda's farm is only a couple of miles from here."

"Like this?"

"She won't mind if her guests have sweaty faces and dirty clothes."

Marla's little cautionary tale popped into her head, but she quashed it. Brett had talked so much about his aunt that Merrideth's curiosity was piqued.

"All right, then. Let's go see Aunt Nelda. If you're sure it's all right for us to drop in on her."

"Don't worry. She and I are close."

She smiled. "I can tell that without even meeting her."

Brett pulled out of the school's parking lot and turned left onto Bluff Road. The limestone bluffs that gave the road its name rose in a 200-foot wall to their left. She had heard that they went on for eighty-some miles. Trees and shrubby plants grew at its base, and their fall foliage was lit up by the sun, adding to the spectacular view. Through the leaves Merrideth spotted a cave and wished they could stop and go exploring. She should have insisted on driving separately. With him behind the wheel it felt like they were a couple out on a beautiful clear Saturday afternoon enjoying the last of the fall color—instead of merely colleagues who happened to be working together on a project.

"There's the barn Glenn told us about." She leaned toward Brett for a closer look out his window. It was a mistake, and she pulled back to the safety of her side of the car.

Brett inhaled suddenly, almost as if he had been as affected as she. He glanced at her briefly and then looked back at the road. "I didn't hear anything about a barn. It is a neat old thing."

"I guess that was last time. Anyway, Glenn said its foundation was made from stones carried away from the ruins of Fort Piggot, at least according to legend."

"And that," Brett said, nodding his head toward the west, "must be your famous American Bottom. Well, not yours, but you know what I mean."

Merrideth laughed. "Yep," she said, gazing out her window. "Only these days farmers no longer have to live in log fortresses, ready to fire at invading Indians."

"I wonder if they complain that all the adventure is gone from farming."

They passed stubbled fields where corn and soybeans had already been harvested. In other fields, fall crops of what looked like cabbage, or maybe broccoli, stretched to the west like green corduroy. Out of sight beyond the last field, she knew the Mississippi River flowed, separating Illinois from Missouri.

"Here's the road," Brett said. After a look in the rearview mirror, he braked and turned left onto a narrow gravel road. He was obviously familiar with it, but it would not be easily seen from the blacktop by the average driver. The road was marked only by a half-rotted wooden sign upon which the words *Sundown Lane, Private!* had been carved.

"It's not much farther."

Sundown Lane rose through a natural cut in the bluffs. As they climbed, it curved sharply to the left, and trees grew nearly up to the sides of the road. Merrideth wondered if it were even wide enough for two cars and where Brett was supposed to go if they met someone coming down.

But it was difficult to work up much worry with sunlight streaming through the half-bare tree branches overhead, turning Brett's silver car to gilt. Soon, the trees weren't hugging the road so closely, and houses on green lawns began to appear on either side. Most were decked out with ghosts, witches, and other Halloween decorations, although some homeowners had gone the corn shocks and pumpkins route.

The road curved again and Brett slowed the car to a crawl. When they came around the bend he stomped on the brake pedal and said, "What is the old fool up to this time?"

CHAPTER 5

Two people stood at a cluster of black mailboxes. The man was red-faced and obviously angry. The woman was smiling, seemingly unconcerned with whatever bee was in his bonnet, as she looked over the mail in her hands. But when the man shook his raised his fist at her, Brett bolted out of the car the moment it stopped moving.

"Aunt Nelda? Is everything okay?"

She looked to be in her early sixties, a lot younger than her old-fashioned name had prepared Merrideth for. Nelda's face brightened when she saw Brett. The look told Merrideth without words how close they were, and she felt a momentary twinge of envy.

She lowered her window in time to hear Nelda say, "Nothing's wrong, Brett. Just having a neighborly chat with Walter."

The mild comment only seemed to make the man angrier. Merrideth wasn't sure if that was Nelda's purpose or only the unintended consequence of her obvious refusal to argue with him. Merrideth got her phone out in case she needed to call 9-1-1.

"Hi, Walter," Brett said, equally mildly. "What's the problem?"

"That is," Walter spat out. He pointed a bony finger across the road where a truck sat idling in the driveway across from Nelda's.

"Your truck's acting up?"

It was a reasonable assumption. Clouds of noxious exhaust came from its tail pipe. But Walter's face grew redder and he said, "Are you mocking me, boy?"

Nelda put a hand on Brett's arm. "Walter is talking about the grass clippings on the road. As I said, Walter, I apologize for letting my mower blow toward the road. I promise to remember the next time."

"See that you do, or I'll report you to the road commissioner." Walter jerked one of the mailboxes open, took a thin pile of mail out, and stomped across the road toward his truck.

"Road commissioner?" Brett said when Walter had driven out of sight.

"He's convinced that grass clippings are bad for the road."

Brett snorted and came around to Merrideth's window. "Aunt Nelda, this is Merrideth Randall."

"Hi," Merrideth said. Nelda didn't seem surprised to see them or surprised by their disheveled appearance. Brett must have told her about the dig. She wondered what else he had told his aunt about her.

"Sorry you had to see that." Nelda stuck her hand in the car and Merrideth shook it. It was a large hand for a woman, and calloused.

Brett opened the back door for Nelda and then got back in beside Merrideth. Nelda's driveway curved through the woods, and Merrideth recognized dogwood trees, lots and lots of them, along the border. The lane would be gorgeous when they bloomed in the spring, but still a long walk for Nelda to get her mail.

"He was really angry this time," Brett said. "Are you sure you'll be all right?"

"Walter's harmless. He just likes to be mad."

"It's always something, Merrideth. Last week he was certain her trashcan was in his spot. Before that, he accused her of making ruts in his yard with her car."

Nelda made a disgusted sound that could only be called a harrumph. "As if I'd want to go down his driveway."

"And who could forget the tree incident?" Brett said.

"He accused Mr. Ashe of cutting down trees on his property. Walter called the sheriff and Mr. Ashe had to pay for a surveyor to come out and prove that he was on his own property. Which he was, of course."

"Well, call me if Walter gets nasty again."

"He'll be back to normal tomorrow." Nelda laughed. "Or what passes for normal for Walter Ogle. Then, if I inadvertently run into him, I'll only be subjected to his usual tirades about politicians and the rag-heads taking over the country." In the rearview mirror, Merrideth saw that she used air-quotes on the derogatory term.

The trees fell away and they came to a sunny clearing. An old, faded red barn sat to the left of the drive, which Brett said was Nelda's workshop. Merrideth wanted to ask what she needed a workshop for. But then Nelda pointed out her fields beyond the barn and explained that she leased her tillable acres to a neighboring farmer. After they passed a small barn, a charming little stone and brick cottage with ivy-covered walls came into view. Holly and boxwood snuggled up to it, and a garden, or what remained of it, was visible through a wooden arbor upon which a smattering of red roses still bloomed. Obviously Nelda Garrison possessed an extremely green thumb.

A huge Rottweiler wearing a red bandana seemed to come out of nowhere and ran alongside the car to escort them the rest of the way to the house.

"Don't worry, Merrideth," Brett said. "Duke's harmless."

"As long as I'm with you," Nelda said cheerfully.

Merrideth got out of the car cautiously. Duke's collar read, "I've been a good boy all year," and he grinned and slobbered all over her hand to welcome her. But seeing the size of his teeth, Merrideth hoped she never had to put his friendliness to the test. Visitors would want to give Nelda a heads up before arriving.

There were no ghosts or goblins decorating Nelda's yard, but when they reached the back door, three tin chickens, imaginatively painted blue with white polka dots, were there to greet them. When Merrideth exclaimed over them, Brett proudly announced that his aunt made them herself and sold them in gift shops. So that explained her workshop.

The dog came in with them, making Merrideth a little nervous.

"Sorry," Nelda said. "Duke's a little intimidating until you get to know him." She pointed to a doggy bed next to the back door and said, "Duke, sleep." The dog obediently went to it and plopped down.

The interior of the cottage was as charming as Merrideth had anticipated. And everywhere her eyes landed she saw more evidence of Nelda's creativity. Jars of homemade raspberry jam served dual duty as light catchers on the kitchen windowsill. On the sofa in the living room her embroidered pillows and a quilted throw added more color. There was an exquisite watercolor of a field of daffodils on one wall and a lovely one of a turtle—of all things—in purples and greens on another.

"If you'd like to freshen up, Merrideth, the guest bathroom is through there," Nelda said. "I'll make tea."

It was a relief to wash her face, even if it meant taking off her makeup. When she got back to the living room, Brett was settled in comfortably on the sofa, his face also clean and his hair a bit damp. He must have washed up somewhere else. He didn't seem to notice that her face was naked. Maybe he was too polite to mention it. Ignoring the subtle hint from Brett to sit next to him on the sofa, Merrideth settled into a comfy overstuffed chair across from him.

The room was pleasantly cluttered with books, and a roll-top desk in the corner overflowed with papers.

"Does Nelda have time for a job between all these artistic endeavors?"

"Believe it or not, her day job is in accounting," Brett said. "Unlike me, she uses both sides of her brain."

"A true Renaissance woman."

Taking his phone out of his pocket he called out, "Aunt Nelda? What's your wi-fi password?"

Her voice came from the kitchen. "It's my pen name, no spaces."

"She's a writer, too?" Merrideth asked.

Brett went to a bookshelf, pulled out a slim green volume, and handed it to Merrideth. The title was *Back Roads*, the author N/A Garrison.

"Nelda Garrison, your aunt, is that Garrison? N/A Garrison?"

Brett grinned. "And all this time you thought the poor woman's parents had named her *Not Applicable*. *Nelda* doesn't sound so bad, after all, does it?"

Merrideth laughed. "No, I guess not. I don't think many people know her first name, so I'm honored. I love her poetry."

"If I'd known you'd be that impressed, I would have played that card right off."

He turned back to his phone. "There's something I want to show you. If I can find it."

Merrideth thumbed through the pages of the book. "Oh, oh, this is one of my favorites." She read aloud:

In Answer to the Sun's Prayers

The forest, where dwell
Many hermits, makes
A bridge between finite
And nonterminating
Series. And love grows.
It grows like spontaneous
Joy, converging rapidly
On peace, and it is not
For yourself you feel
This music to come.

You raise your eyes
To the night sky, clusters
Of galaxies emitting so
Much cosmic background
Radiation – it might as
Well be Time saying
Maybe, sometimes, or
The possibilities are endless.

But it's not Time saying
Anything. It's your own
Two hands, waving
Goodbye to the pain.
It's your own two feet,

Dancing several inches
Off the ground, one
At a time. In time.
In space. In twenty-
Five static projections
Per second. Still, your
Heart doesn't fail.

Who is alone? Not
The Virgo cluster. Not
The supergalactic plane.

Look at all this dark
Matter filling the sky.
Is it dark so that you
Cannot see it or so that
You know it is all just
Prayers, prayers and more

Prayers. More prayers than
People to pray them. More
Prayers than numbers to
Count them with. More
Prayers than stars to fill
The empty spaces between
So many prayers.

"Isn't that just pure genius?"

Brett looked guiltily toward the door through which his aunt had gone. "If you say so."

Merrideth looked at him in amazement. "For all your brilliance, you, Dr. Garrison, are a cretin."

"Guilty, as charged. But I am proud of her."

Nelda came in, carrying a tea tray. "Proud of whom?"

"You." Brett handed his phone to Merrideth. "Here, I found it. This is Aunt Nelda accepting the T.S. Eliot Prize three years ago."

Nelda set the tray on the low table before the sofa. "Oh stop." She seemed embarrassed by the attention. "Here, put a cookie in your mouth. I made your favorite."

Brett laughed and took the cookie she handed him. "I won't turn that down."

Merrideth took pity on her and decided to change the subject. "So, I hear you're working on your family tree."

"It's my latest little hobby. I haven't been able to get far, but that's no wonder. I'm not even sure what the family name actually is. Some people spell it Garretson, others Garrison. I'll have to figure out which one is the original variant."

"You should let Merrideth help. She has an amazing ability to ferret out historical information. She's done genealogies for lots of people."

"Oh, that would be wonderful," Nelda said.

"I'd love to," Merrideth said. "But I'm too busy to take on more projects right now. Sorry."

"That's quite all right. Understandable with your new job. Besides, I love a good puzzle. I'll figure it out somehow."

When Nelda looked away, Merrideth glared at Brett. He made a face at her. She couldn't tell if it meant he was sorry or amused at the joke he'd played on her.

"Brett says you teach history at McKendree College. How do you like my old alma mater?"

"I love it. But I'm still getting used to the job."

"So tell her about the history of the house," Brett said.

"Since when have you gotten interested in history, Brett? I've been trying for years to…." Nelda stopped and looked first at Brett and then at Merrideth. She grinned, obviously having just come to the same conclusion Merrideth had. Brett wasn't any more interested in history than *she* was interested in the quadratic equation. Clearly he thought talk of old houses and history would impress her.

Merrideth shot another sour look at Brett, and this time he had the grace to look embarrassed.

"Well, then," Nelda said with a cough into her napkin. "He's not referring to this house, Merrideth. It was the original Garrison house that was historic. It sat farther to the east past my vegetable gardens—where the chicken house is now."

"You have chickens?" Merrideth said.

"It's a whole menagerie out there."

"Brett's exaggerating. It's just my chickens and Maybelle and Morrie."

"They're the pigmy goats, in case you were wondering," Brett said. "And she forgot to mention Puff, Sally, and Jane. They're the cats. Where are they, anyway?"

"Oh, they're around. They're shy of strangers."

"Sorry for the interruption," Merrideth said. "Tell me more about the old house."

"It was a wonderful old thing. I'm sure you would have loved it. Unfortunately, there was a fire in 1973, and it was destroyed one year shy of its 100th birthday. Later, my father built this cottage, using the foundation stones from the old house. They had been hewn from the bluffs. You see, the Garrison's property used to extend all the way down to the river. During a financial down-turn, my grandfather sold all but the forty acres I'm sitting on to the Ogles."

"The current owner being Odious Ogle," Brett said.

"Behave," Nelda said. "Walter's not that bad."

She told several interesting stories about the family, and Merrideth found herself wishing she did have time to take on the project. But Brett's eyes had glazed over, and Merrideth decided it was time to put him out of his misery even though it was his own machinations that had brought them there.

She stood, and naturally Brett and Nelda did as well. "Sorry," Merrideth said, looking at the clock. "I've got to get back. Duty calls."

"And I've got to get back to my new project," Nelda said.

"What is it?" Brett asked, hugging her. "An early birthday present for me?"

Nelda laughed. "Not unless you've suddenly decided to start

35

wearing pearl earrings."

"You make jewelry?" Merrideth said.

"Just one of my many hobbies. You want to see?"

"I'd love to see your designs."

"Come on then. You can give me a lift to my workshop, Brett."

Duke beat them there and stood wagging his tail in anticipation. Merrideth didn't share his high expectations for the workshop. The barn's faded red paint was peeling, and the planks were curled with age. But when Nelda flipped on the light switch inside, it was a different story. She had poured a concrete floor, stained in shades of green. And the walls and ceiling were bead board painted a cream color, which gave the interior a fresh, spacious feel. But Nelda had kept some of the barn's original stalls and mangers, which now served as whimsical room dividers. One stall was outfitted as a small kitchen. Another was a bedroom. A bathroom had been installed in what had once been a granary.

"At first I thought Aunt Nelda was nuts for sinking so much money into a barn."

"If the zoning board hadn't been so incalcitrant, I would have put up a new building. Anyway, it wasn't so much money since I used slave labor." She patted Brett's arm. "The professor here did most of it, including the wiring and plumbing."

Merrideth almost blurted out, "So that's how you got your muscles," but stopped herself in time. For her, intelligence in a man was always a major lure, and Brett Garrison had that in spades. But that he could use his hands for practical work had just doubled his attractiveness. Drat him.

She pulled herself together and said, "Nelda, you've made this barn nice enough to live in."

"I told Brett if he ever gets tired of that horrid condo of his he could always live here."

"I would if it weren't for the commute time."

"Look closer at the bathroom door, Merrideth," Nelda said. "It's part of the original barn."

The door was rustic and scarred, but it had a cute vintage china knob. The scars turned out to be names carved into the wood in different sizes and styles and with varying degrees of talent.

"Every scalawag boy that ever passed through here made his mark on that door."

"Where are you, Brett?"

He leaned in and pointed to the lower right panel where *BRETT GARISON* had been neatly carved in a tidy Roman font.

Merrideth laughed. "You misspelled your name."

Nelda laughed delightedly. "I love it when people point that out to him."

"Well, I was seven at the time. I got nervous."

"I shouldn't laugh," Merrideth said. "I had a hard time with my name, too. I usually wrote my nickname because it was easier."

"Ah, another clue," Brett said. "Was it *squirt*? No, that's too hard to spell. *Half-pint* maybe?"

"Leave the poor woman alone," Nelda said. "She's probably sick and tired of the short jokes."

"Thank you, Nelda. For that, I'll tell you. It's *Merri*. Like Merry Christmas, only with an *I*."

"Oh, I like it."

"Me, too," Brett said. "It suits you."

"You are not to tell anyone, Brett. I mean it."

"Don't worry. I'm good at keeping secrets."

Nelda snorted. "About like a second grader, you are."

She took them around to show Merrideth her various artistic projects that were in progress on well-lit work benches, including more of the tin chickens. And then she showed them the jewelry designs she was working on. Like everything she made, they were original, quirky, and fun. When Merrideth complimented her, Nelda promised to make her something.

"Thanks for the tour," Merrideth said at last. "This place is wonderful."

Nelda and Duke saw them to the door. When they got in the car she waved and called out cheerily, "Take Merrideth to dinner, Brett."

"Hope springs eternal, Aunt Nelda." He glanced at Merrideth as they drove away. "I'm sorry about my big mouth back there."

"Why on earth did you tell Nelda that I could help with her family tree? I told you I don't have time for any more projects right now. You have no idea the work it takes to construct an accurate, detailed genealogical report."

"I didn't mean for that to pop out. Sorry. It's just that I can't stand to see Aunt Nelda the least bit unhappy. I feel terrible every time I leave her here alone."

"I have to admit that the thought of living in the country as isolated as she is kind of creeps me out. She must be lonely." Even introverts needed a certain amount of social interaction, and although Merrideth paid little attention to the tenants in her apartment building, it was nice knowing other human beings were nearby.

"She keeps busy—very, very busy, as you must have noticed. But still, I know she has to be lonely."

"I'm surprised she never married."

"She was engaged once years ago, but her fiancé died in the Gulf War. As far as I know, she's never had a serious relationship since." He smiled. "Other than Duke. He's a real member of the family, you know. He and I are the last of the Garrisons around here."

"Garrison? Or Garretson?"

"Hopefully, Aunt Nelda will find out."

"All right," she said.

"All right, what?"

"I'll help her. Once I finish Jillian's."

"She won't mind waiting."

"Have her email me as many names and dates as she knows, and I'll take it from there."

"Will do. And I'll pay whatever you say, Merri."

"It's not a matter of money."

"Of course it is. And you'll make a lot of it once you get your little business going."

"That would be nice."

"Just let me know what your fee is."

In truth, the money would be more than just nice. He didn't say anything more, and as the silence grew, she began to worry that any minute he really would ask her to dinner. It was past time, and she was starving, but surely he wouldn't, would he? She had made it perfectly plain that she wasn't interested in seeing him.

Yeah, and look where that got her. She had just spent the day seeing him. And it occurred to her that since his aunt was like a mother-figure to him, he had essentially just taken her home to meet the parents, which, of course, hadn't been his intention, but still, it was another stop on the slippery slope.

So if Brett asked her to dinner, she would not cave in like she had when he asked to come today. As for agreeing to help his aunt, she would work with Nelda directly, so there was no reason she'd have to be around him any more than usual.

Merrideth's phone rang just as they reached the outskirts of town. "What's up, Abby?"

"Can you talk? I know you're busy with the dig."

"No, actually we're finished. You sound rattled."

"I'm definitely rattled. John's mom is in the hospital. They think it's pneumonia. And his dad can't be left alone, so we're going over there to take care of things. We'll stay the night. Maybe all weekend. And our regular babysitter—"

"I can be there in an hour."

"Are you sure?"

"I just need to get a shower, and then it's Aunt Merri to the rescue."

"The girls will be thrilled."

"Me too. I miss the little critters. See you in a bit."

Brett gave her a sly smile. "If you have nieces or nephews, then I deduce that you must also have—"

"Sorry to disappoint you, Sherlock." The smile she gave him was no doubt more of a smirk. "They're honorary nieces, only. I get to babysit them tonight."

"Will you take them trick-or-treating? Or stay home, safe from goblins and witches?"

"I'm sure there will be nothing the least bit spooky about our evening together. They're not much into Halloween."

Merrideth was concerned for John's folks, but she couldn't help feeling a sense of relief that her resolve with Brett wouldn't be put to the test. But when he drove away after dropping her off at the curb in front of her apartment house, she perversely wished that Abby's call had come a few minutes later. Now she would never know if he had been planning on asking her to dinner.

CHAPTER 6

Warm happiness washed over Merrideth as she stepped up onto the front porch of the beautiful old Victorian house where Abby and her family lived. Eulah and Beulah, or the "Old Dears," as they had fondly called them, had specified in their wills that John and Abby were to be given first option to buy the house. At the time, Abby was a brand new elementary school teacher, and John's law practice was in its infancy. It had taken some doing for them to get the financing, but thankfully it had all worked out.

The Old Dears had been identical twins, and their house and the one next door were twins, too, both built by their great grandfather. John and Abby's was buttery yellow with a gray slate roof and had white gingerbread trim dripping from the eaves and front porch. They kept it in tip-top condition.

John's cousin Lucy had owned the twin house next door, alike in every detail, except painted a dusty blue. But eventually she had sold it to the Wilson family who were not very interested in the chores that came with being the owner of a vintage Victorian house. Every time Merrideth came to visit Abby and John and saw their peeling paint and torn screens, she shuddered, hoping Eulah and Beulah couldn't see it from heaven.

They had been gone for ten years, and memories of them still permeated Abby and John's house. She had first met the ladies fifteen years ago, that horrid summer she was eleven, when her mom, after years of loud marital skirmishing, had finally retreated from the field of battle, uprooted Merrideth from their home in

Chicago and dragged her, metaphorically kicking and screaming, to that shabby old house in Miles Station. Merrideth had finally understood why she had taken such drastic measures later that summer when her dad was arrested on drug and weapons charges.

Merrideth's heart had nearly broken. Her mom had been too wrapped up in her own problems to notice, but Eulah and Beulah had appointed themselves her dual grandmothers, and in doing so, had generously filled a gaping hole in her life. Abby had come to be her tutor that same summer, and she and John had also been there for her when her own mother was too busy and self-involved to bother. In her emotional pain, Merrideth had certainly not made it easy for Abby. But in spite of her brattiness, Abby had lovingly persevered. She and John eventually became her friends and treated her as a peer, even though they were ten years older than she was.

Abby refused to celebrate Halloween on religious grounds, so there was nothing the least bit scary on her front porch. Bright leaves littered the floor, and pots of mums and a plump pumpkin sat next to the door. As for Merrideth's opinion of Halloween, well it didn't take a degree in psychology to understand why it was her least favorite holiday.

The door opened before she could knock, and Lauren and Natalie launched themselves at her. Merrideth set her overnight bag down and enveloped them in a three-way hug.

She drew back and took in their sweet faces. "I've missed my little bugs. Well, not so little now, but I'll refrain from making those embarrassing comments aunts always do."

"Come on," eight-year-old Lauren said. "We've got everything ready."

"What are we making this time? Guitars out of cereal boxes? Alien spaceships out of Styrofoam bowls. Bracelets out of rubber bands?"

Lauren laughed. "Don't be silly, Aunt Merrideth. We made those last time. We're going to make dolls."

"Outta clothespins," Five-year-old Natalie explained.

John opened the door wide and smiled a welcome. "Girls, let your Aunt Merri get settled before the crafting marathon begins."

Abby joined her husband at the door, leaning into John's side as if she still couldn't get enough of him even after ten years of marriage. Merrideth's heart lurched every time she saw them mooning over each other. Their marriage was the standard that she had set for herself, the reason none of the men she dated ever turned out to be good enough.

"Okay, you two," Merrideth said. "You're making me a little nauseous. Get out of here and leave us girls to our fun."

Abby left John's side and pulled Merrideth into a hug. "Thanks for helping out, kiddo."

"Are we mentioning the pneumonia?" Merrideth asked softly when the girls had run on ahead.

"No, we are not," Abby said.

"We decided to wait until we've got a better idea about how serious it is," John added.

As usual, Abby had a long list of "guidelines" to go over with her. Merrideth always tried to comply with the rules, even though in her opinion most of them were needless. But, they were not her children, after all.

Thirty minutes later, Abby and John finally kissed the girls and left. One minute after that, Merrideth was ensconced with Lauren and Natalie at a table in the sunroom ready to make clothespin dolls.

The table looked like a small tornado had passed through, leaving behind piles of calico scraps and bits of lace. Some of the fabrics looked familiar. Abby had told her the best birthday gifts Merrideth could give the girls were craft supplies and fabrics—lots and lots of fabrics.

At first she was terrified to see Natalie handling a hot-glue gun. But when she realized it was the low-temp type and that both Natalie and Lauren were old hands at it, she settled down to enjoy making dolls with them.

Lauren, always the serious big sister, made tailored school clothes for her dolls. They were nicely color-coordinated and exquisitely detailed with darling little collars and belts. Natalie's creations were, like her personality, more flamboyant. She made fairies—not mere dolls—complete with wings and dresses in sparkly purple, hot pink, and teal.

The two dolls Merrideth managed to construct looked like clothespins with fabric stuck to them. Her attempt at creativity was, as usual, woefully inadequate. The girls' kind comments, clearly meant to bolster her confidence, only made her feel worse.

Their neighbors were mostly elderly, and Abby had told Merrideth not to expect many trick-or-treaters. So it was no surprise that the doorbell only rang three times throughout the evening. Three times Lauren and Natalie left their crafting and rushed to the door to admire the kids' costumes and hand out miniature candy bars from the bowl Abby had set by the door.

Eventually, they all grew weary of making dolls and went to the living room. Each of them chose three candy bars, per Abby's "guideline," and sat together on the floor to eat them. Merrideth told them a silly story about the adventures of a doll named Betty Broccoli Head while they tried to make the candy last as long as possible. The girls laughed at the story, and Merrideth felt vindicated in the creativity department.

She had planned on "forgetting" the time so they could stay up a little later, but at nine o'clock Lauren dutifully announced that it was their bedtime.

Although Merrideth personally had never seen the point of celebrating death, demons, and ghosts, it seemed wrong not to do something at least a little Halloweenish with the girls.

"I have an idea," she said. "How would you like to have a Halloween camp out? You still have your Cinderella tent, don't you?"

"Can we, really?" Lauren said. "That would be so cool. We could scare people when they walk by the house."

Merrideth smoothed the girl's blond hair. "So you wouldn't be scared?"

"No."

"Me either," Natalie added.

"Anyway, it's fun to be scared," Lauren said. "Only Mom doesn't get that."

"Good," Merrideth said. "But it's a little too cool to camp outside. Besides, your mother would kill me. So I have a better idea."

CHAPTER 7

Yawning, Merrideth put aside the novel she had been reading by the light of her flashlight and got up from the air mattress to check on the girls. Their Cinderella tent glowed from within, a bright beacon in the attic's gloom.

When she was eleven, the Old Dears had let her play in the attic whenever she came to visit. And the girls had been delighted with her suggestion that they camp out there. That didn't mean Abby wouldn't get her feathers ruffled when she found out. But better to apologize later than to risk asking permission first. Lauren and Natalie were intrepid girls who wanted to have a little excitement. How scary could it be with her sleeping next to their tent?

She poked her head in and saw that they were conked out, flashlights lying loose in their limp hands. She brushed a golden strand of hair from Lauren's face, kissed each smooth forehead, and switched off their flashlights and her own.

The nearly full moon shone through the dormer windows, and the light she'd left on at the bottom of the stairs spilled through the doorway. There would be plenty of illumination if anyone needed to go down to the bathroom during the night. But it was still a little spooky. She smiled to herself. If she had Brett's phone number, she would call him to let him know she was having a proper Halloween after all.

Yawning again, Merrideth checked the time on her phone. Eleven o'clock. It had been a long day. She sank back onto the air mattress, pulled the blanket to her chin, and promptly fell asleep.

And then Charlotte Miles was there in her quaint nineteenth century clothes. Merrideth knew that it was a dream. But it was so good to see her again that she willed herself not to wake up. And Charlotte's house in Miles Station was there, too, fresh and brand new, not at all like the shabby place it had been when Merrideth and her mother moved into it 150 years later.

Then Charlotte was at the depot waiting for the two o'clock train to arrive. But she wasn't there to meet someone. No, this time she would be a traveler herself. She would board the train and go to Chicago. Merrideth could go too—go home at last. She started to follow Charlotte into the passenger car. But then, panic filling her chest, she took her foot off the step and set it back on the depot's boardwalk. The girls! What was she thinking? She couldn't leave Lauren and Natalie alone. They'd be frightened.

A beam of blue light lasered past Merrideth's eyelids, and she sat up and blinked. The light came out of the darkest corner of the attic. The sight of it filled her heart with a rush of joy. But it couldn't be. Could it? Not after all these years. A blue light had wakened her at the ancient house in Miles Station on more than one occasion. Now it did the same here in John and Abby's Victorian house. The common denominator was that they were both old houses—old houses with soul. That was how the program worked.

Switching on her flashlight, she rose from the air mattress, then peeked into the tent and was reassured that the girls slept on, oblivious to the world.

The blue light was still there. Actually there, definitely not part of a dream. But she was being a fool. The light was probably only a smoke or radon detector that she had somehow overlooked earlier.

She crept on stocking feet toward the light, until she saw that it came from a set of metal shelves that stored various abandoned household goods. More specifically, the light came from a hole on the side of a box that had originally held printer paper.

Merrideth set her flashlight on the shelf next to the box and lifted the lid. The light poured out, turning her hand neon blue. Inside the box, sat John's old laptop, instantly recognizable by the distinctive label he had affixed to it back in the day. She cleared a place on the shelf and then lifted the laptop out and set it there. Thumbing the release button, she opened it and saw that somehow, some way, *Beautiful Houses* was working again, the slideshow of houses scrolling by like old times. The program's banner at the top invited her to take "Take a Virtual Tour."

She laughed out loud, but then muffled it with a hand to her mouth so she wouldn't wake the girls. For one thing, they needed their sleep. For another, it was best they didn't see what was on the laptop. When the program had stopped working fifteen years ago, the three of them had agreed that it was probably for the best. It had seemed entirely too risky to let word of it get out. John had insisted that if *Beautiful Houses* fell into the wrong hands—even their own government's hands—a clever programmer would eventually find a way to adapt it until every detail of every citizen's life was available for scrutiny. Uncle Sam would make Big Brother look like a kindly Wal-Mart greeter in comparison.

At first look, *Beautiful Houses* was a rather simple program that allowed viewers to ooh and ahh over fabulous award-winning houses around the world. None of the houses scrolling by now looked familiar to Merrideth. Then, just like old times, Eulah and Beulah's Victorian house slid into view. She hurried to click on it before it could be replaced by another house.

The image on the screen went crazy for a moment, and then there it was—the attic in which she now stood.

Only instead of moonlight, it was sunlight that came from the dormer windows. A girl of eleven or twelve walked into the attic, humming under her breath. Judging from her hairstyle and low-waisted lavender dress, not only was Merrideth seeing the attic at another time of day, she was seeing it at another time entirely. She remembered the time counter at the bottom of the screen and saw that it read *October 30, 1922.*

Her stomach somersaulted. It had to be one of the Old Dears. She zoomed in closer to study the girl's face and then laughed softly. It was probably Beulah, although she'd always had trouble telling the twins apart unless Eulah was grousing about something.

The program was nothing short of miraculous. She saw that now even more clearly than she had as an eleven-year-old. They had never had a clue about how it worked. There hadn't been time to find out before it went kaput. That it was working again after all this time, was equally miraculous.

The low-battery indicator flashed. The miracle was about to come to a crashing halt. Merrideth looked in the box and found the electric cord there. She snatched it and the laptop and hurried to plug it into the wall outlet near her air mattress. The indicator light stopped flashing, and she was able to breathe again.

She settled cross-legged on the mattress with the laptop on her knees and draped the blanket around her shoulders. The girl in the attic was kneeling in front of a large wooden steamer trunk, rummaging through what looked like cast-off clothes.

The attic door opened again, and another girl wearing an identical lavender dress came in. Now that the twins were together, Merrideth was sure she was right. It was Beulah at the trunk.

Beulah looked up at her sister and said, "I can't find it."

"Drat," Eulah said. "I can't go as Schéhérazade if I don't have a long veil."

Beulah held up a pink tutu. "How about a ballerina?"

"I did that two years ago."

Merrideth grinned. How cute. They were planning their Halloween costumes. The screen flickered, and her stomach bottomed out. It would be too cruel to have *Beautiful Houses* stop working again now! Not after seeing Eulah and Beulah again. But after a minute or so, the screen settled down, and with it her stomach.

Back then, she and Abby and John had jokingly called themselves the Three Musketeers. They had set several rules for themselves, one of which was that they would never "time-surf," as they called it, in bedrooms or bathrooms, like peeping toms. But the first rule in their pact, the cardinal rule, was that they would always time-surf together, never alone.

But Abby and John wouldn't be back until tomorrow night—or maybe even Sunday. What if she shut down the program and it never worked again?

Inside the Cinderella tent, one of the girls mumbled something, and Merrideth stopped to listen. When no other sounds came, she went back to watching Eulah and Beulah pick through the clothes in the chest.

Surely Abby and John would want her to take the opportunity, before it was lost forever, to see their old friends one more time. She wouldn't even set the program to go virtual. She could just tag along with them as they were for a while.

Merrideth set the dial to slightly faster than real time, knowing that she would use up her own life if she didn't skip over at least some of theirs. Eulah and Beulah stood up and race-walked toward the door, each carrying a pile of clothes. Merrideth tried to remember which dial she needed to set in order to lock onto one of them. If she didn't, she wouldn't be able to follow them out of the attic. At last, she managed to lock onto Beulah just as the last of her dress was visible in the doorway.

Merrideth went with them downstairs and then watched in amusement as they fussed over their Halloween costumes. Afterward, she followed them into the kitchen and watched as they made popcorn balls with their mother.

Merrideth increased the speed again, and then again, until the screen became a blur. Every few minutes she slowed to real time to see what they were doing. Most of it was the mundane stuff that made up the bulk of people's lives. But it was fascinating to watch the Old Dears grow from adolescents into beautiful young women and then eventually into the spunky eighty-five-year-olds they had been when she first met them.

She slowed to real time again and saw that now they sat on their front porch, looking older still and so tired, as they had in the last months before they died, one sister after the other. It wouldn't do to fast-forward now. Eulah and Beulah didn't have a lot of time left. She had no wish to re-live those last sad days, and certainly not to experience their deaths again.

She had to stop anyway. She was so tired she could barely hold her head up. She would just have to hope the program would restart in the morning. Mentally crossing her fingers, she shut the laptop, and put it into her overnight bag on the floor beside her air mattress.

But, no matter that her body needed sleep—craved it—she was too wired to settle down. She turned over, and then over again. The top sheet came loose, then the bottom one. She hated loose sheets, but she tried not to think about it. At last, she found the perfect position. Her muscles began to relax, and she felt herself drifting off to sleep.

Until the blue light came on again.

"Okay. Okay." She sat up and took the laptop out of her bag.

Fifteen years before, when the computer had insisted on coming on at odd hours of the night to wake them, she had proposed the theory that it wanted them to time-surf, to discover specific things. It seemed to actually have a mind of its own. It was a crazy idea, of course. But even Abby and John had half-believed her theory by the time they had finished using it to uncover genealogical information for Abby's friend Kate.

With trepidation, Merrideth opened the laptop. The monitor flickered and then stabilized. Hand to her chest, she exhaled the breath she hadn't known she was holding. Not only was the program still working, Eulah and Beulah were still chatting on their front porch swing on a summer evening. It was a sign, wasn't it?

With that settled, she un-paused and waited to see what the twins would do next. But then, without any help from her, the scene dissolved into a blur, and time began to race by. She tried to slow it, but the program refused to cooperate. Finally, it slowed on its own, and the colorful blur reconfigured into the Old Dears standing at the bottom of the stairs, paused in mid-step. The time counter at the bottom of the screen read October 31, 2005.

The date filled her with dread, and her first instinct was to shut the laptop and pull the blankets over her head. But she also had a strong feeling that there was something she was supposed to see. She took a deep breath and switched to virtual mode.

Beulah took her twin's arm and steered her back toward the dining room. "Let's not go to the attic, okay?" When Lucy got back she'd be mad that she had let Eulah get off the couch. Well, not mad, because Lovely Lucy never got mad at them. But she'd be worried that Eulah would fall and break another bone. But who could stop Eulah once she got something into her stubborn old head? The best she could do was try to distract her.

"We've got to get ready." Eulah's mouth turned down on the left side and her speech was so garbled that nobody could understand her. Except for her, of course. Beulah smiled fondly. They'd been thinking each other's thoughts too long for a stroke to get in the way.

"Ready for what, Yoo?"

"I get the tutu this year," Eulah said petulantly. Then her expression turned kindly. "But I'll help you find the veil."

Beulah had no idea what on earth she was talking about, but she led Eulah to her usual chair at the table. Her sister obediently sank into it and put her thin wrists on the table in front of herself. Then

Beulah realized what her sister had meant and laughed. "You want to go trick-or-treating, is that it, Yoo?"

Eulah grinned and said something that even a twin couldn't decipher. Well, if she wanted to dress in a tutu and go trick or treating in the neighborhood like a child, then that's what they'd do. Not that Eulah needed a costume. She was a ghost of herself, so thin Beulah could nearly see through her. She chuckled at the thought and immediately felt guilty. But then she reminded herself that dear Eulah would want her to keep her sense of humor. Anyway, Lucy would know what to do when she got back from Walgreens.

Beulah sat down in her own chair and picked up the lined yellow tablet on which she'd been writing earlier. She pushed her glasses up where they belonged and squinted at the paper. "Now, where were we, Yoo?" When her eyes focused, the best they could anyway, she saw that the next item on the list was the tea set.

Just thinking of the ivory cups and plates with their pretty pink roses around the rims made her smile. It was too bad they hadn't thought of it back in June, or they could have given the tea set to Abby and John as a wedding present. They appreciated old things.

And the tea set was very old. She and Eulah had always believed their mother had bought the set, that is, until Abby and John went on the World Wide Web and found out that the tea set was much older than they had realized. In fact, they discovered that it had been in the family for four generations.

Dear Abby and John. They had helped her and Eulah find their Buchanan roots. She turned to look at the family tree hanging on the dining room wall and smiled in satisfaction at the names she'd hand painted on the little apples. Yes, Abby and John should have the tea set.

But then Lucy's sweet face came to her—kind and generous Lucy, their next-door neighbor who had taken care of them all these years. She was out this very minute buying Depends for Yoo. Beulah picked up her pen and wrote Lucy's name on the tablet. Then she wrote the name again on a matching pink Post-It note.

Next to her, Eulah attempted to rise from her chair. "Tutu," she said.

Beulah put a restraining hand on her shoulder. "Not yet, Yoo. You have to stay here and help me."

With the sticky note in hand, Beulah pushed herself up from

the chair and went to the china cabinet against the wall. The door always stuck a little, but she tugged and it came open. She carefully lifted one of the rose teacups from the shelf and stuck the Post-It on its bottom. "There," she said. After a last look, she put it back. Then she picked up their father's pocket watch from its position of honor on the top shelf.

"This will be the toughest one to decide," she said, carrying it back to the table. "Who did you have in mind, Yoo?"

Eulah didn't have an opinion, or at least didn't care to express one. Beulah studied the watch in her hand. The fob kept coming off the chain when she polished it each week with Silver Cream. Just picking it up now, it came off again, drat it. Lucy would know where to take it to be repaired.

The extra loud doorbell that John had installed for them clanged, and they both looked up. Perhaps Lucy had forgotten her key. Glad she hadn't sat down yet, she put the watch and fob in the pocket of her sweater and turned to her sister. "Stay there, Yoo. I'll be right back."

The bell clanged again before she could get the door open. She turned on the porch light, and there was their sweet Merri, teary-eyed and disheveled.

"Grandma Beulah? Can I come in? I know it's late, but…"

Beulah opened the door wide and her arms wider still. "It's never too late for you, honey."

Shocked to her core, Merrideth dragged herself out of the past and paused the program. She had never run across herself while time-surfing. They hadn't realized it was possible. And they had been so fascinated by their trips to the past that they had never gotten around to fast-forwarding up to the present or trying to see into the future. She, for one, wouldn't want to.

On the monitor, her sixteen-year-old self was captured in all her teenage angst, ready to fly into Beulah's comforting arms to weep out all her anger and shame.

That Halloween night was burned into her memory. She had made an awesome zombie costume for herself and left early, planning to put it on before the party at her best friend Jenna's house. But when Jenna answered the door bell, she informed Merrideth that she had been un-invited to her party. Somehow she had found out that Merrideth's dad was not deceased as she had told everyone, but very much alive in Joliet Prison, five years into a twenty-year sentence for making and distributing methamphetamine and possessing a boatload of unregistered firearms. When Merrideth had tried to explain, had begged to be let inside, Jenna had threatened to tell everyone she knew about her father if she didn't leave. Merrideth had never found it easy to make friends and treasured the few she did have. Jenna's defection that night had been an arrow to her heart.

Her present self was nearly as frozen with indecision as the image on the screen. She could shut down the program and go back to bed. It was surely the most sensible thing to do. Or she could un-pause the action and let the scene play out. She would hear again the wise advice and comfort Beulah had given her that night, words that had shored up her wobbly confidence and helped send her down the path to where she was today. She would watch as Eulah, not quite understanding what the fuss was all about but wanting to help, gave her one last big hug.

Or, she could change the settings, switch the lock from Beulah to the young Merrideth, and presumably watch herself grow up. What new insights would she gain if she revisited all the key events of her life from the perspective of time and maturity?

But no matter what she decided to do, there was no changing the fact that at a few minutes before ten o'clock as they sat waiting for Lucy to get back from Walgreens, a third stroke would come and take Eulah away forever. The loss had been a second, even more devastating, arrow to the heart in a single night.

Setting the laptop beside her pillow, Merrideth lay down and stared at the frozen scene. Finally, she decided that the thing to do was go forward for just a few more seconds. Then, after she'd seen the Old Dears' sweet faces one last time, she would shut down the computer before it went too far. The sky was lightening. It would be dawn soon, and she knew from experience that Lauren and Natalie were early risers—very early risers.

She was surprised to find that tears were dripping onto her pillow. She couldn't remember the last time she'd cried. Maybe at Eulah's funeral. She wiped her eyes with the corner of the sheet, then sat up and put the laptop on her knees. She clicked the dial, and sixteen-year-old Merrideth flung herself into her Grandma Beulah's waiting arms. Beulah staggered a little, and as she did, a shiny coin dropped out of nowhere onto the porch floor and rolled away, unnoticed by either of them. Arm in arm they started down the hall toward Eulah.

Merrideth clicked to stop the action. The wooden porch floor had acted as a drum, amplifying the sound of the coin's landing. Of course, Beulah couldn't hear very well, but her own hearing had been keen. Yet wrapped in her misery, she hadn't even noticed. It just went to show how much sensory information the brain tuned out during moments of stress.

She zoomed in close and studied the wooden floor. The porch light was plenty to see by, but the coin had disappeared. It was stupid to get obsessed with it, but somehow she couldn't bear to go on without discovering where it had gone. She rewound, and played again, this time in slow motion, and saw that the coin had come from Beulah's sweater pocket. Her pulsed kicked up as she realized that it was the medal, not a coin at all.

She stopped the action with the shining disk in mid-air. Merrideth laughed out loud and hugged herself. She clicked and the medal continued to fall in slow motion. At last it landed and rolled across the porch. Then it hit a crack in the floor at just the right angle and fell in. She shook her head at the wonder of it, then clicked to allow Beulah and her young self to continue walking into the house. She would let the scene play out only a little, just until they reached Eulah.

CHAPTER 8

Grandma Beulah took her arm to hurry her along. "Got to get back to Eulah quick. She's had it in her head to go up to the attic all evening."

Merri, in spite of her misery, wondered why she would want to go up there. And then a spurt of worry hit her. Grandma Eulah would fall again if she tried to climb all those stairs.

"To be honest," Grandma Beulah said, "there are a few un-Christian words wanting to come out of my mouth about that so-called friend of yours, Merri. But I'm not going to let them out. Of course," she added thoughtfully, "since the Lord already knows I'm thinking them anyway, maybe I should go ahead and speak my mind."

Merri was amazed to find that she was smiling. In the dining room, Grandma Eulah was writing something on a yellow pad at the table. She looked up and smiled sweetly, albeit crookedly, at her. When Merri got to the table, she saw that Grandma Eulah had written *Merri* in her spidery cursive.

"Sit down here and let's talk, honey," Grandma Beulah said. "When Lucy gets back in a few minutes, she'll watch after Yoo, and you and I'll go to the icebox and get us some Coca-colas."

54

Merrideth stopped the scene from playing out. There. That was enough. It was all she needed to see. She'd remember the three of them that way, sitting together at the table.

Then, what she had just seen sank in, and she zoomed in close to the tablet in front of Eulah. Then the tears started up again. The Old Dears had wanted her to have one of their most valued possessions. Was the medallion still there under the porch after all these years? Surely *Beautiful Houses* wouldn't have insisted on showing her the scene if it weren't. She pictured the ladies up in Heaven smiling happily that she'd finally figured out where it was. Well, Beulah would be smiling. Eulah would grouse, "It took you long enough." Merrideth laughed at the thought.

"What's so funny, Aunt Mewwi?" Natalie stood outside the Cinderella tent, rubbing her eyes. In the pink-tinged light streaming into the attic, her hair and nightie glowed as if some fairy godmother had sprinkled fairy dust on them.

"What's so funny?" Merrideth slipped John's laptop into her overnight bag, and then pulled Natalie down to sit beside her. She kissed her turned up nose and said, "Life, little bug. Life."

"Can we make more faiwies, Aunt Mewwi?"

"We can after we eat. I'll fix breakfast for you and Bug Number One in just a minute. But first I'm going on a treasure hunt."

Natalie's eyes lit up. "Can I go too?"

Lauren came stumbling out of the Cinderella tent. "Me too!"

"Of course. How could I manage without my sidekicks."

"Come on, Lauren," Natalie said. "Let's go get our Dora the Explorer boots."

"I wish *I* had some," Merrideth said.

Natalie laughed.

Lauren frowned. "Mine don't fit any more."

"Never fear. I will buy you another pair, Bug. But you won't really need them for this treasure hunt. We don't have to go far— just to the front porch. Hurry and get dressed."

When Merrideth and her two fellow explorers opened the front door a few minutes later, they were met with the brilliance of the morning sun reflecting off the frozen coat that Jack Frost had put on everything within his reach during the night.

Natalie ran to the porch rail and scraped up some of the frost. "It snowed, Aunt Mewwie!"

"It's frost, Bug. Let's hope we don't get snow for a while yet. It would really mess up a project I'm working on."

"Where's the treasure, Aunt Merrideth?" Lauren said.

"Under the porch. Come on. But be careful. The steps will be slick." Merrideth went carefully down the steps, and the girls gamely followed. Natalie's Dora the Explorer boots thumped loudly on wood.

As she had figured, the lattice that formed the porch's skirt was well maintained. And firmly attached with bright new screws, drat John. They knelt and each put an eye to an opening and looked in. Rays of light speared in through the lattice, making a checkerboard of light and dark and revealing all the spider webs and filth Merrideth had feared would be there.

"That looks disgusting," Lauren said. "I don't think I want to be an explorer."

"Me neither," Natalie said.

"Don't worry, Bug One and Two. I'll do it. Lauren, can you go upstairs and get my flashlight? I'll go find a screw driver, and then we can…" Kneeling as she was, her eyes were level with the porch floor. A bit of sunlight winked off a spot just in front of the door. Merrideth hurried back up onto the porch. There it was, still in the crack! Why had no one seen it before?

"Never mind the flashlight, Lauren. Instead bring me your mom's tweezers."

Lauren was back in a flash and handed the tweezers to her. She looked worried.

"It's all right, Lauren. I'll get your mom new ones if I mess these up." Merrideth carefully inserted the tweezers. The medal slipped out easily, as if it had just been waiting for her to come get it from its hiding place. She rubbed off as much grime as she could on her jeans and then held it out for the girls to see.

"Is the rest under the porch, Aunt Merrideth?" Lauren said.

"The rest?"

"The pirate chest."

"Oh. Sorry. No, this is it. It's not that kind of treasure, sweetie. It's a historical treasure. I thought it was lost forever, so I'm really happy to have it back. It's a Lewis and Clark Peace Medal made back in 1802."

It had been Eulah and Beulah's ancestor Nathan Buchanan's, a memento of his participation in the expedition, although no one had known its historical significance until Abby and John time-surfed back and saw what it actually was. And then the medal had been passed down through the generations. The Old Dears' father had used it as a watch fob. Suspicions had run high after Beulah's death, everyone assuming the valuable artifact had been stolen.

Merrideth handed the medal to Lauren, and she and Natalie studied it with interest. "Who's that man?" Lauren said.

"That's President Jefferson. Turn it over." When Lauren complied, Merrideth said, "That's an Indian peace pipe. This medal went on the Lewis and Clark Expedition all the way to the Pacific Ocean and back."

"Cool," Lauren said, showing no disappointment in not finding a pirate's treasure under her porch. Merrideth smiled. The girls had already shown a remarkable interest in old things and history. She loved teaching them. It was so nice to have such eager students for a change.

It *was* cool to have found it. The actual monetary value of the medal was slight. The historical value was immense. But the sentimental value to her personally was beyond calculation. Her throat knotted. Without *Beautiful Houses*, she never would have known that her "grandmas" had wanted her to have the treasure that had been in their family for generations.

And then it hit her—the fort! With the *Beautiful Houses* software she could find out where Fort Piggot was. Better yet, she could virtually visit it! Glenn, Eugene, and all the volunteers would be so pleased. And it would be a boost to her career as well. She could publish a paper which would keep President Peterson happy and, more importantly, add valuable information to the body of knowledge about southern Illinois' past.

And with the software now working again, genealogy consulting was suddenly a very practical idea for a paying sideline business. Following leads would not take nearly as long, and she could give her clients so much more in-depth information than had ever been possible before. Brett would be her first paying client. She could practice on him, working through the logistics, figuring out her fee schedule, and all that. She would have to have business cards. But those were pretty cheap. If she were lucky, word of mouth advertising would be enough to keep the clients coming in without her having to spend a dime.

And then her excitement dissolved like a sugar cube in hot coffee. What was she thinking? *Beautiful Houses* wouldn't work unless she could find a suitably old building in which to run it. Nelda's house was not nearly old enough to work. Nor had Jillian never mentioned any old houses belonging to her family.

And there sure weren't any buildings out in Mr. Schneider's bean field to yield clues about where Fort Piggot was.

But then a new thought had her heart pounding. The old barn on Bluff Road! If its foundation really had been made from stones from the ruins of Fort Piggot, it might possibly work. It was a long shot, but Abby and John had once been able to pick up enough vibes from the basement of an old house to successfully time-surf even though the house itself was no longer there and a modern museum had been built over the spot where it had once stood. But would *Beautiful Houses* be able—and willing—to do its thing with foundation stones that were no longer in their original location?

She would be at the barn at first light tomorrow, ready to find out.

"I'm cold," Natalie said.

Merrideth snapped out of her happy thoughts and saw that the girls were shivering. The light jackets they wore were no match for the frosty air.

"I'm sorry, girls. Let's go in and I'll tell you about the peace medal while we make breakfast."

CHAPTER 9

When Merrideth got home that evening she propped the Lewis and Clark medallion next to the clothespin dolls on her faux mantel. Then she sat down on the couch and slipped John's purloined laptop out of her tote bag. She set it before her on the coffee table and stared at it.

Abby and John had been so happy to know that she had found the medallion. And the whole time her friends were congratulating her, Merrideth hadn't said one word about how she had done so. Some Musketeer she was. But what if Abby and John, fearing the repercussions—and grown stuffy in their old age—refused to let her use *Beautiful Houses*? And even if they agreed, everyone's schedules were full. The logistics of getting the three of them together for the work Merrideth needed to do would be nearly impossible.

She should just go to the barn in the morning as she had planned. If the program worked, she would take that as a sign that it was okay for her to proceed without Abby and John.

And then reality hit. Before she went trekking around the countryside with John's laptop, she had to insure the safety of the software. She didn't even want to launch the program again until she had a new computer to run it on. The laptop was a veritable dinosaur on borrowed time. That it worked at all after all these years was a miracle. If it crashed, the *Beautiful Houses* program would be lost forever.

And she would need an internet connection. There sure

wouldn't be any signals to pick up at the barn on Bluff Road. Back in the day, John's friend Tim Skyzyptek , A.K.A. "Timmy Tech," had transferred *Beautiful Houses* from the computer her dad had sent her onto John's laptop and then lent them a gizmo he had designed that allowed them to piggyback off of other people's wi-fi signals without having their passwords. She didn't have it now, but she could probably get Tim to make her a new one. These days, he ran a wildly successful computer consulting firm in Alton. But it wouldn't be open on a Sunday night, and even if she wanted to call him at home, which she didn't, it was too late to do so.

But she wouldn't have to wait for business hours to get her new computer. She spent three hours online comparison shopping, and then ordered a high-powered laptop equipped with the most RAM she could find. She smiled, remembering that back then Tim had been impressed with her new computer, pronouncing it in geek speak a "flaming sweet beast." The one she had just selected probably had a thousand times the memory. She also ordered an industrial-strength metal case to carry it in, an external back-up drive, just in case the laptop got overloaded with data, and a power cord adaptor, which would allow her to plug it into her car's cigarette lighter. She winced at the total cost, and then winced again when she checked the box for two-day express shipping.

There was nothing else to do but wait for her goodies to arrive, so she spent an hour prepping for her Monday classes and then went to bed.

Merrideth did everything possible to have loose ends tied up so she could leave as soon as her last class ended. Even so, she arrived at Tim's shop with only minutes to spare before closing time. Merrideth had seen him a number of times through the years since that long ago summer when he had repaired her computer. Hopefully, he would agree to stay late for old time's sake, sell her what she needed, and not be overly curious about why she wanted it. After all, it was not exactly something he could sell to the general public.

Pterodactyl Technologies was painted on the glass door along with a cartoon version of their namesake. It was a ridiculous name for a serious company, but she supposed it was better than using his unpronounceable last name. She'd heard him tell John that *Pterodactyl Technologies* stood out among the stuffy, look-alike company names in the yellow pages. Besides, he happened to like pterodactyls.

Merrideth opened the door and went into the reception area. No humans were in sight, but computers of various types sat on the floor and on shelves around the room, waiting either to be repaired or picked up. There was a doorway to another room on the far wall, but it was curtained off. As cluttered as the reception room was, there was no telling what kind of condition it was in. At least the front counter was neat and bare of extraneous computers. On the wall above it, a colorful sign announced that *Pterodactyl Technologies* specialized in customized networking solutions for small to medium businesses, but that they also sold and maintained computers for the individual, ending with the statement, *No Repair Job Too Small.*

Merrideth started to call out, and then saw the bell on the counter. She rang it, and after a moment Tim stuck his head out from the curtained doorway. "Hold on a sec," he said. "All my techs are gone for the day, and it's just me."

"No problem."

He smiled distractedly and disappeared behind the curtain.

There had been no recognition on his face. It was true that it had been three or four years since she'd last seen Tim. They had both attended a party at Abby and John's house, and despite her efforts to discourage him, he had hit on her all evening until, to her mortification, John had gone all big brother and told him to knock it off. Apparently, the incident wasn't as etched on Tim's memory as it was hers. Maybe she was more unmemorable than she realized.

He came out of the back room, this time wearing horn-rimmed glasses. A smile of recognition lit up his face and he hurried toward the counter. So he was near-sighted, then.

"Merrideth Randall, how in the world are you?"

"Fine. How about you?"

"I was having a bad day, but it's looking good now. I hear you're a professor over at McKendree now."

"I am."

He leaned down, putting his elbows on the counter and his face alarmingly close to her chest.

61

She took a step back and plastered on a smile. So that was still there. She glanced down at his left hand and verified that as she had heard, he did indeed now wear a wedding ring. "I hear congratulations are in order."

"For my new store? That's old news."

"For your new wife."

He stood upright and replaced his overly friendly smile with a bland look. "Oh, that. Thanks. What can I do for you today?"

Now all she had to do was ask him to build a piggyback gizmo similar to the one he'd given them fifteen years ago without stirring either his libido or his curiosity, and without showing her disgust. She made the request sound like no biggy, and he seemed to have no ethical qualm about making the gizmo for her. Fortunately, he was his usual oblivious self and didn't ask uncomfortable questions about why she wanted it, just promised to get it done pronto.

Relieved, she smiled at him. It was a mistake.

An unpleasant degree of eagerness appeared on his face. "I just need your number so I can call you when it's finished."

She gave it to him, trying not to show her reluctance. If he decided to pester her, she could always get a new number, as annoying as that would be. She wondered if John knew about his friend's propensity for marital unfaithfulness. If not, she'd just as soon not be the one to disillusion him. But if she had to, she would, and she knew John would come riding to the rescue. It was just one of the many perks of having a pretend big brother.

Merrideth left the store as soon as she could, hoping her new computer would be waiting for her when she got home. She reached Lebanon in record time and parked behind the apartment building. Quickly gathering her things, she got out of the car and started toward the door. Tires screeched behind her. Heart stuttering, she pirouetted faster than a ballerina. The red convertible that belonged to the Oswald sisters in apartment B was still quivering to a stop.

Merrideth had met them briefly her first week there. She didn't remember their first names, but one was a junior and the other a senior at McKendree. They wore identical looks of horror over the close call.

The driver said, "I'm so sorry, Dr. Randall. I thought you saw us."

"I didn't. But even if I had…well, you know pedestrians have the right of way, right?"

The younger sister in the passenger seat said, "They do?"

"They do," Merrideth assured her. Of course, she thought, pedestrians should avoid being so distracted that they failed to watch where they were going.

"Well, I'll be more careful."

"Good idea." Merrideth smiled to let them know there were no hard feelings, and the girls pulled into the parking spot next to hers. Her poor old Subaru probably suffered from insecurity. Or maybe loneliness. The red convertible was seldom there. The girls didn't have jobs, so presumably their parents were bankrolling their education. Merrideth was glad they were having a more care-free college experience than she'd had. The Oswald sisters didn't have to wear themselves out working at minimum-wage jobs with no time left for any fun.

The package she'd nearly gotten herself killed over was not waiting for her in the hall. She shouldn't have expected it to be. But it wasn't there when she got home Tuesday or Wednesday either. So much for "express" shipping. But Tim had left a message saying he had finished making her gizmo and that the store was open late on Wednesdays. Or he could bring it to her if she gave him her address. She shuddered at the thought, and hurried to go pick it up.

She fully expected Tim to be waiting for her alone in the store, but he hadn't lied. Other techs were still there working, and happily Tim kept things business-like. She wondered if she had imagined his come-on the other day.

He told her he had named the gizmo Frankenstein because it was made from bits and pieces off several old computers in the back room. Frankenstein, like its namesake, wasn't very pretty. But Tim assured her that it would give her a range of over 700 yards without worrying about pesky passwords. This time she remembered not to smile, but happily paid him, knowing that with Frankenstein, she would be able to time-surf almost anywhere. On the way home she stopped at Walmart and bought two 150-foot heavy-duty extension cords and a backpack to carry all the equipment in.

The computer was still not there. But finally after dark, when she'd resigned herself to another day of waiting, the UPS guy arrived with a large box. She ripped into it the moment he was gone.

The new laptop looked good, really good. And it didn't take as long as she feared to complete the set up. When she was sure it was ready to use, she connected it to John's old laptop via a USB cable and then, using the technique she'd learned fifteen years before from Tim, began the process of transferring the *Beautiful Houses* program files onto the new computer. She figuratively held her breath while the computers did their thing. It was taking so long that she finally went into the kitchen to do some cleaning, figuring if she didn't watch, the process would go faster.

When she got back to the living room an hour later, the monitor was black, and she had a moment of panic. But then she put her hand on the touchpad, and the *Beautiful Houses* home page filled the screen in living color. She let out the breath that had been locked in her lungs. And then she smiled.

She itched to run the program. Her apartment house was certainly an old enough building for it to work in, and it was sure to have an interesting past worth exploring. But she resisted the temptation. She and Abby and John had agreed long ago that it wasn't ethical to use the program where they were likely to run into people they knew, at least not people currently living. They would be the worst sort of creeps to do so. Mr. Haskell and the other tenants in her building deserved their privacy. Fear of compromising the whole nation's privacy was why they had guarded the program's existence so fiercely back in the day and why she would continue to keep *Beautiful Houses* safe when she used it for her research.

So she shut the computer down and loaded everything into the new backpack, reminding herself that tomorrow wasn't that far off.

CHAPTER 10

Merrideth got to her office early and then concentrated on doing her job. And the morning went well, despite the fact that adrenalin bombs kept going off in her stomach every time she thought about what she was going to do at the end of the day. On Thursdays she had a late class, and so she wouldn't have a lot of time for time-surfing before it got dark. But she had her equipment near to hand in her office and her Subaru waiting in the faculty parking lot.

She taught two sections of American history, which went amazingly well despite her distraction. She got caught up on her grading, which had fallen a little behind in recent days due to all the time it had taken to equip herself.

And she took the time to find Marla and apologize for being snippy with her. She was gracious, and Merrideth was glad to have things right between them again. Both refrained from mentioning Brett.

But Marla was right, and Merrideth knew it. Therefore, not mentioning Brett, not thinking about Brett, and especially not seeing Brett would be her best course of action. And she succeeded fairly well in accomplishing those all morning.

But then she ran into him, literally, in the waiting line at the 1828 Cafe.

"Sorry, Merrideth," Brett said with a grin. "I didn't see you down there."

"Very funny," she said. "And so original. I've never heard that joke before."

He laughed. "It's either short jokes or your nickname."

She sputtered, and he quickly apologized.

He actually looked and sounded sincere, so she decided not to be mad. Two students in front of them glanced back at her and then Brett with a speculative look. Merrideth put on a serious face and said, "How are your classes going, Professor Garrison?"

Brett's eyes sparkled with amusement, but he answered equally seriously. "Quite well, Professor Randall. And yours?"

"Splendidly."

Merrideth ordered a chicken Caesar salad, and after she'd paid for it, Brett ordered the same. When she got her lunch, she turned, tray in hand, to look for a table. And then she realized she didn't know what to do. Just because they happened to be in line together didn't mean Brett wanted to eat lunch with her. It would be presumptuous to assume so. But it would be rude to go her separate way, choosing a table just for herself as if they were strangers.

She was standing there feeling foolish when he said, "There's one," and led the way toward a table in the corner.

He was stopped three times on the way there by students wanting to talk. Each time, she stood behind him, tray in hand, waiting to proceed and feeling even more foolish than before. A number of her own students were in the crowd, but without her roster in front of her, she couldn't put names to faces. Several looked up when she approached but then turned back to their friends and food.

When they finally reached the table, Brett grinned. "I usually brown bag it in my office."

"So do I." She avoided crowded places like the Cafe but was surprised that he did. Didn't he enjoy basking in the admiration of his fans?

"So, how are your classes really going, Merrideth?"

"Fine, really. My students are more engaged, and I'm getting good work from them."

"I knew you'd settle in. I have to give Peterson points for being smart enough to snatch you out of your cradle and make you a faculty member. The youngest ever, I hear."

"Said the second youngest ever, so *I* hear." Piecing together things Marla and Jillian had said, Merrideth had deduced that Brett was thirty-one and that he had never been married. She wondered why. Of course it was none of her business if he wanted to play the field—until he was a senior citizen, if that's what floated his boat. She smiled at the thought of the Great One, wrinkled and pudgy around the middle, still drawing women like moths to candle light.

Beyond Brett's right shoulder, she caught one of her students staring at her. Dane Walters, that was his name. He was a freshman in one of her Illinois History classes. He smiled at her and then turned red and looked away. He had probably just realized that Merrideth's smile had been for Brett, not him. It was possible Dane had a crush on her. He was the nerdy sort of boy she had dated in high school and college. In a few years, he'd be the sort of man in her dating league now. Like a bowling league, she thought. She smiled at the image of the various men she had dated, wearing matching yellow shirts with *Fred's Towing* on the back, or maybe *Merrideth's Merry Men*. And they'd have pocket protectors. Definitely, pocket protectors.

"What's so funny?" Brett said.

Merrideth coughed into her napkin. "Nothing."

"Have you had a chance to work on the Garrison family tree?" Brett said.

"I haven't gotten far with it." Actually, she hadn't spent a single minute thinking about his genealogy, or Jillian's either, because she had made finding Fort Piggot her primary goal. But it was only a small lie. The bigger lie—one of omission—was the existence of *Beautiful Houses*.

As an expert on quantum physics, he would be fascinated by the program. He might even be able to explain how it worked. The urge to tell him about it had grown the more she had gotten to know him. Now, it welled up so that she could barely keep her mouth shut.

Brett studied her face. "I didn't mean to put pressure on you."

"You didn't."

Even if she could reveal the secret to him, the cafe wasn't the place to do so. It felt like a thousand eyes were watching their every move. Two tables over, three girls, one of them Alyssa Holderman, were sitting, heads close, in the classic boy-do-I-have-juicy-gossip pose. They were taking turns looking their way and snickering in a manner only slightly more sophisticated than that the girls at Merrideth's junior high had employed.

"What is it?" Brett said.

"I think we're causing a commotion." She indicated the source of the disturbance with a slight nod of her head. She had a tendency for social anxiety—which her therapist had told her stemmed from the time her father had been hauled off by the police in the middle of dinner at the crowded Brown Cow Restaurant—so she wasn't sure if she could trust her own senses on that.

He glanced back briefly and then sighed. "I should have known they'd be curious."

So it wasn't her imagination, after all.

Brett rolled his eyes. "You do realize we're the only unmarried teachers on campus?"

"We are?"

"Yep. Let's take our lunch to go. We can hide out in the faculty lounge to finish eating."

The afternoon passed slowly, but finally four o'clock came, and her last class ended. She left on the heels of her students and hurried to her office to retrieve her equipment. She was just locking her door when the phone on her desk rang. It was President Peterson. During the fifteen-minute phone conversation that ensued, she found out why certain members of the faculty privately called him "Publish-or-Perish Peterson." At last, after she promised to keep him apprised of her progress on her journal article on Native American tribes in Illinois during the War of 1812—a topic she had invented on the spot—he ended the call. Marla's little cautionary tale was starting to sound like non-fiction after all. She pushed it all to an unused compartment in her brain and hurried to her car.

A mile down from the dig site on Bluff Road, Merrideth turned into the driveway of a very cool old house. Glenn had said it was built in the late 1890s. She promised herself she would check it out some day when she had more time. Today, it was the barn fifty yards to the left of the house she wanted to explore.

Fortunately, the property was vacant. It was owned by the city of Columbia, and Glenn had told the volunteers that plans were in the works, assuming they could get the funding, to convert the house into a small museum and tourist information center that explained the importance of the Kaskaskia-Cahokia Trail in Illinois history. In ancient times, Bluff Road was only a buffalo track that ran beneath the bluffs along the Mississippi River. In the early 1600s, it became known as the Kaskaskia Trail when French explorers began building their little villages along it, including, among others, Kaskaskia and Cahokia. Later still, the American settlers built their blockhouse forts there.

Cars rushed by on Bluff Road, but as long as the daylight remained, no one would think anything of her being there. Unfortunately, there wasn't as much light left as she had hoped, and, once it grew dark, her car would look suspicious to passing motorists. They would likely think kids were messing around in the barn, up to no good. Some good citizen might even call the police.

She got out of the car and retrieved her backpack then hurried to the barn, eyeing its stone foundation. She squatted on her heels and studied the stones. It was a silly waste of time, because no one had labeled them "Fort Piggot stones." She rose and went to the barn door, only then wondering if it would be locked.

It wasn't. There was little need. The barn was completely empty of anything worth stealing or even dust and cobwebs. Someone had recently cleaned it. Maybe it, too, would be used as part of the tourist center. It was dim, but some light was managing to sneak in between the warped boards, reminding her of the old barn she had played in as a child at her mother's house in Miles Station.

There was no place to sit other than on the dirt floor, so she went back to her car and got the sturdy computer box she had put there to be recycled when she got the time. It made a pretty good stool.

She plugged in Frankenstein, then opened the laptop and turned it on, half expecting to find that *Beautiful Houses* had disappeared or that Tim had lost his techy touch and the gizmo didn't work. But after only a momentary swoosh of colors, the program launched faultlessly, inviting her, as always, to *take a virtual tour*. The houses started scrolling by.

It was a tempting selection, and they looked great on the computer's high definition screen. But all of the houses existed in the here and now. None looked even remotely like it could be a

69

circa 1783 blockhouse fort, James Piggot's or anyone else's.

So that was that for the barn. And if the program didn't work there, it surely wouldn't work in Mr. Schneider's bean field. Her dream of being the one to find Fort Piggot deflated until it was a drooping birthday balloon three days after the party. But there was no sense wasting time moaning and groaning about it. She shut down the computer and packed her equipment. Outside, the sun was at the horizon, and typical of fall, the warm day was turning into a cool evening.

On the way home she considered the possible reasons why time-surfing hadn't worked in the barn. She had told herself that if the program worked, it would be a sign for her to continue without Abby and John. But there was a fatal flaw in her logic, because, of course, the program not working did not necessarily mean the opposite. Maybe it hadn't been triggered into miracle mode because Fort Piggot's foundation stones had been disturbed and recycled into a completely different structure. Or maybe the legends were wrong about the stones being from the fort at all. So, in order to know if she could give herself permission to continue using *Beautiful Houses*, she would have to try it out somewhere else.

And there were lots of historic buildings she would love to explore, some right there in Lebanon. No telling what she could learn in them. Later, she could travel, go see all of her favorites. There was no use even thinking about the White House. It was so heavily guarded she'd never get past the door with her laptop. But what about Jefferson's Monticello or George Washington's Mount Vernon? And in New England she could "tour" the oldest buildings in the country, some built as early as the mid-1600s. The Jamestown Church came to mind. There were so many others to explore, and that wasn't even considering Europe. She would have to make a "bucket list" of buildings to see.

Meanwhile, she could get her genealogy consulting business off the ground, starting with the Garrisons. In view of her failure with the barn, it was highly unlikely that Nelda's house would work any better. And even if it did, there was no easy way to time-surf there without being discovered. Of course, solving the Garrison/Garretson question wouldn't require the use of her software anyway. All she would need was Google's minions and maybe the assistance of one or two of her genealogy subscription sites. It wouldn't be nearly as much fun as time-surfing, but it would get the job done. And in the future, she could limit herself to clients for which *Beautiful Houses* would work.

When she got inside her apartment, she regretfully set aside Frankenstein and her other gadgets and began the online hunt to determine the original variant of the Garrison name. She lucked out. In just under an hour she had the answer to that question and a lot more. Nelda would be happy to know what she'd found. Merrideth dialed her number, hoping she wasn't one of those early to bed, early to rise types. She wasn't and answered on the second ring.

"I hope it's not too late to call."

"Heavens no, Merrideth. I'm a night owl. I was just sitting at the kitchen table sketching my first jewelry design."

"I wanted to let you know I solved the Garrison/Garretson puzzle. Plugging in the information you sent me, I found your relative Cornelius Garrison, who is listed as the son of Garret Garretson, born in Monroe County in 1823. To me, that's a pretty good indicator that whoever recorded Cornelius' birth misspelled *Garretson* as *Garrison*, a common word people would have been more familiar with. Maybe at some point the family got tired of everyone misspelling it and just went along with Garrison. Anyway, Garret was your fifth great grandfather."

Nelda gasped into the phone. "I had no idea I could get that far back. Brett was right. You really are good. Tell me how much I owe you."

"Don't worry about that. Brett's paying for this. And I've only just begun the hunt. I hope we can go back much further, maybe even to when the family immigrated from Europe. I have a feeling *Garretson* is Irish."

"I can't wait to hear what you find. I'd like to put everything together into a nice format, a little book or something, for Brett."

"Maybe I can help with that," Merrideth said. "It would be a nice service to offer all my clients."

"Hopefully, Brett will start taking more of an interest in the family history." Nelda chuckled. "A genuine interest, that is. It will be to him to preserve the information and pass it on to his own children one day. And speaking of which, I want to apologize to you, Merrideth."

"What on earth for?"

"For sounding like an old busybody the other day. When I told

Brett to take you out to dinner, I didn't mean it in a matchmaking sort of way. The last thing I'd want is to be that sort of interfering aunt—I mean, what a cliché, right?"

"That's a relief. Not that your nephew isn't a nice guy, and all."

"And you are a wonderful woman, Merrideth. And it's clear that you and Brett have a lot in common."

With that last statement, Merrideth's suspicions flared up again. "Thanks, Nelda. Well, I'd better let you get back to your jewelry."

"Actually, I was just about to call *you*, Merrideth. I have something I want you to see. I think you're going to find it very interesting. Could you come over Saturday?"

"Sure. I guess."

"Be here at two o'clock. Don't tell Brett. I love him to pieces, but I wasn't kidding. He's terrible at keeping secrets. Be sure to dress warmly—something bright. I'd hate for you to get hit."

Could the woman be any more mysterious?

"Oh, and do you prefer gold or silver jewelry?"

Apparently she could.

When Merrideth turned onto Sundown Lane, Nelda and Duke were waiting in her car by the wooden sign. She got out wearing a neon orange jacket and pointed where she wanted Merrideth to park.

The dog tried to get out of the car, but Nelda shoved him back in. Duke whined his disappointment. No doubt he sensed there was an adventure afoot. Nelda was revved with whatever it was she wanted to show her.

"Where are we going?" Merrideth said.

"For a walk in the woods. Here, put this on." Nelda handed her a bright red stocking cap. It was too warm for it, but apparently Merrideth's purple jacket hadn't passed muster in the brightness department. "And this too," Nelda said, giving her a stretchy bracelet of silver jingle bells that matched the one making a racket on her own wrist. It wasn't what Merrideth had hoped for when she told Nelda she preferred silver jewelry.

"Over this way. It's not far."

"So, why all the gear?"

"Because it's deer season. And I don't want Walter to be the least bit confused."

The thought of Odious Ogle with a gun in his hands promptly cancelled Merrideth's enjoyment of the sound and smell of the crunching leaves. "We're trespassing on his property?"

"Technically, yes. But it used to be Garrison land. It ran from my house all the way down the bluffs and across the Bottom to the river. Sort of a split-level property." Nelda grinned. "I figure I still have certain rights."

Waving her bracelet from time to time, Merrideth concentrated on looking conspicuous as she followed Nelda's orange back down what looked like a deer path. Indeed, a whitetail deer flashed by just then. Merrideth wondered how many irate hunters were cursing them from their deer stands. If she and Nelda got shot, it would be on purpose, not an unfortunate hunting accident. After a couple of minutes, they came to a little creek.

"It meets up with the Mississippi eventually," Nelda said. "But we only have to follow it a little way to get to what I want to show you."

Only a short time later, Nelda stopped. Grinning at Merrideth, she pulled back a still-green branch of some hardy bush. "There. See? Is that cool, or what?"

Stones jutted out of the side of a small hill. Merrideth thought at first that Nelda was showing her a section of the bluffs. They had to be nearby. But this was not Nature's handiwork. A second look told her that she was seeing a corner section of a stone wall four courses high. Soil had filled in behind the wall, covering whatever it had originally been meant to enclose. The mossy stones were uncut and irregular in size, but there was no way their arrangement could have occurred randomly in nature. Someone had purposely stacked them there.

Nelda was wearing a satisfied smile. "It's old, right? I've been traipsing all over these woods and never noticed it until after part of that hill broke away during a heavy rain last month. I've been wanting to find someone to check it out, and then you came along."

"Really?" Merrideth studied the stone wall again. Her heart galloped, and she suddenly felt like sitting down, which she did. After wandering around in the woods, it was difficult to estimate how far away Bluff Road was, but she could hear the traffic from where she sat. That put the ruins only a short distance from the

Kaskaskia Trail. Maybe the creek Glenn and Eugene had pinned their hopes on was the wrong one. Maybe the one she and Nelda had just followed was the one the French had called *Grand Ruisseau*.

"Do you think it could be an old house?" Nelda said.

"No. I do not." After another minute, Merrideth looked up and smiled at Nelda. "To think of all those hours and days we wasted digging in Mr. Schneider's bean field, and here it was the whole time."

"Fort Piggot?"

"Fort Piggot. I think this is the foundation of one of the blockhouse forts."

"What's a blockhouse?"

"Think of it as a log cabin on steroids. They were fortified beyond the norm, two stories tall with thick puncheon doors. There were portholes in the walls from which those inside could shoot at attackers. For the same reason, there were holes in the floor of the second story where it projected over the first. Anyone trying to come through the door would get it. Some were single-family dwellings. In bigger forts there was a blockhouse at each corner of the stockade. When danger threatened, the settlers ran inside—much like European peasants ran for cover inside Medieval castles when Vikings attacked. In this case it was white settlers versus indigenous Indian tribes. And sometimes," she said, pointing at the wall before them, "they were built on stone foundations."

And, unlike the barn, the foundation Nelda had found was intact, the stones unmoved from their original use. Merrideth felt certain of it.

"How about that? A fort. That is so cool."

"I think so. But we'll have to do lots of work to find out for sure. Have you told anyone about this?"

"Not yet. I didn't want the place swarming with people. Who knows what Walter would do?"

"Good. Let's not mention it quite yet. You'll have to alert the authorities eventually. But since you've waited this long, let me see what I can find out from my sources first."

No doubt Nelda thought she was referring to human sources, like her history colleagues, for example. But the source Merrideth had in mind was in a backpack locked in her workroom closet, and she intended to go get it as soon as Nelda was gone.

CHAPTER 11

She returned as fast as she could manage, this time parking her Subaru completely off Sundown Lane and down among the trees where it wouldn't be easily seen by the casual observer. The day was still unseasonably warm, but still she wished for summer. If only it were June or July, she would have until nine o'clock or later before it got too dark to work. But it was October, and even though it was only four o'clock, the light would be gone soon. But she had come prepared. A little thing like darkness was not going to prevent her from time-surfing –or trying to—at the stone ruins.

It was not far, but she was huffing, more from excitement than exertion, when she reached the site. She had feared that a closer inspection would reveal that it was only a curious rock formation and not a man-made construction at all. But the evidence was just as compelling as she had first thought. Smiling in satisfaction, she climbed up onto the wall and set her backpack down.

Beautiful Houses booted up without a hitch, the homes scrolling by across the screen in their normal fashion. She waited, trying to be patient, but it failed to launch into miracle mode. She let out a disappointed sigh. Had she been wrong about the antiquity of the stone wall she sat on? Was it possible she had dreamed the whole thing in the attic, and *Beautiful Houses* was still dead?

With that worrisome thought, she looked at the date indicator and saw that it was set to Sunday, May 12, 1667. No wonder it wasn't working! James Piggot hadn't arrived in the Illinois Country until the next century. She couldn't remember the exact year. She was terrible with dates, a handicap for a historian, to be sure.

In any case, she knew it was shortly after the Revolutionary War that James Piggot had led somewhere around fifty settlers, including his wife and children, up the Mississippi to Fort Kaskaskia. They had stayed there one season, and then after they'd harvested their crops that fall, had travelled overland up the Trail through the American Bottom and built their fort not far from present day Columbia.

She changed the date to 1783, the year the war ended, but still nothing happened on her screen. She tried the next year and the three subsequent years, and still there was no fort and no miracle mode. The houses continued to scroll by. The time was still wrong, and her own time was running out.

She skipped ahead to the year 1795. The screen scrambled, and she felt her heart drop. But then the program snapped out of its funk, and a log cabin filled the screen. A rush of adrenalin made her hand tremble on the touchpad.

From time to time, *Beautiful Houses* had featured log cabins—the huge, fancy kind rich people built so they could "rough it" in the country. But the log cabin on the screen was no modern structure. It was more primitive in every way than anything a contemporary homebuilder would put up. And it was built on a stone foundation very similar in style and proportion to the one she now sat on. The only thing missing was the green moss.

But was it really the original of the ruins beneath her? Merrideth slid down from the wall, careful to hold the laptop as level as she could. The screen scrambled again. After a few more steps, it settled, but the log cabin that had been there was gone. A Victorian house in San Francisco was being featured, and when it slid out of view, a contemporary concrete and glass mansion in Chicago took its place.

Merrideth reversed her steps, and the screen went crazy, only stopping its mad roll when she reached the wall and set the laptop down. The log cabin was back! Laughing with relief, she climbed back onto the wall and sat down. She felt like hugging her computer.

In Abby's attic she had used only the most basic of the program's features. It had been fifteen years since the last time she had fully utilized *Beautiful Houses*. But before she tried out her rusty skills on the advanced features, she had better go get her equipment before it got too dark to see what she was doing. Besides, the laptop's battery would be drained soon. Going virtual always took a lot more juice than normal computer use.

For a moment she was disoriented and didn't know which way her car was. But then she saw the faint trail. When she started forward, a deer went crashing away. "Stay safe, Bambi." Hopefully it would, because if there were any hunters in this neck of the woods, it would soon be too dark for them to continue.

The car was where she left it and in one piece, apparently undiscovered by hunters, Nelda, Walter Ogle, or anyone else.

She got her high-powered flashlight out of the trunk and, after checking to make sure it worked, put it in her backpack along with a couple of the Mylar thermal blankets she had added to her kit. Once the sun set, it would get cool fast. She took out the adapter and inserted it into the cigarette lighter, and then got the two orange extension cords and connected them.

It took her several minutes to snake the stiff new cord down to the stone wall, only to find that it was a few feet short. She went back up and drove the Subaru farther down into the woods, knocking over a few scrubby bushes along the way. *Ooops, sorry, Mr. Ogle*, she thought.

Finally she got the cord into position. She set the laptop on the stone wall and plugged it in, then smiled when the log cabin came back up on the screen right where she'd left off. She sat on one Mylar blanket and draped the other over her head and shoulders, creating a cocoon for herself. It was a bumpy seat. Maybe next time she'd bring a folding chair. She chuckled at the image she made, sitting alone in the woods. Actually, she probably looked more pathetic than funny. It would be so nice to have a fellow adventurer to keep her company and share the excitement. The face that came to mind was Brett.

She zoomed out a little and then a little more until the whole cabin fit on her screen. She let out a little excited yip. This was clearly no average settler's log cabin. It *was* a blockhouse! An honest to goodness fort! It was two-stories tall with its upper floor projecting over the lower just as she'd described to Nelda. Zooming out farther, she saw that on both sides of the cabin was a stockade wall of upright saplings still wearing their bark. Yes, it was definitely a fort, but a small one, not nearly as large as Glenn and Eugene had thought Fort Piggot had been.

Brushing that thought away for the moment, she zoomed out to get the big picture. The fort sat in the open under bright sunlight, not in the woods as its ruin did now. The men would have cleared all the trees away for the stockade pickets, but also to give them a clear view of anyone approaching, friend or foe. She zoomed out even more until the fort was tiny, and there was the Kaskaskia Trail, evident by the tracks of horses and wagons in the dust, and where today she could hear cars and trucks going by. Beyond the cleared area, prairie grasses grew taller than two men. She would have thought that the image on her screen was a photograph except that the wind blew over the grass, creating shushing waves in infinite shades of green.

She zoomed back in and saw that an American flag fluttered from the corner of the stockade. Her own heart fluttered, too, when she went in a little closer and saw that there were only fifteen stars on it.

With the closer view came the sound of the wind whipping the flag and faint singing from within the stockade. She turned up the volume but still couldn't make out the words or recognize the tune. It was time to go inside and meet the pioneers.

Merrideth toggled from *Exterior* to *Interior*, and in the blink of an eye, she saw the inside of the stockade. A couple dozen singing people stood facing a man behind a makeshift pulpit. Even though they wore rough homespun and deerskin and there were no pews to sit on, it was clearly a church service, only without a church. She still couldn't catch the words of the hymn, and then it was over.

The man at the pulpit was very young, much younger than most of his congregation. He smiled at the people before him and then opened a large Bible. After a short time thumbing to the page he wanted, he looked up, wearing a serious, almost sad expression. Then he looked down at the Bible and read:

Ye have heard that it hath been said, 'Thou shalt love thy neighbor, and hate thine enemy.' But I say unto thee, love thy enemies, bless them that curse you, do good to them that hate you, and pray for them which despitefully use you, and persecute you; That ye may be the children of your Father which is in heaven: for He maketh his sun to rise on the evil and on the good, and sendeth rain on the just and on the unjust.

The congregation's reaction to the Scripture reading was

startling. Merrideth heard the buzz of people speaking, and then a man shouted angrily and made his way to the front, thoroughly interrupting the service. Apparently, the flock didn't take their young shepherd very seriously.

She paused the action again. There was some brouhaha about to break out, so it wasn't the best time and place to be scouting for James Piggot. She could let it play out and maybe someone would call him by name. But it was unlikely they'd call him by his full name. She couldn't very well use up a month of her own life waiting for someone to say *James Piggot*. When she'd been a kid her mother called her by her full name only when she was mad at her. "Merrideth Ann Randall, get in here this instant and clean your room."

If she switched to virtual, she'd be able to hear more clearly and know what was going on. And whoever she locked onto would give up his thoughts and emotions to her. It would be like being in his head. If James Piggot was there the person would think it.

But if she went virtual, she would get so into their world that she might forget her own. It was getting darker by the minute, and even with her high-powered flashlight she had absolutely no desire to spend the night in the woods. She would have to wait until tomorrow to find out who the people were, specifically whether James Piggot was one of the members of the congregation. Sighing in frustration, she made a mental note of the date and then closed down the program.

She put her things in the backpack and, flashlight in hand, began following the orange extension cord back to her car, gathering it up the best she could with only one hand. As she had hoped, it made a great trail marker, working ever so much better than breadcrumbs had for Hansel and Gretel.

The cord came to an end, and she found herself holding its bulky plug. It should have been inserted into the second of her 150-foot extension cords. Or, if she had somehow passed the junction of the two cords, it should have been inserted into the adapter in the cigarette lighter of her car. But the cigarette lighter was not there for it to be plugged into, because her car was not there. She trained the flashlight ahead. It did not reveal her Subaru, nor any other vehicles for that matter.

She had been feeling proud of her resourcefulness and bravery up to this point. Now, the hair on the back of her neck stood on end. Reining in the irrational urge to run screaming through the woods, she started toward where the cord, and her car, should be. Hopefully. Nothing looked familiar, but she reminded herself that darkness often had that effect even on streets that she was familiar with.

And then her light winked off something metallic. A wave of relief washed over her. It was the bumper of her car. She adjusted the backpack on one shoulder and the loops of the cord on her other and started toward it. Then her light picked up something else. Something orange. Her second extension cord lay in a neat coil beside the car. She swung her flashlight in a wild arc.

An answering light appeared, and then a man stepped from behind a tree. The light came from the cap he wore, the kind hunters were fond of. An even bigger clue that he might be a hunter was the shotgun he was pointing her way.

The man cursed. "I figured if I waited long enough I'd catch a fish on the end of that line." He pulled a phone out of his coat pocket and tried to dial while juggling the gun. "I'm calling the sheriff."

"Mr. Ogle?" her voice came out as a squeak. "Don't do that. Don't you remember me?"

"Get your flashlight out of my face." When she lowered it, he looked her up and down and then said, "You're that girl."

She ignored the flare of annoyance over the noun he'd used. It wasn't the time to worry about the finer points of women's rights. "Yes, Nelda's friend."

"This is my land. Mine. Did Nelda Garrison tell you it was hers?"

"No, of course not. I was taking a walk in the woods, and—"

"In the middle of the night? Are you crazy or just stupid?"

"It's not the middle of the night, and I'm not..." The look on his face grew even more alarming, so she decided that she had better take a more conciliatory tone. "I guess the time just got away from me."

He snorted in disgust. "And you just happened to be carrying a flashlight for your stroll through my woods. And extension cords. No one needs extension cords to walk in the woods."

He wasn't pointing the shotgun at her, not exactly, but he waved it in her direction. "What's in the backpack, girl? Explosives? Drugs?"

The ends justify the means. That's what she'd been telling herself when she did her little song and dance for Mr. Ogle. She had spent five minutes spinning a tale about recording night sounds in the woods for a class she was teaching. It was disturbing to discover how good she was at coming up with a lie on a moment's notice. She had shown Mr. Ogle her college I.D. and invited him to call the president's office. If he did, Peterson was going to wonder what she was up to. Since when did history professors do science experiments in the field? In the end, she had been able to calm Walter Ogle's paranoia. He had even given her grudging permission to return to make more recordings "for science."

It was pure situation ethics, and she wasn't proud of herself. But even though her work wasn't for science, the information she could uncover did have the potential for changing the history books. Mr. Ogle probably wouldn't care, but the history world, her world, would. So she would come back to the ruin and do her work. Hopefully, she wouldn't run into him while she did it.

CHAPTER 12

Adding more guilt to that lingering from the night before, Merrideth packed her equipment in the Subaru for a Sunday drive that was not going to end at the church. She made the effort to attend as much as possible, but it just wasn't going to work out this time.

She shut the back hatch and then jumped in alarm before she realized it was Brett Garrison standing beside her car and not some Sunday morning rapist.

"Sorry, Merri. I didn't mean to startle you."

"That's all right," Merrideth said with a breathless laugh. "I'm always looking for ways to give my heart an aerobic workout." Then remembering her backpack and other equipment, she positioned herself in front of the rear window so he couldn't see in.

"Where are you off to?"

"You first."

"Sunday School."

Merrideth laughed. "No, really."

"What's so funny about Sunday School?"

"Oh. Sorry, I shouldn't have laughed. It's just that I thought Sunday School was for kids."

"Don't you have adult Sunday School at your church? Sorry, I'm making the assumption you go to church."

"I go to church quite regularly. Since coming to Lebanon I attend services at Bothwell Chapel on campus. As far as I know, there are no Sunday School classes there, for kids or adults." In case that had made it sound like the chapel was not a real, full-service church, she hurried to add, "Reverend Dupont is really good. I always enjoy his sermons."

He smiled. "I suppose it's only natural that a historian should go to an antique church."

"Bothwell Chapel amazing," Merrideth said. "Did you know it was built in 1856? The best part, really, is the bell. It was cast in Spain over a thousand years ago. Some say it is the oldest bell in the country. I get chills every time it rings."

"Ah, the ghosts of Bothwell Chapel."

"Ghosts?"

"Students would say you get chills because the chapel is haunted. Supposedly, a student back in the college's early years hanged himself from the bell tower. When we get a little closer to Halloween, Peterson will begin with the flyers and announcements to reassure everyone that those legends are nonsense."

Merrideth had already added Bothwell Chapel to her bucket list of places to time-surf in. She didn't expect to find ghosts, but it would be easy enough to see if the suicide were true.

"I thought Bothwell's service was at ten o'clock," Brett said. "It's only eight-thirty."

"It is. But I'm not going today. I have a good excuse, really."

"So your ox is in the ditch?"

"What on earth does that mean?"

"It means you have a really good excuse for not going to church. The saying is from the Old Testament."

In that case, she did have an ox in the ditch, because today was the only full day she'd have to explore her find until the weekend rolled around again. And anyway, she thought with a grin, she'd be attending a church service at the fort.

Before she could stop him, Brett moved to the side of her Subaru and looked in the window. "Looks like you're going camping," he said, his nose fairly twitching with curiosity.

"No, not camping."

"An alfresco breakfast for one in the park?"

"No."

"A hike down scenic Route 66?"

Ignoring him, she opened her car door. "Goodbye, Professor Garrison. Have fun at Sunday School. If that's at all possible."

"I will. Goodbye, Professor Randall. Have fun with whatever

you're up to." He walked off grinning good-naturedly.

She got in and started the car. For all his smiles, he was probably annoyed by her secrecy. Too bad. It couldn't be helped. Besides, she the one who should be annoyed by his nosiness and the grilling he'd just subjected her to.

And a grown man going to Sunday School, really? Once again, he made her think of her freshman roommate Emily. Even though she had stopped spouting Bible verses, she had continued to hound Merrideth about coming to her Bible study until she had finally given in just to shut her up. Emily's friends had all sounded like kooks, and they had an extreme degree of reverence for the Bible that screamed *Cult! Run away!* For crying out loud, people should worship God, not a book. So she hadn't gone back.

Granted, Brett Garrison didn't give off kook vibes. Nevertheless, it would be a good idea to stay alert. She pulled into the street and put thoughts of him aside. Now for the project at hand.

Nelda's find was a huge discovery, because otherwise there was no physical evidence left to show where any of the forts that had sprung up along the Kaskaskia Trail had been. She had read somewhere that the raw timber from which they were constructed only lasted thirty years or so. Most were not built on stone foundations, and for those that were, the stones had been carried away to be used for other buildings.

Except for the fort Nelda had found. If it was Fort Piggot, it was a lot smaller than historians had thought it was. If it was someone else's smaller family blockhouse fort, it was not listed in any of the documents Merrideth had been able to uncover, and so it was impossible to know who the people she had seen there were. That was where *Beautiful Houses* would come to the rescue.

She parked the Subaru out of sight in her usual spot and went to the back to unload her stuff. It was another beautiful day for a walk in the woods. If she hadn't wanted to go unnoticed, she would have sung for happiness. Maybe she should. She definitely wanted any hunters out there to notice her. She donned the bright hat and jingling bracelet Nelda had given her and crunched her way through the fallen leaves to the ruins. Once there, she launched *Beautiful Houses*, happy in the knowledge that she would have all day to work.

She had whispered the date to herself all the way home last

night and then jotted it in a notebook, knowing full well she'd never remember it otherwise. After consulting the notebook, she entered it into the program and found her way back to that Sunday in 1795. She debated for a moment over whether she should lock onto the young preacher or his angry parishioner. But since Piggot hadn't been a man of the cloth, at least as far as she knew, she chose the angry man.

And then she clicked *Virtual.*

Filled with rage, William Whiteside felt like the top of his head was going to blow clean off. Martha pulled at his sleeve, but he swatted her hand away and rushed to the front, intent on getting to the preacher boy. At the last minute before he would have grabbed James Kyle Garretson by the throat and shaken some sense into him, he stopped and made the effort to calm himself. Martha was always warning him that his temper would be his downfall. He stood there heaving until the red haze cleared a little. He was relieved that he hadn't strangled the little fool. It would hardly do to kill a preacher in church.

He contented himself with glaring at him. "I may not have as much book learnin' as you, James Kyle, but I'm not stupid. I don't need you to spell it out for me, boy. I know what you're sayin'."

James Kyle closed the Bible and came to stand in front of him. William thought it was a stupid thing for the preacher boy to do, given his murderous rage. But even in the midst of his fury, he gave credit to the boy's father: he certainly hadn't raised a coward.

"I was just preaching the Word, Captain Whiteside," James Kyle said mildly. "You know that. You have no call to disturb the service."

William snorted. "You stand behind that pulpit using the Good Book as a weapon, then I'm goin' to have somethin' to say." He turned to the people. "You all know me. I deal squarely with every man I meet. If a man is honest, I want to be his friend. If I see someone in want, I help him. But if a man comes to my home set on killin' me and takin' what's mine, then I kill him first, no doubt about it."

Shadrach Bond made his way toward the front. The people

85

respectfully gave way until he stood next to James, clearly aligning himself with the boy. "Sounds like you're a might defensive, William," Bond said. "Maybe you're remembering, like I am, that peace treaty we all signed over two years ago after the Battle of Fallen Timbers. You had no call to kill those Potawatomis last month. They weren't at your door. They were sleeping in their lodge over on Shoals Creek. I hear you left sixty dead Indians, including women and children, lying where they fell."

"If I was wrong to kill those Injuns, seems like you're the only one that thinks so, Bond. Judge Piggot couldn't find a single man willing to sit on a jury."

"That doesn't make what you did right, Captain Whiteside," James Kyle said.

"Right? Of course it was right."

Benjamin Ogle called out from the rear, "We ain't never killed anyone that didn't need killin', Bond." His father Captain Joseph Ogle shushed him, but William knew for a fact that he agreed wholeheartedly with him. William had seen Joseph kill a dozen of the Injuns himself. And he hadn't said a word when Benjamin went a little crazy and took a few scalps.

"Maybe next time, Preacher boy, you should sermonize about all the folks that's been killed," William said. "Have you forgotten so soon?"

"I haven't forgotten," Joseph Ogle said. "There's only one way to deal with an Injun, Preacher. That's kill him. They're heathens. When I was just a lad back home in Virginia I saw a dozen heads stuck on pikes. The Injuns put 'em there to warn us off their huntin' ground. Some of those heads belonged to people I knew."

James Kyle frowned and put up a hand. "Please, there are children here."

William Whiteside pounded his fist into his left palm. "You should care as much for the children that got killed, Preacher. My two boys, my brother, my nephew. But not just my family. Pick whichever massacre you want. How about Captain Ogle's niece's family out on Andy's Run? You might mention, Preacher, that the last thing those folks saw before they left this world was the savages tomahawkin' their baby girl in her cradle. At least they didn't know the Injuns carried away their other little girls to give to their filthy chief. And if Captain Ogle hadn't gone after his nieces and ransomed them back, they'd still be there growin' up heathens.

And the captain's son, Benjamin there, nearly died, too. He carries a ball in his shoulder to this day. We've all suffered losses, only I ain't forgot, nor am I goin' to until the day I die."

William saw that James Garretson, senior, had finally hobbled up to stand next to his preacher boy son. People said he didn't have much time left. Whatever was ailing him, he looked near the end, and William felt a momentary pang that he had riled him up.

Garretson leaned on James Kyle and looked up at William from under his pain-furrowed brows. "I came up here to say Judge Piggot is not the only one sayin' you're wrong, William," he said in his croaky voice. "And I'd have been on that jury to say so, if I hadn't been stuck in bed at the time." He reached out his skeletal hand toward William. "Whether we like it or not, God says we're to forgive, no matter how hard it is. Vengeance is mine, he says."

There was no reasoning with soft-hearted fools. William grunted, put his hat back on, and headed toward the corral for his horse. He slowed when he remembered Martha. She caught up with him, as did the Ogles. Benjamin pulled something from his pocket and waved it, tauntingly, with his gimpy arm at the people. William saw then that it was one of the Indian scalps he'd taken. The wind blew the long black hair and it caught in his beard. He pushed Benjamin away in disgust. Captain Ogle slapped his son on the back none too gently and said, "Put that away, fool, before Shadrach Bond sees it. They're fixin' to make him judge. Then we'll have two addlepates on the court."

With considerable effort, Merrideth pulled herself out of William Whiteside's mind, out of 1795 and back to the present. Her head hurt with his residual emotions and those of the people near him. It was difficult to think clearly. The clock on her computer said 9:38, and that was crazy. She'd been time-surfing much longer than that, surely.

The aftereffects of the virtual trips had always varied so much, depending mostly on whose head she had spent time rummaging around in. Her trip down memory lane with the Old Dears in Abby and John's attic last week had given her happiness, overlaid with a poignancy, at seeing them again after so long.

But this trip left her sorting through a much darker brew of emotions. Whiteside had been filled with anger and vengefulness against the Indians. The young upstart preacher had been firmly put in his place for presuming to tell others to forgive that which he himself had not had the misfortune to experience. And from the congregation, Merrideth had picked up a whole cauldron of confused emotions: fear of the Indians, relief at their deaths, disgust with how it had been accomplished, and horror at the scalp the man carried in his pocket as a barbaric trophy.

Merrideth shut the laptop and set it to the side. She got awkwardly to her feet, stiff from sitting on the wall, and stretched out the kinks in her neck. Then, wading through the fog in her brain, she finally remembered the names she had heard. Someone had mentioned Judge Piggot! It had to be the James Piggot she was looking for. And the young preacher and his father were Garretsons. And the other father and son duo had been Ogles. She had hit the jackpot.

She laughed softly. She had told Brett that she too busy looking for Fort Piggot to help Nelda with their family tree. But in looking for James Piggot's fort, she had discovered James Garretson's. She felt sure of it now. The one she had just seen was too small and too far away from the dig site to be anything but one of the small family blockhouses.

Fort Piggot had been the largest of the forts in size and population, but William Whiteside also had a substantial one south of Columbia. He had led a large party of pioneers, including mounted and armed men, from Pennsylvania and built a blockhouse, stockade, and underground powder magazine. They were considered some of the bravest and most daring of all the settlers in the region, and had quickly stepped into the role of Indian fighters and peacekeepers at a time when there were none. She hadn't known anything about the Ogles, but it sounded like they were also Indian fighters. Ruthless ones, she thought, remembering the scalp.

Perhaps William Whiteside had been on his way to somewhere—the seat of government at Kaskaskia, for example, or even to Fort Piggot—and stopped at the Garretson's blockhouse to spend the night within the stockade's protection. His visit must have left him feeling unappreciated for all he had done for the welfare of the people there.

All her thinking had made her headache worse. And there was no sense going back to 1795 without a clear head. She lay down on a thick layer of leaves, closed her eyes, and tried to relax away the pain. The wind blew in the trees, and she pictured the colorful leaves falling around her. One fell on her face and she wiped it away.

CHAPTER 13

The leaves were still falling, only now they were weird leaves that clinked as they landed near her ear. Merrideth reached up to brush them away and her hand came in contact with something furry. Her eyes flew open. Duke was licking her face, his name tag clinking as he moved. She sat up and wiped her face on her flannel sleeve. Duke grinned happily.

Patting his head, she scanned the woods but saw no one. "I'm glad to see you, too, buddy, but you know you're not supposed to come without Mom. Is she out there?" Duke didn't answer. Other than the rustling leaves, the woods was quiet.

It was warmer now, so she took off her jacket and hung it from a conveniently placed tree branch. She hadn't slept long, and there was still plenty of time to work. Actually, she was surprised to see that it was only noon.

Thankfully, her headache was gone. Now hunger was her most pressing problem. She took out the peanut butter sandwich she had brought and ate it, amusing herself by throwing occasional bits of it for Duke to snap up mid-air.

With her head clearer, she began to think. Undoubtedly there would have been interaction between Fort Piggot and the other smaller forts. As members of the tiny population of white Americans who had settled there—the Indians would have said *trespassed* there—they would have been keen to stay in contact with each other and share in their common defense.

So if she went back and locked onto James Garretson, he was

bound to lead her to Fort Piggot, eventually. And while she was time-surfing, she would surely pick up information that would fill in the blanks on Nelda and Brett's family tree—like how the two James Garretsons she had just met were connected to the Cornelius Garretson she had found online. She smiled. It would be a win-win: she would garner both a feather for her career cap and a boost to her genealogy consulting job.

Or was she jumping to conclusions that they were Nelda and Brett's Garretsons? No, surely not. After all, their blockhouse fort was on property that Nelda said used to belong to her family. That, together with the other father/son duo of Joseph and Benjamin Ogle, who had to be connected to her odious neighbor Walter Ogle, was just too much to be a coincidence.

She wiped her hands and patted Duke. "Okay, boy, what to you say to a little time-surfing?" Hopefully, Nelda wouldn't come looking for him while she was zoned out in the late 18th century. She took his doggy grin as a *yes* and opened her laptop. The scene popped up right where she'd paused it at the open-air church service.

By the body language, James Garretson was the owner of the blockhouse, and it was confirmed when the gathering of worshipers left except for him and three woman, presumably his wife and two teenaged daughters. James Garretson was staying put, but the Whitesides and Ogles were leaving—hopefully for a visit to Fort Piggot.

She decided to keep the lock on William Whiteside. She would have to run on fast speed if she didn't want to use up *her* whole life watching his unfold. But on fast speed it was easy to miss things and then have to go back. And the virtual feature only worked in real time. It was a tedious business. She'd been good at it when she was eleven. She hoped she still had the knack.

She set the speed fast enough to get through a lot of time quickly but not so fast that the scene became a blur. She watched as William Whiteside and his wife mounted their horses and left the stockade in company with the Ogles. Unfortunately, they went south, away from Fort Piggot.

She rewound back to the fort, took the lock off Whiteside, and put it on the younger Garretson, James Kyle, as they called him to distinguish him from his father. As she figured, he didn't live with his parents, but rode out of the stockade with another departing group of worshipers.

She tracked his movements on fast speed for the next several weeks of his life, slowing from time to time to listen in on his conversations. He lived with his wife in another settlement a few miles away, but he spent most of his time traveling between settlements, where he ministered to the people and conducted church services in homes. Merrideth didn't slow enough to listen to his sermons. She wondered if he used the same Bible passage that had stirred up so much trouble at his parents' home.

Finally, one day he traveled north, and Merrideth was sure he was heading to Fort Piggot. But instead, he veered off onto a trail through the woods and ended up in a small Indian camp. She knew that hostilities in the Illinois Country for the most part ended after the Treaty of Fallen Timbers, but James Kyle Garretson wouldn't have known that yet. And in view of William Whiteside's recent attack at Shoals Creek, it was brave of him to go alone into the Indian camp. Brave, but foolish. She had never understood why missionaries risked their lives to take their religion to people who had their own and didn't want or need someone else's.

As for the Indians, in a few years war would break out again and not come to an end until every last Native American had been killed, driven west of the Mississippi River, or assimilated into the white culture. The U.S. government would use religion as one tool for the latter option. Whether he knew it or not, young Reverend Garretson was in the vanguard of missionaries who would convert the Indians to their brand of Christianity and attempt to destroy every last vestige of Native American culture.

She slowed a little and saw that he was well received by the Indians, as if they were familiar with him. He ate and talked with them. He got out his Bible and read to them, and they talked more.

It was quite apparent that James Kyle Garretson didn't share the attitude of Whiteside and the Ogles. But then he obviously hadn't personally suffered at the hands of the Indians the way they had. The Bible's command to forgive one's enemies was a tough one to follow. Merrideth knew that if someone killed anyone she loved, she would have a hard time forgiving them. Her natural inclination would be to want her enemy dead, preferably after long, painful hours of suffering. She would definitely not sit down to tea with them as Garretson was essentially doing.

She had no stomach to listen to his preaching, but she wanted very badly to slow to real time so she could experience the Indian culture up close and personal. Wouldn't Publish-or-Perish Peterson be thrilled at a paper on that subject!

But then a new thought ruined her good mood: no matter how amazing the things she learned about the past were, she wouldn't be able to share them, much less write about them, if she couldn't find an outside source, some kind of documentation for what she discovered. How horrible it would be to know incredible details from the past, like the fact that Odious Ogle's great, great however-many-greats grandfather had scalped Indians, and yet not be able to tell another living soul about it. What if one day she discovered that...that...George Washington had a love child with Martha's sister, or that a chest of gold was buried under the Lincoln Monument, and she couldn't reveal it.

She put aside that discouraging thought and focused on the task at hand: finding Fort Piggot. It meant foregoing a virtual tour of the Indian camp, because she knew from past experience how easily it was to get lost on rabbit trails while time-surfing. On more than one occasion, she, Abby, and John had completely forgotten what they were supposed to be searching for. But she did get out her notebook and jot down the date and time so she could find her way back to the Indians when she had more time.

She upped the speed and watched Garretson's meanderings continue. But still he didn't go to Fort Piggot. She sped up even faster until the screen was a blur of pixels. Or were they pixels? Wasn't that only something photographs and other digital images had? It was real life unfolding on her screen, not a photograph or video. Wasn't it? She set aside that puzzle and concentrated on Garretson.

A high-pitched whistle rang through the woods, and Duke perked his ears and got to his feet. Merrideth looked up in alarm. She had almost forgotten he was there. Another whistle sounded, and then Nelda called, "Here, boy. Come, Duke." He barked joyously. Merrideth assumed he would run off to meet her, but he stayed at her feet, as if waiting for Nelda to join the party in the woods.

Feeling all thumbs, Merrideth managed to get her laptop shut and back in her pack just as Nelda came over the rise.

"Hi, Nelda. Duke was helping me study the ruins. I hope you don't mind."

Nelda was all smiles. "Aren't you a good boy?" she said, kneeling to pet him. "But you're naughty for going in the woods without permission." She looked up at Merrideth. "I'm not entirely sure that Walter Ogle wouldn't shoot him if he thought no one was looking."

"Surely he wouldn't kill a dog," Merrideth said. But then again, if Walter was descended from the Ogle she had seen waving an Indian scalp around, maybe he would.

"I hope you're right. Have you made any progress with our mysterious stones?"

Merrideth wanted to say, "Holy cow! Have I ever!" But since she didn't have any way to give Nelda proof of what she now knew, she restrained herself. "I'm pretty sure these are the remains of a fort, but I don't believe it was Fort Piggot."

"Oh, that's too bad."

"Don't worry. Even if it's not, it's a big find." She took her phone out of her pocket and snapped several photos of the foundation. "Silly me, I forgot to get pictures when I was here before." Photos were a good idea, although they seemed a bit redundant under the circumstances and totally lame compared to the real deal. "There, that should do it."

"Since I'm here, I might as well let Duke chase a few squirrels. You want to join us?"

"No thanks. I need to get back to some things I'm checking on. And I haven't forgotten your family tree."

"Don't feel like I'm pressuring you on either of the projects, Merrideth."

"I don't."

"Then you should take time for a walk in the woods while it's so nice."

Merrideth grinned. "Is that a variation on 'take time to smell the roses'?"

"It is. And get Brett to go with you. He loves the woods in the autumn."

"Thanks. Maybe I will," Merrideth said, thinking *not in a million years, thank you very much.*

After Nelda left Merrideth pondered the woman's suggestion. It was just ambiguous enough that she wasn't sure if she were matchmaking or not. In any case, with Nelda likely to come upon her again at any time, she couldn't continue her virtual tour of

James Garretson's life. It was a shame to waste so many valuable hours of daylight, but there was no help for it. She might as well go home and see what, if anything, she could find out about Garretson, the hard way—in a library.

Merrideth went straight to McKendree College without stopping to change out of her jeans and sweatshirt, or as she thought of them, her Dora-the-Explorer clothes. She was not surprised to find Holderman library nearly empty. It usually was on Sundays. But there were always a few students who hung out there to read, some with good posture at the tables and others slouched in the overstuffed chairs by the windows.

In her experience, college students who spent their Sundays in libraries while everyone else was out having a social life did so for one of two reasons. Either they knew that it was the best time and place to study. Or they were introverts and had discovered that the library gave them the modicum of human interaction they required in a non-threatening environment. Both had been true of her when she was an undergraduate. And she had definitely been in the slouching category.

Meghan, a friendly senior who had looked up things for her on more than one occasion, was manning the circulation desk and smiled as she approached. Her eyes flitted to Merrideth's outfit, but she didn't comment on it.

"Hi, Dr. Randall. Can I find something for you?"

"Thanks, Meghan. I'll let you know if I need help."

Holderman Library was small and its holdings limited, but it had subscriptions to all the best research databases. If there was information to be had about James Garretson, she should be able to locate it. She went to one of the computer stations and logged in with her faculty I.D. and password. She entered the name in the Boolean search bar, and variations of *James Garretson* popped up in a surprisingly long list of documents. Most of them were not useful, so she refined the search. And then she began wading through the most promising of the hits to find pertinent information.

Bellefontaine kept coming up in connection with him. She had already known that Bellefontaine was the first American settlement in the new Illinois Country, earlier by several years than James Piggot's. The French, who had lived there first, had given it the name, which in English meant *beautiful fountain*, for the natural spring there. It had been a popular stopping point for travelers along the Kaskaskia-Cahokia Trail. But she had not realized that Bellefontaine was now known as Waterloo, a town not far from where Nelda lived. She probably even did her shopping there.

And she had already known that the Americans who settled there after the French left were veterans of the Revolutionary War, having seen and admired the country when they had served under Colonel George Rogers Clark in the 1778 campaign that had secured the Illinois Country for America under the auspices of the state of Virginia. The newborn United States government had no money, but lots of land. So after the war, the soldiers were paid in land grants. And five men chose the land in and around Bellefontaine. They arrived with their families in 1782, the first of the Americans to come to the Illinois Country. Their leader was Captain James Moore who had been charged by Virginia governor Patrick Henry to establish a military post for the protection of the Illinois Country.

But what she had not known until now was that one of the five men with him was James Garretson from Pennsylvania! Furthermore, Captain James Moore's original log cabin, now known as Bellefontaine House, still stood and was open to tourists on weekends.

It was after two-thirty and the website said Bellefontaine House closed at four o'clock, but if she hurried—and found a suitable place to set up her program there—she might get a chance to learn a whole lot more about James Garretson.

When she stepped out onto the sidewalk, Brett nearly walked into her.

"Hey, I saw your car. I was just coming in to find you." He gave her casual attire a surprised look.

"What? I'm not allowed to wear jeans?"

"Of course you can wear jeans. With a figure like yours you should wear them on all possible occasions. So where have you been hiding? I haven't seen you since Thursday."

She didn't know which was more flattering, the compliment or the fact that he remembered how long it had been since they last met. It made her nervous. "I wasn't hiding, just busy with things."

"Things like the Garrison family tree, perchance?"

"Didn't Nelda tell you? It's *Garretson*."

"No, I haven't talked to her. What else did you find out?"

"Sorry, I can't talk right now or I'll be late." Merrideth continued to walk toward her car.

He loped alongside her. "For what?"

"A museum."

"Cool. I love museums."

"I thought you said...never mind. Just hurry and get in, if you're going."

"I'm going."

"I'm sorry. That was rude."

He smiled, apparently unfazed. "After a while you forget about it."

"What?"

"The ever-present eyes watching your every move."

"I hope so."

Fortunately, she already had her car door open, so there was no worry that he'd do it for her. It would have immediately signaled *This Is A Couple On A Date* to the students on the quad watching them with interest. But who was she kidding? Just the fact that they drove off together would start the tongues wagging.

Sighing, she pulled away from the curb and headed out of town.

"So tell me about this museum we're racing off to see."

"Sorry. If Nelda hasn't seen fit to tell you what I've uncovered, I don't think I should say more. She probably wants to keep it a secret until I'm finished."

"I deduce that the museum has something to do with our genealogy, then."

"I'll give you this much: your ancestor James Garretson, with a *T*, may have lived there for a short time back in 1782."

"In a museum?" he said with a grin.

"In Waterloo."

Waterloo was a pretty town, and small enough that it shouldn't have been too difficult to find the street she was looking for. But she spent several precious minutes driving around before Brett resorted to the GPS app on his phone to navigate them there.

Bellefontaine House looked like a residential home in every way, except for the bronze sign in the front yard that said it was the site of the first American settlement in Illinois and owned by the

Monroe County Historical Society.

"Where's the log cabin?" Brett said.

"I hope I didn't get that part wrong. I *was* reading everything pretty fast."

It was an elegantly proportioned brick house shaded by an ancient elm tree that had somehow managed to survive Dutch elm disease. Everything about the style indicated that it was very old, but it was certainly no log cabin.

"Well, since we're here, we might as well try to find someone to ask about it," she said.

There was no parking lot so she parked on the street. The front door looked too imposing, too closed to outsiders, to be a tourist entrance, so they walked around the house hoping to figure out where they should enter. At the edge of the side yard a little creek flowed, and they went to take a closer look. The stream was weed-choked and unpleasant.

"If this is the *Fontaine*," Brett said with a grimace, "I'd have to say it's not too terribly *Belle*."

Laughing, Merrideth continued on to the back of the house. There was a single car parked on a little lane they hadn't noticed from the front. So at least one person was there. The back door didn't have a tourists-enter-here sign of any kind either, but there was a donation box beside it, so it looked like the right place.

Brett opened the door and she stepped into the house. It was dark inside after the brightness of outdoors. They stood in a hall that went all the way to the front door. At the other end was a staircase to the upper floor. The ceiling was at least ten feet high, maybe more. The walls were papered in faded cabbage roses and the woodwork was stained dark walnut. To their right was an archway leading to a parlor set with beautiful antique furniture and accessories.

"Do you think they're authentic?" Brett said.

"They look it. And accurate for the age of the house."

They heard footsteps coming down the stairs and went back into the hall. A young man dressed in khakis and a dress shirt appeared at the bottom of the stairs.

"Oh, sorry," he said. "I didn't hear you come in. I was upstairs shutting windows."

"Are you closing, then?" Merrideth said.

He smiled at them. "Not now, I'm not. We don't get many

tourists, so we grab the ones we get."

"Really?" Merrideth said. "This is an awesome house. I expected to have to fight the crowds to see it."

"Allow me to give you your very own personal tour."

He was a knowledgeable guide. The house had been built in the 1870s by one of Captain James Moore's grandsons. He started first with the parlor and then took them through the rest of the house. Each room was fully dressed. Every piece of furniture and every accessory now in it was authentic to the period, although some of it had been donated and was not original to the house.

It was fascinating, and the guide was a fount of information. But Bellefontaine was just another distracting rabbit trail. When they got back to the hall, Merrideth thanked him profusely for staying open for them and tried to make a graceful exit.

"I'll be sure to leave a donation in the box," she assured him.

"You can't leave until you've seen the piece de resistance." He gestured to a small door to the left of the hall. It seemed out of scale with the rest of the house, and when he opened it, she saw that the room was a step down. "Voila," he said. "Captain Moore's log cabin."

"Really?" Merrideth said.

"Really."

When Brett saw the room he laughed. "Now this really surprises me. I had no idea the pioneers were into avocado green appliances."

Their guide chucked. "You won't often find a circa 1970 kitchen completely intact. It should be a museum display in its own right, but we use it for the volunteers and our historical society meetings. Believe it or not, behind the ugly wallpapered walls is Captain Moore's log cabin. Thankfully, his grandson had the sense to keep it. He just built the house around it. One day, when we have the funds to hire experts do it safely, we'll restore it to its original glory."

Merrideth nearly stumbled in her excitement. Oh, what stories those ugly walls could tell if only she got the chance to set up her program there!

But then the guide glanced at his watch, and she knew that the tour was over. She and Brett stepped out onto the stoop. The man didn't follow them immediately. Then she heard a beeping sound coming from behind the door and realized he was setting an alarm system. Even John, who had on more than one occasion been willing to trespass for a good cause, would not consider trying to get inside for a little extracurricular tour of Bellefontaine House. If there were crowds of tourists to melt into, there might be a remote chance of getting a few minutes to set up *Beautiful Houses* but that didn't seem likely. Besides, what good would so little time do them?

The guide locked the door and followed them down the steps.

"What about the fort?" Merrideth said. "Do you know how it lay?"

He pocketed the key and turned to her. "Fort?"

"Yes, according to Baldwin's book, Moore and the others built a blockhouse fort here. It was a small military base. There would have been several log cabins. And a stockade wall."

"I'm sorry. I don't know anything about that. I only know about Bellefontaine House itself. You could try calling our president. She may know." He pulled a business card out of his pocket and handed it to her.

"Thanks. And thanks again for the tour."

"You're very welcome."

She and Brett walked to the front and got in her car then sat there for a moment admiring the old house.

"Sorry about that," Merrideth said. "I had hoped to learn more about your ancestor James Garretson."

"Hey, it was a pleasant way to spend a Sunday afternoon."

True, Merrideth thought, but it hadn't advanced her knowledge about the Garretsons at all. And it sure hadn't done a thing to help her find Fort Piggot.

It was getting dark by the time she drove into Lebanon. Brett directed her to his condo one block over and down from her apartment. It was an ugly, utilitarian structure lacking all charm, a rarity in Lebanon.

She must have shown her surprise. He laughed. "As Aunt Nelda said, it's horrid. But it makes up for a complete lack of architectural interest by being brand new and including a weekly cleaning service."

She laughed. "Lucky you. 'Bye."

"See you, Merrideth."

CHAPTER 14

When Merrideth got to her own apartment, she remembered that she hadn't checked her mailbox on Saturday. She unlocked the box and took out a circular for cable TV. Under it was her father's monthly missive. She was in no hurry to open it. It would contain the same empty promises and self-justifying whining that all his letters did. When she got inside, she tossed it on the couch to read later while she ate her dinner in front of the TV. It would cap off the wasted day perfectly.

Merrideth picked through the contents of her refrigerator and pantry and found that both were dismally lacking in anything interesting to eat. She should go get groceries and then prepare herself something healthful and low-calorie. It was adult thing to do. But she was too hungry to wait that long. Besides, the thought of eating alone again was disheartening. Of the restaurants she'd tried, the Tapestry Room was her favorite, but they were already closed, as was the campus dining hall, but that was a moot point because she wasn't desperate enough for company to eat there anyway. The 1828 Cafe was nice, but they were closed on Sundays.

As she went through the other possibilities in Lebanon, a loud buzzing noise startled her. It must be her door bell. Having rung only a handful of times since she'd moved in, it was still a new sound for her.

She went to the fish-eye peep hole and saw that it was the same face she'd just seen only a few minutes earlier, although distorted almost beyond recognition. She admired confidence in other people, really she did. She wouldn't wish her damaged self-esteem on anyone. But coming to her door unannounced as if he just knew she'd want to see him again went beyond confidence. The fact that she *did* want to see him was beside the point. She should feel safe from his wiles in her own home.

She opened the door, and the distortion turned into Brett's normal face. "So you really are a stalker after all, then?"

"What? No! Sorry. I would have called but I don't have your number."

"What do you want?" Merrideth said ungraciously.

"There you go again being all sweet. And cheerful, too. No wonder they call you Merri. Aren't you going to invite me in?"

"It depends. Is your car out front?"

"No, I walked. Why?"

She opened the door wider. "Okay, then you had better come in before someone sees you."

"What is this, a ladies' boarding house where men are strictly verboten?"

"Not hardly. The Oswald sisters below me have male visitors at all hours of the day. And night."

"You, however, are more concerned with your reputation than they are."

"I have to be, even in the 21st century. Besides, I detest having people know my business. But since you're here, you might as well sit down on my horrible couch and try to make yourself comfortable. Notice I said *try*. Here," she said, handing him a throw pillow. "This might help." While he was positioning the pillow behind his back, she saw her father's letter with its tell-tale return address and snatched it up and put it in her pocket.

She sat in her one easy chair and waited to see what he would say. He sat there rubber-necking at her apartment without saying a word. Seeing her apartment through a visitor's eyes, especially his eyes, reminded her how shabby it was. Well, it was as good as it was going to get until she got her debts paid down.

"Sorry it's not up to your standards," Merrideth said. "I wasn't a trust fund baby."

"What?"

"You're obviously disgusted by my apartment."

Brett looked outraged. "I am not."

"You aren't?"

"Merrideth, I was just admiring your flair for decorating. Your apartment makes my condo look like a doctor's waiting room."

"Oh. That would be my friend Abby. She did most of it."

"Does the friend live here in Lebanon?"

"No."

"If not a trust fund baby, what kind were you? A Seattle baby? A Detroit baby? I know. A Poughkeepsie baby."

"I was born in Chicago, if you must know."

"I don't detect a northern accent."

"Mom and I moved downstate when I was eleven."

"Ah, so Professor Randall does have a mother. I was worried that you were spawned by an alien life force and sprang up like a mushroom in the woods."

Merrideth rolled her eyes and kept her mouth shut. She put her hand in her pocket to reassure herself that her father's letter with its incriminating return address was still safely tucked away out of his sight. She had no intention of telling Brett another word about her family. Even his own aunt said he couldn't keep a secret. The very last thing she needed was for her colleagues to learn that her father was in prison. It was bad enough the mailman knew.

Brett didn't seem concerned by her silence. Finally, she said, "If you're here to ask me about your family tree, forget it. As I said, I'm not saying anything until I'm done."

"And when do you think that might be? For some reason, I have become very curious to know."

Merrideth pursed her lips. "Hmm. I remember a professor I once had. Whenever a student made the mistake of asking Dr. Richardson when she would be finished grading his paper, she would inform him that his paper had just gone to the bottom of her pile."

He put his hands up in surrender. "All right. All right. I won't badger you." He paused. "And, anyway, that's not the reason I came by." Amazingly, he suddenly sounded almost shy. "I was wondering if we could go grab a bite to eat."

"Really. How odd. I could have sworn that I told you that I don't—"

He put his finger up. "Shhhh. Don't say it."

"Well, I don't. Surely you remember what happened the time we ate a meal together in public."

"I know. I know. It's just that my condo suddenly seemed

so…sterile. The cleaning service was there yesterday, and—"

"And it hasn't had time to devolve into its usual chaos yet?"

"Exactly! Stupid entropy must have gone into slo-mo. How am I supposed to eat under such conditions?"

Beyond his silly grin, he looked genuinely lonely, and how could she hold out against that? "I'd offer you something to eat here, but my cupboards are bare. I've been busy with things, history things, not genealogy things, and definitely not domestic things like grocery shopping."

"I've got lots of good stuff at my place, but I didn't figure—"

"You figured right."

In the movies during situations such as this, the heroine, or these days the hero, always whipped up a tasty omelet from various items that just happened to be in the fridge. But since the only things in hers was one egg, a partially eaten deli container of mashed potatoes, an onion with brown spots, and a few condiments, an omelet wasn't on the menu.

However, the mental accounting of her refrigerator's contents gave her an idea. "I just remembered I have a can of tuna in the pantry. How do you feel about that?"

"I love tuna."

"Good," she said, hopping up from her chair. "Because that's what's for dinner."

Brett came to the counter and watched as she worked. First, she drained the can of tuna, beat the egg, chopped the onion, and rolled a sleeve of saltines into crumbs. Then she stirred it all together with the mashed potatoes and the last of the pickle relish in the jar.

"Very interesting," he said. "Now what?"

"Now we make patties and fry them in butter. It's not exactly a balanced meal. Sorry I don't have vegetables."

"Hey, onions count. Do you want me to set the table?" he said, looking doubtfully at the piles of student essays covering it.

"Is the counter all right?"

"I'm not picky."

She slid two of the browned patties onto a plate and set it and a fork before him. He didn't waste time. "I don't suppose you'd help me edit Bill's book? By the way, this is excellent."

"Thanks," she said, sitting down beside him. "It's one of the few things my mother ever makes from scratch. So Bill's writing a book?'"

"Oops. I don't think I was supposed to let the cat out of the bag yet. But since I did, yes. It's a sci-fi adventure novel."

"I had no idea Bill could write."

"He can't. It's horrible. Hence, the need for editing. Lots and lots of editing."

"And he asked you."

"I sort of have an eye for details."

"What's it like? The book, not your eye."

"There's much heaving of sweat-glistened bosoms and prancing about with light sabers. I swear there's a fight scene on every page."

"Starring Science Man Bill?"

"No, the main character is female. He refers to her as an 'Amazon warrior-ess.' I'm not kidding. And she sounds suspiciously like Marla."

She laughed at the image. "Does she know of this great honor?"

"I don't think so."

"Well, I'll pass on the editing, but have fun. And speaking of implausible plots, I was thinking about something you said the other day. About cell memory."

"So you were listening. What did I say?"

"You said we inherited memories from our parents. Do you really believe that or were you just kidding? I mean, it sounds crazy."

He smiled. "Out of all that stuff I was blabbering about, that's what you remember? Most physicists dismiss it as pseudoscience. But topics like that get my students thinking. What do *I* think? I don't know enough to make a reasoned judgment. But as Shakespeare said, 'There are more things in heaven and earth, Horatio, than are dreamt of in your philosophy.' Ever since Einstein came up with $E=mc^2$, most of what we thought we knew about the world was turned upside down. Things that used to sound like science fiction are now common knowledge."

"You'll think I'm stupid, but I've never even taken the time to learn what that equation means."

"The E stands for energy. The stuff on the other side of the equal sign is everything else. Einstein was saying that everything is energy. That includes every cell in the human body. It sounds deceptively simple, but the ramifications are immense."

"What does that have to do with cell memory?"

105

"It means that even our memories are energy, each one with its own electrical wave pattern. The Defense Department did an experiment back in 1998. Scientists scraped cells from the mouths of test subjects and put them in test tubes. They hooked polygraph machines to the people and to the test tubes. Then they had them watch violent TV shows."

"The people or the cells?"

He laughed. "I love your sense of humor, Dr. Randal. Their polygraph output showed the wild spikes in electrical energy that you'd expect. And here's the kicker: so did the cells in the test tubes."

"You're saying the people's negative thoughts emitted damaging energy," Merrideth said. "That passed through the glass."

"Yep. In another study, researchers put DNA material in the test tubes they gave subjects to hold. Then they told them to think about negative, painful memories from their pasts. When they checked the DNA in the test tubes, it was damaged."

"So the DNA that parents pass on to their offspring contains their memories, or at least the effects of the memories. The sins of the father are visited upon the children."

"Exactly." Brett looked proud of her answer. It gave her a taste of why his students were so eager to please him.

She, however, felt a black wave threaten to swamp her. It was no wonder, with her dysfunctional family, that she had turned out to be a social misfit with a tendency toward depression. Who knew what kind of damage she had sustained from her parents, including their warped DNA? Worse, what kind of defective DNA would she pass on to her own children one day? It would be criminal to bring any into the world. Not that she'd live long enough to have any. Cancer cells were probably already running amok in her system. *Her* family tree would come to an abrupt end at her stubby branch.

"Merri, are you all right?"

She was startled to find that Brett had risen from the couch and now crouched beside her chair, looking at her with concern. She must really have been zoned out there for a second.

"Sorry. I'm feeling a little tired."

He continued studying her face. The intelligence in his green eyes was a bit frightening. "I don't think so."

"What do you mean *you* don't think so? I should know whether

I'm tired or not. And I say I'm tired."

"We were talking and joking and suddenly you got this sad look, so sad I can't stand it."

"I'd hardly call discussing human genetics joking around."

"We were earlier. What is it, Merri? Did I say something stupid? I'm sorry if I did. Only please smile again. 'A merry heart maketh a cheerful countenance; but by sorrow of the heart the spirit is broken.' Proverbs 15:13."

"Please do not start quoting Bible verses at me, Brett." For Pete's sake, he sounded just like Emily.

"Just trying to help."

"Well, it's not helping. I don't even know why you're here. I cannot, for the life of me, figure you out."

"It's not complicated, Merri. I like you."

"Well, you shouldn't. You didn't say anything stupid, Brett. But you're *being* stupid to hang around me. You should stop hovering. It's annoying."

"I changed my mind. You *are* tired. You've been working far too hard. I'll leave so you can rest."

At the tone of his voice, she turned and saw that his face had gone stiff with anger. He went to her counter and wrote something on a scrap of paper and then thrust it at her. "Here's my number. Call if you need me. What am I saying? Merrideth Randall doesn't need any help, does she? She prefers to go it alone. Don't worry, Merri. I won't bother to ask for *your* number. It would be far too much sharing for you to manage, I'm sure."

And then he left, closing the door quietly behind him.

Good! Now that he and his huge ego were gone, the apartment—her little refuge from the world—was back to normal, quiet and peaceful, just the way she liked it. She could tackle the stack of essays that needed to be graded. She could make a grocery list and go to the 24-hour supermarket. No, she would write off the day as a total waste and go to bed early. She was, in fact, tired and could use the extra sleep. Then tomorrow, she'd be ready for the new school week. And she had the fort to look forward to after class.

But once she had tucked herself into bed in her blue flannel pajamas with the snowflakes, she was no longer sleepy. The evening played over and over in her head. She could almost hear Brett's sarcastic comment still reverberating through the apartment.

She hated that he was mad at her, but when was he going to get it through his thick skull that she wasn't going to date him? Her impulse was to go to him and apologize, but wouldn't that just keep him coming around? So he liked her, did he? Well, it was better if he realized right off that a romantic relationship between them was doomed. If he knew her well enough, he would understand that. She was doing him a service, saving him from wasting a lot of time on her when he could be looking for someone normal.

Her apartment had never sounded so quiet. Around two o'clock she got up and went to the kitchen to turn on the little radio she kept on top of the fridge. There was a late-night talk show in progress. She turned the volume down until the voices were low and murmuring, and then she got back in bed and tried to sleep.

CHAPTER 15

The unusually warm fall came to an end during the night, and Merrideth woke to a cold Monday morning. At least the sky was clear and would give her the most hours of light a November day had to offer while she worked at the fort. She gathered a change of clothes suitable for field work, gloves, and her down coat. Hopefully, it would be enough to keep her from freezing in the woods. Maybe during her lunch break she'd pick up some of those hand warmers hunters used.

It took two trips down the steps to get all the gear and her classroom materials loaded in the car. She tried, unsuccessfully, to convince herself that the extra exertion would offset the fact that she wasn't walking to school.

With nothing in the apartment to eat, she had to stop at a drive-thru for breakfast and arrived at McKendree with barely enough time to get set up in her classroom— and a grease stain on her pants.

There was nothing to do about the stain. So she tuned it out and got on with the day. Stray thoughts about the blockhouse fort and the people she'd seen there came to her periodically throughout the day. Which of them should she lock onto this time? Which one would lead her to Fort Piggot? But she tuned all that out, too, and concentrated on her classes.

But thoughts of Brett weren't so easily kept at bay. She fretted over what she would say when she saw him. He probably wouldn't even talk to her anyway. It was a distressing thought, but she wasn't caving to his attempts to bulldoze her into something she didn't want. If he chose to be angry with her, there was nothing she could do about it.

In the middle of her second lecture, she suddenly remembered that he had called her *Merri*. It had sounded so right, so natural, that she hadn't even noticed or thought to scold him for it.

In the middle of her third lecture, it occurred to her that the look on his face when he left her apartment might have been hurt, not anger. Presumably even the super stars got their feelings hurt. Of course they did. And that was an even more distressing thought.

She mentally composed an apology to make when she saw him. It was a masterpiece of breezy wittiness that expressed regret without actually apologizing for anything. But he didn't come by, so her apology remained unused. As the day wore on, the fear that Brett was purposely avoiding her out of hurt made her feel a little sick to her stomach, and by the end of her last class, it was nearly the only thought left in her head.

As she was setting up her equipment at the ruin, she heard the sound of someone running through the leaves and nearly had a heart attack. Then she saw a flash of color in the distance and realized it was only Duke, wearing his red bandana as he happily chased squirrels. Fortunately, she was upwind of him, so he didn't get her scent and come to her. Then she heard Nelda calling him in the distance, and Duke, the naughty boy, went running for home.

Merrideth found her way back to the church service at the fort and then scanned the people milling around after the Whitesides and Ogles had left in a huff. She turned the volume up and listened as they continued to discuss what had happened. But the wind had picked up, and much of what they said flew away before she could understand it. But from what she could make out, no one was addressed as *James* other than the two Garretsons, nor was the name *Piggot* spoken. Of course, that didn't rule out the possibility that he was there. But there was no good reason for James Piggot to come to church at the Garretsons' small family blockhouse fort, because surely his much larger fort had its own church services.

So she was back to hoping James Garretson would lead her to Fort Piggot. But it might be weeks or months before he had an occasion to go there, assuming he ever got well enough to travel. Merrideth would have to scroll through all that time, hoping not to miss it. She could literally be there until Christmas, freezing her patootie off in the woods, hoping not to be shot by hunters—or Odious Ogle.

After their guests were gone, the Garretsons went to sit on benches in front their cabin. The view from there was not picturesque. They had traded the beauty of the countryside for the safety of the stockade walls. All Merrideth could see from her vantage point was a small log barn, a smaller log shed, and a few chickens scratching in the dust.

She zoomed out until she could see the land outside the stockade. Several head of hobbled cattle and horses grazed nearby, and hogs rooted about within a split rail enclosure. In another enclosure a vegetable garden grew luxuriantly in the rich soil. She zoomed out further still and saw a field of tall, green corn and another of hay. Given the sort of tools available to them, even such a small homestead represented a colossal amount of hard labor and fortitude. The plowing, harvesting, and other endless chores would have been difficult enough for a healthy man. And James Garretson wasn't well at all. Perhaps their neighbors had helped. Pioneer life was harsh under the best of times, and survival depended on collaboration.

Merrideth zoomed back in and found the stockade empty except for the chickens. The family must have gone inside. She set the controls to fast-forward and watched the sun of that day move across the sky until it was dusk. Then James and the women came out of the cabin. He hobbled to the gate of the stockade, his wife and two daughters alongside him. One of the girls climbed a ladder onto a shelf-like observation post on the wall. James picked up a musket that leaned against the wall and handed it up to her. The girl was a pretty little thing, but she aimed the musket over the wall like she knew what to do with it. Then, picking up another gun for himself, James opened the gate and he and the other girl went out. His wife quickly shut and latched the gate behind them.

As if the work wasn't back-breaking enough, they had to do it while carrying weapons, on guard against Indians. It was a brutal life. Perhaps the relentless stress of living under fear of attack had contributed to James Garretson's illness.

Merrideth fast-forwarded, and soon the woman opened the

gate, and James and the girl came in, leading five horses and one mooing cow, which they led into the barn. Apparently, they weren't as worried about the Indians stealing their other livestock. After a while they all came out of the barn, the girls carrying a pail of milk and a basket of eggs. Then they went inside the cabin for the night.

Merrideth paused the action. There was no sense in fast-forwarding any further. She would have more luck rewinding James Garretson's life to a time when he was healthy enough to make a visit to Fort Piggot. Or she could rewind back to the church service and lock onto each of the other men in turn, until one of them led her to Fort Piggot.

Either plan would mean sifting through a lot of time. And there was no sense even beginning now. Dusk was nearly there. Besides, she had tons of work to do to prepare for her classes, including all those essays she had put off grading. And if she didn't intend to starve, she'd have to stop for groceries. Also, she'd have to get to the laundry if she wanted to wear clean underwear, which she most certainly did. So she packed up and went back to her car, telling herself that good things come to those who wait.

CHAPTER 16

After four hours and forty-five minutes of restless sleep in which she'd fought off attacks from hostile Indians, co-workers, and students, Merrideth sat on the side of her bed, trying to convince herself that it really was time to get up. The stress and lack of sleep were finally catching up to her. She wasn't surprised to see a haggard old wino staring back at her from her bathroom mirror. She'd need a gallon of eye drops and another of industrial-strength under-eye concealer to make her look the least bit normal. Or lots of cucumber slices. They were supposed to remove bags under the eyes.

By the time she got to McKendree she felt better, but any hope that her fatigue didn't show was quickly abandoned when two different people asked in concerned tones how she was before she even got to her office. The two cups of coffee she had drunk had given her a boost, but it was fading fast. Taking her empty travel mug, she went to the faculty lounge. Fortunately, it was empty. She refilled her mug from the coffee maker, and tried not to look at the Krispy Kreme box that some evil person had left on the table.

She hurried to the door before her self-control faltered. Before she could escape, the door opened and Brett Garrison and two other men from the math department came in together talking animatedly about something all math-y. It made her head hurt. Out of the gobbledygook she heard *quantum indeterminancy*, which she wasn't sure she'd know how to spell even on a good day.

Nevertheless, she felt her heart jump at the sight of Brett. He didn't look mad. And he sure didn't look hurt. In fact, he looked disgustingly cheerful and well rested. She was annoyed to think of all the hours she had wasted worrying that she had hurt his feelings.

"Hi, Merrideth," Brett went to the table and took a donut from the box. "Bill, here," he said, gesturing with the donut, "was just telling us he agrees with Stephen Hawking about Schrodinger's cat. That is, just hearing about the experiment has him looking for a gun to shoot himself. I'm concerned because, unlike Hawking, Bill has full use of his limbs."

Kevin laughed. "I'd help him find a gun if it meant I wouldn't have to hear him complain about Schrodinger."

Merrideth should have just said a cheery *good morning* and left. But for some reason, she was standing next to Brett watching him eat a glazed donut. It was a double temptation on a morning when she was weak.

"I know I'm going to regret asking, but what does a cat have to do with physics?"

"Well, you see, according to Schrodinger's wave function theory, everything in the universe exists on a continuum of quantum states, and when a system reaches a certain critical point, it both exists and doesn't exist. To prove his theory, Schrodinger proposed putting a hypothetical cat into a hypothetical box with a hypothetical—" Brett frowned and dipped his head to look into Merrideth's face. "You don't look so good. Are you sick?"

"Maybe she's sick of hearing about Schrodinger's cat," Bill said drily.

"No, I'm fine," Merrideth said, wiping her bangs out of her eyes. "Do go on, Brett. I can't wait to find out what happens to the hypothetical cat. Hypothetically speaking."

"No, it's too early in the morning for quantum physics anyway. Have you eaten, Merrideth? You should have a donut."

"Get thee behind me, Satan."

Just as she feared, the blatant show of familiarity had Bill and Kevin metaphorically perking up their ears and watching with interest to see what their single, rock star colleague would say to the new girl on campus.

Brett took her arm and steered her away from their avid stares and eager ears. "You look haggard, Merri."

"Thanks. Thanks a lot." She lowered her voice to a fierce

whisper. "You should get your hand off my arm before Kevin and Bill get any crazy ideas. And do not call me *Merri*." She paused and then added, "At least not in public."

At Kevin and Bill's curious looks, Brett removed his arm. But he still stood in her personal space. "I was hoping you'd feel better after you slept."

"I feel fine. In fact, I can barely keep myself from bursting into a rousing rendition of *Zip-a-Dee-Doo-Dah*."

"No, you are not fine. Any fool can see that. If that brat Alyssa Holderman is giving you grief again I'll have a talk with her, whether you want my help or not. No, it's Peterson, isn't it? He's pressuring you to get something published. I could explain to him that—"

"No! Are you trying to get me fired? Whatever you do, do not say anything to President Peterson. If you must know, I just haven't been getting enough sleep."

"Not because of the other night, I hope."

"Don't flatter yourself."

As soon as the words were out of her mouth, she realized how that little interchange could be misconstrued. She looked past Brett and saw with relief that Kevin and Bill were concentrating on their donuts. But then Bill looked up and smiled brightly at her, and Kevin coughed and turned abruptly away. Yes, they heard it all right. But before Merrideth could think of what to say to correct their misinterpretation, the door opened and Marla breezed in.

"Bonjour, bonjour."

Bill gave her a wide smile. "So how was *your* weekend, Marla?" he said, glancing at Brett and Merrideth.

Merrideth took a step away from Brett the same moment he took one away from her. She wondered if Marla had warned him with the same scenario of doom she had given her.

After a quick scan of the room, Marla's gaze went to Brett and then to Merrideth. "I see I'm just in time." Marla paused. "Looks like Humanities is outnumbered by Math and Science." She smiled at Brett. It was a strange and not entirely friendly smile. Merrideth felt certain now that she had spoken to him about the danger of fraternizing with the new, untenured teacher. "Are you giving the poor woman your famous arrow of time lecture?" She turned to Merrideth. "Brett insists on telling anyone who'll listen all about it. Especially, the new staff."

"No, Mademoiselle White," Brett said with an equally strange smile. "We hadn't gotten that far. But Merrideth is a grown woman. If she doesn't wish to...discuss physics with me, she can always tell me so."

"Actually," Merrideth said defiantly. "It sounds fascinating. I'd love to know about the arrow of time." If anyone were going to insult Brett, it would be her, not Marla White.

"Oh, dear," Marla said. "Now you'll never get him to stop. Don't say I didn't warn you, Merrideth. As Brett will explain, once the arrow's out, it's impossible to reverse its course." Marla took a donut from the box and left.

Bill and Kevin came over to stand by Brett. "What did you do to hack her off, Brett?" Kevin said. "I've never seen Marla so...so icy."

Brett looked unperturbed. "She informed me of a new rule of hers. I'm choosing not to comply with it."

Kevin clapped him on the shoulder. "Way to go, man. She's not the boss of us."

Bill grinned at Brett. "Yeah, way to go, Garrison. See you at the marathon." Then he opened the door and Kevin followed him out.

"That went splendidly," Merrideth said, rolling her eyes. "You know what they think, of course."

"What?"

"Surely you noticed that they——. Never mind." If he hadn't picked up on it, she wasn't going to tell him. There was no sense sending his thoughts down that path. Besides, he'd feel obligated to go try to set Bill and Kevin right, and the more he tried to convince them nothing was going on between them, the more they would believe that there was. The best thing to do was ignore Bill and Kevin and hope they had enough character not to spread rumors on such flimsy evidence.

"Do you run?" she said instead.

Brett chuckled. "I do, but Bill wasn't talking about that kind of marathon. The annual *Back to the Future* movie marathon is tonight at the Hett. We all dress in 1950s get-up. The kids love it. I don't suppose you'd want to go. There are three movies to get through."

"Will other faculty be there?"

"Lots of them will be there. Even Peterson usually comes. But if you mean will Marla be there, no, you're safe from her disapproving eyes."

"Then I'll be there." Merrideth knew full well that it was Marla's bullying that had triggered her contrariness, or she would never have agreed to go. Besides, knowing that Brett wasn't mad at her had made her a little giddy.

"I'll pick you up at 6:45."

"Oh, no, you won't. But thanks."

"Because that would be a date."

"You are such a fast learner, Professor."

Even if they didn't arrive at the marathon together, Bill and Kevin and everyone else were bound to pair them up in their minds and watch their every move with eagle eyes for things to gossip about. But Brett was right to stand up to Marla. As long as Merrideth was careful to maintain appearances—and watch what came out of her mouth—there was no reason they couldn't attend the same school function if they wanted to, for Pete's sake.

It was time she lightened up a little, anyway. She couldn't spend all her free hours hunting for Fort Piggot. If she weren't careful, she'd turn into an obsessive-compulsive nut, and she already had enough issues without adding more. Besides, rushing there after school each day for such a short amount of available work time was foolish. She'd wait until Saturday and then have a marathon of her own.

Merrideth hadn't had time to come up with a really good costume. But she put her hair in a ponytail and crammed herself into a pair of skinny jeans. Together with bobby socks and sneakers, it would have to do. She figured she'd feel like a fool, but once she walked into the Hettenhausen Center for the Performing Arts, popularly known as the "Hett" on campus, she saw there were plenty of other faculty members getting into the spirit of the '50s. Dr. Peterson was channeling Elvis and Jillian, Marilyn Monroe. She couldn't figure out what Kevin's costume was supposed to represent. A sociopathic Albert Einstein, maybe?

The place was crowded but no one was sitting yet, even though the first movie was scheduled to begin in ten minutes. Instead, everyone was walking around in their costumes for the admiration of their friends. The students had gone all out. Every other girl wore a poodle skirt. The guys favored greased back their hair, leather jackets, and tight jeans.

"Nice costume, Professor Randall." Dane Walters was smiling at her, and Merrideth felt stupidly proud of herself for coming. It was the first time she had heard him speak without first being prodded to do so.

"Thanks, Dane. I love yours, too." Merrideth would have said more, but she wasn't sure if he was trying to be ironic or not. He wore over-sized glasses, a narrow tie, and a plaid shirt buttoned to his chin. It was the quintessential nerd costume, but it wasn't that far off from his usual attire.

"What's the movie about, Dane. I've never seen it."

He seemed shocked. "But it's a movie classic, Professor."

"I've been meaning to see it. It's on my list."

"You'll love it. See, there's this guy named Marty McFly. He has this friend Doc Brown, who's a freakin' genius scientist, and he modifies a fabulous DeLorean sports car with flux capacitors, which of course he also invented. Doc Brown gets plutonium to power it from Libyan terrorists, but then they steal back the plutonium and then—"

"What does it do? The DeLorean?"

"It's a time machine. Wouldn't you just love to have one, Professor Randall?"

"Yes, I would, Dane." In the face of such enthusiasm, she felt selfish for not sharing *Beautiful Houses* with him.

"What?" Brett was suddenly there at her side, wearing horned-rim glasses, a narrow tie, and a gray cardigan, a complete opposite of his usual sartorial panache. In short, he looked like an older version of Dane.

Merrideth laughed so hard she snorted.

Dane smiled happily. "A time machine, Dr. Garrison. Wouldn't it be cool?"

"Yes, but don't get your hopes up, Dane. If you think of time like an arrow flying forward—"

"Ah, the famous Arrow of Time lecture," Merrideth said, grinning.

"Oops," Brett said. "There I go again."

"No, really," Merrideth said. "I wasn't just saying that to irk Marla this morning. I want to know."

"Me, too," Dane said.

"Okay," Brett continued. "Time is like an arrow let loose. It only goes one way. It can't reverse itself back into the archer's hand. That's because of the Second Law of Thermodynamics."

"Entropy," Merrideth said.

"A gold star for you, Professor Randall."

"Stop patronizing me and tell me what entropy has to do with time travel."

Brett grinned. "Entropy is disorder. And it's always increasing. Any housewife knows this. As a matter of fact, it was my Aunt Nelda who first explained the Second Law to me when I was eight. She said that no matter how hard she worked to clean the house and keep it repaired, the moment she stopped working, everything immediately started getting dirtier and messier, worse and worse. If enough years went by with no further effort on her part, the house would eventually fall down and decay, completely reverting to chaos. Which is why she claimed she was not allowed to ever get sick. Unfortunately, the process of entropy is not reversible. You'll never see a pile of rotten boards start forming themselves into a little hovel, much less a nice new house. For all of us, entropy, that is disorder, is increasing. We're all dying and will never be able to revert to a younger stage of our lives."

"Well, that's encouraging," Merrideth said. "Thanks."

"Sorry, Professor Garrison. I don't get what you're saying," Dane said.

"I'm saying that time travel is impossible, Dane. At least not back to the past, like Marty McFly does. You'd be going toward a more ordered state, and that would defy one of the immutable laws of physics."

Dane looked like Brett had just announced that Santa Claus and the Easter Bunny were fakes. Smiling sadly, Brett put an hand on Dane's shoulder. "Sorry. Disappointing, isn't it?"

Dane's face brightened. "I noticed you didn't say anything about traveling to the future being impossible, Dr. Garrison."

"No, I didn't. So keep the faith, Dane."

"Okay." Dane's face suddenly reddened and he glanced apologetically at Brett. "Oh, sorry, man. I'm right in the middle of your date."

Brett grinned. "I wish."

"What Dr. Garrison means," Merrideth said firmly, "is that of course we're not on a date."

"Dr. Randall's right." Brett said. "That's what I meant to say."

Merrideth shook her head. "Come on, Dr. Garrison. They're going to start. We'd better find seats."

Dane started to turn away and Brett said, "You coming, Walters?" Dane smiled happily and followed her and Brett to a section near the front of the auditorium. When they were settled in their seats, Merrideth leaned toward Brett and whispered, "Good save, Science Man."

"I thought you'd approve."

Dane said something and Brett turned to answer him. She couldn't hear what they said for the crowd noise. Then Brett looked back at Merrideth and said, "You're smiling mysteriously. What are you thinking?"

"I'm thinking how grateful I am that I don't have to understand physics for the world to keep on turning."

The lights went down, and the movie began, but she continued to smile at the thought that the Second Law of Thermodynamics wasn't so immutable after all. And apparently her *Beautiful Houses* program had never heard about the famous Arrow of Time.

CHAPTER 17

Merrideth paused the computer then rubbed her cold hands together, pulled the red stocking cap farther down over her ears, and took a sip of hot coffee from her thermos. It was now 10:45. The sun was bright, but despite that and her preparations, the cold was beginning to seep into her bones.

For her own back-to-the-past marathon, she had arrived Saturday at sunup, dressed in layers and with enough food to keep her fueled, all night, if need be. If only she'd remembered to get the hand warmers to put inside her gloves. She had parked herself, virtually speaking, outside the stockade walls and then rewound for several years, waiting to follow anyone who headed north toward Fort Piggot. There had been a couple of times when she'd thought she was about to get lucky, but each time, her hopes were dashed. Neither James nor anyone else had gone to Fort Piggot. Their unending labor to make a life for themselves on the Illinois frontier kept them close to home.

The late 18th century farming and household practices were fascinating even at the fast rate they flew by. She badly wanted to slow down and study all that more closely, but, reminding herself of rabbit trails, she had sped past all that in her quest for Fort Piggot. And it had gotten her exactly nowhere.

Why not take a few minutes to indulge her curiosity about the Garretsons' personal lives? For one thing, she hadn't yet even seen what the inside of their cabin looked like. She took another sip of coffee then put away the thermos and glanced at the time indicator.

It read November 21, 1788.

She set the controls to *Interior* and found herself in a much darker space than she expected. But then the windows were small. Most of what light there was came from a fire in the fireplace. James Garretson's wife sat near it working a spinning wheel. She had a dreamy look on her face and was humming quietly.

"It's about time I find out more about the woman of the house," Merrideth said, switching to *Virtual*.

Isabelle hummed as she spun her wool. Part of her mind was occupied with spinning a smooth, consistent thread. The other part was trying to untangle the words to the third verse of a hymn she used to know back in Pennsylvania.

They had sung it nearly every week, and now she couldn't remember how it went. Maybe James would know. A wave of sadness came as she thought of family and friends they had left behind.

Oh, how carefully they had prepared for the trip west! It had taken months to gather the essential tools, supplies, and livestock and for her to dry game and beef into jerky and make enough journey cakes to see them there and settled. But even with all their wise planning and hard work, they had been unprepared for the loneliness and hardship of life on the frontier. Even after six years, James still fretted about whether he had done right to bring them there.

But when the army had granted him his 100 acres for services rendered, he had wanted the rich land of the Illinois Country. James had seen what a good land it was when he and the other men had come with Captain Clark during the war. They and the other four families traveling with them had been the first Americans to settle in the Illinois Country. As far as Isabelle knew, her little Mary was the first child born there.

James had not exaggerated. It was a good land, a land of plenty, if a body was willing to work. And they were a family of hard workers, every one of them. The sound of hammering underscored that fact. James was outside the walls building another split-rail hog pen. Samuel and James Kyle, already doing a man's work at sixteen and fourteen, were helping. Jane was on the stockade wall, supposedly on the watch for danger, but mostly watching for Benjamin Ogle, whom James had finally given permission to come calling. Sarah was churning butter in the yard.

Yes, they were good children, although James had inherited a bit too much of his Grandfather Kyle's sense of humor and had a propensity for playing tricks on folks. Isabelle smiled contentedly. She had much to be grateful for. Plenty of hay was stooked in the field, and their storeroom and root cellar were full to bursting. And once James and the boys did the butchering, they'd be ready to face the winter.

She glanced away from her spinning to the corner where Bella and little Mary were giggling over their sewing. She smiled. On Christmas she would pretend to be surprised by the handkerchiefs they had made for her and their older sisters. The girls would be so proud.

The cabin door opened and Sarah came in, holding the corners of her apron in one hand and brushing a dusting of snow from her hood with the other. The wind came in with her and made the fire dance in the fireplace. Isabelle smiled. Her firstborn's cheeks were rosy, both from the cold and from her churning.

"It smells wonderful in here, Ma."

"The meat is coming along nicely. You'd best hurry with that."

The little girls left their sewing in the corner and ran like curious little goats to see what their big sister carried in her apron. "What did you bring from the root cellar, Sarah?"

"Sweet potatoes, Bella." She tumbled them out of her apron onto the plank table.

"Pa loves them so," Mary said.

"Yes, and I must hurry and get them into the ashes to roast."

Isabelle smiled, happy that her efforts had made it possible for the treat. James did indeed love sweet potatoes, although after the way he had teased her, he did not deserve to have any for his supper.

He had thought it foolish when she had insisted on bringing the sweet potato slips with them from Pennsylvania. But she had faithfully kept their roots moist the whole time their family, along with four others, had crossed the Allegheny Mountains, gone down the Ohio River, and up the Mississippi to Kaskaskia. They had stayed there for a while, but not long enough for her to plant them.

Finally, when they reached Bellefontaine, while James and the other men had repaired the abandoned French fort they were to live in, she had planted her sweet potato slips in the rich Illinois soil.

The harvest had been good, enough to share with the other families that winter. But James said that the soil in the bottom near the river was even richer than that in Bellefontaine, and so with the help of the men, he built their own cabin and stockade there. He had been right about the soil. It was easy to till and their first crops had been wondrously bountiful.

Sarah gently pushed her little sisters toward their corner. "You had best get back to your work," she whispered, "or you will ne'er have your gifts completed in time."

Isabelle pretended not to hear. When she looked back down at her own work, she saw that the little distraction had caused a small irregularity in her thread. Her mother would have scolded her for her carelessness. But she did not let a few nubs concern her. When the thread was woven into cloth, each tiny lump would be a reminder that life was made up of all the moments along the way.

Badger commenced barking, and the girls looked to her in alarm. But then they heard Jane call out a friendly greeting and knew that all was well.

"Sounds like we have company," Isabelle said.

The little girls squealed with excitement and went to stand by the door.

Sarah smiled. "I'll put on extra potatoes, then."

Isabelle eased her spinning wheel to a stop and went to look out the window. Jane had come down from the wall and was opening the gate. The first through was young Benjamin Ogle. Next came James Lemen. Even from where she stood, she recognized his Roman nose and curly auburn hair. He had led a group up from Virginia two years before, saying that for their settlement he wanted a new design, on the order of Williamsburg. The name had stuck and now New Design was a small settlement to the south of them.

"Who comes?" Sarah said.

"It's Mr. Lemen and Benjamin. Jane is over the moon."

James and the boys came into the stockade, closing the gate behind themselves. The visitors dismounted, and Lemen pointed to his horse. The men talked, except for Benjamin who stood a short distance away, making calf eyes at Jane. Then they all walked toward the barn. When she saw that his horse was limping badly, the purpose of Lemen's visit became clear to her. Likely he had lost a shoe along the way. James was an excellent farrier. Folks in the Bottom often asked him to shoe their horses.

"Come away from the door, girls. They won't be in for a while."

The girls' faces fell in disappointment.

"Come on, Bella and Mary," Sarah said. "You can help me set the table."

Isabelle checked on the roasting pork and then went back to spinning. Soon she had the rhythm again, and with it her thoughts turned to the rhythm of a poem she had been working on earlier. When she was girl, her mother had complained about her poetry, said it was a foolish waste of time. Maybe so, but back in that life she had had the time to spare. Now, the only time she composed poems was as she sat at her spinning wheel. She let the words of her latest poem wander through her mind:

Sing: sing in the grey rain,
sing a song of dreams,
of roses and moonlight.
Lonely nights spent in waiting
and hoping.
Where is my love?
He hides himself from me.
Hair of gold and bright silver has he
my favor lies velvet at his waist
upon the gleaming mail.

It didn't even rhyme. But even so, it felt right to her. Maybe she would find a scrap of paper upon which to write it before the thoughts skittered away. She chuckled softly, imagining the way James would tease her. He'd say, "For pity's sake, Isabelle. Are you not a happily married woman? Why are you composing love poems about a knight in gleaming mail?"

"What makes you laugh, Mother?" Sarah was watching her curiously.

Isabelle laughed the more. "Nothing I can possibly explain, dear." She turned her attention back to her proper work.

Then there were voices from outside, and the door flew open. Jane came in, cheeks rosy and eyes bright, ahead of her beau and the others.

"Come in, Mr. Lemen, Benjamin," Isabelle said, stopping her wheel again.

Jane, with a shy smile at Benjamin, took his coat and hung it on a peg by the door. Benjamin nodded his head respectfully toward Isabelle, and the young couple went to warm themselves at the fireplace.

Isabelle took Mr. Lemen's coat. "You must be frozen."

"Not too badly, ma'am. Compared to being baptized in Fountain Creek last December, this seems positively balmy. The preacher had to chop the ice away to get me dunked."

"I imagine right about then you were considering switching to Presbyterian," James said with a grin.

Lemen laughed. "I was, James. I was." He joined the others at the fire. "We are most appreciative of your hospitality, Mrs. Garretson," Lemen said, holding his hands out to warm them. He smiled kindly at Bella and Mary who had come up to stand shyly looking at him from beneath their lashes.

"You are most welcome. Supper will be ready soon. Where are you bound, Mr. Lemen, home or someplace else?"

"For home."

"How does New Design fare?" James said.

"We are well, God be praised. He gave us bountiful crops this year. It is most heartening after our first season here."

"It was a sad time, to be sure," Isabelle said. Mr. Lemen and the other poor people in his party had journeyed from the Ohio to Kaskaskia in mud and standing water. And then the rest of that summer had stayed wet. Disease had desolated nearly every household, and swept many of them away.

"What's the news from Great Run?" James asked. He turned to Isabelle and added, "They've just come from there."

"I don't like to say," Mr. Lemen said, glancing meaningfully at the little girls. "I planned to tell you later."

James studied his guest for a moment. "Bella, Mary, go up to the loft for a spell," he said. "You, too, Sarah and Jane."

The girls obeyed their father, although Sarah and Jane didn't look too happy about it. They were sure to remind him later of their advanced age and maturity. Benjamin watched Jane's progress up the ladder until she was out of sight.

Samuel put on a solemn expression and puffed out his chest to demonstrate that he was old enough to hear the grownup's conversation. "Go on, Mr. Lemen," he said. "What happened."

"Yes," James Kyle said. "We want to know."

"No, you don't," Benjamin said. "It was awful."

Mr. Lemen sighed. "Yesterday John Dempsey was scalped and left to die in in the weeds alongside the trail. Frances Ballew and one of her children found him."

"That's the second attack in a month," James said, glancing at Isabelle.

"Dempsey looked near to death, but the woman set in caring for him right away. Seemed to know what she was doing, too. She says he might make it."

"Mr. Dempsey is fortunate to have her skillful hands," James said with a sidelong glance at Isabelle.

Isabelle doubted Mr. Dempsey's wife felt fortunate that the one caring for her husband was Frances Ballew. For all her skills at doctoring, most of the settlers, especially the women, saw her as a loose woman with three bastard children hanging on her skirts. To Isabelle, it hardly seemed fair to condemn Frances Ballew when no one held Captain Piggot in any less esteem, even though he was the one living in sin with her. Of course under the circumstances, there wasn't much they could do about getting married.

Isabelle was torn. She wanted to be kind to the poor woman, and especially to her children, bless their little hearts, but she did not wish to appear to condone fornication.

Isabelle turned to her guest. "We'll pray, Mr. Lemen, that she'll be able to save poor Mr. Dempsey."

Merrideth popped back to the present and paused the scene. She would need a few minutes to sort out her own reality before going back to theirs. The first thing that came to her in all the haze was that she was sitting like an idiot in the middle of the woods during deer season. The second thing was that she had just met James Lemen.

He apparently wasn't a Baptist minister yet in 1788, but he would become one. James Lemen was considered one of the fathers of Illinois' so-called Free-State Constitution of 1818. He had been instrumental in making sure that it had included provisions excluding slavery and that the revised constitution of 1824 had retained them. His success in doing so was largely attributable to the eight anti-slavery Baptist churches he had founded in Illinois. Before coming west, Lemen had been a friend of Thomas Jefferson, and one of his sons became a friend and colleague of Abraham Lincoln.

The Jameses were piling up. Piggot, the two Garretsons, and now Lemen. Merrideth stretched and took a deep breath to dispel the last of the stray thoughts and emotions from her mind. She took out her notebook and wrote down the time coordinates, as it were, of the spot she'd left off. Then she jotted down the names of James Garretson's wife and their six children. With those details and a little research, she'd soon figure out where they fit in on the Garretson family tree. On another page, she jotted down Dempsey's and Frances Ballew's names in case they turned out to be historically significant to her Piggot research.

She put her notebook and pen away and then wondered what to try next. As cool as it was to meet James Lemen, he wasn't going to help her find Fort Piggot. If she had time, she'd follow him home to see New Design or rewind and go to Great Run, wherever that was. Then it sank in. Great Run. *Grand Ruisseau.* Of course they would refer to it by the English translation.

Merrideth un-paused the scene in the Garretson cabin and transferred the lock to James Lemen. She felt a momentary qualm about not letting the poor man eat his supper before she rewound his life, then chuckled at her foolishness.

"Sorry, sir, but I need you to retake your trip to Great Run, A.K.A. Fort Piggot so I can go, too."

She did a slow rewind, stopping to check a couple of times until she had Lemen and Benjamin just past the Garretsons' hay field, riding north on the trail, heading for Fort Piggot. She let it play forward in real time so she could study the surrounding terrain.

Other than the bluffs on their right, nothing looked like the present. It was still morning, because the bluffs were in the shadows, and she couldn't see much detail. A little fox crossed the road not far in front of them and disappeared into the rocks. They seemed amazingly unconcerned, but, of course, back then seeing wildlife would not have been an unusual event like it was for her.

The prairie grass on either side of the trail, being dormant now, wasn't as tall as when she'd seen it before. That made it less likely to hide lurking men intent on killing them. But still, Lemen and Ogle stayed vigilant, holding their muskets on their laps and constantly looking around as they trotted at a pace meant, no doubt, to get them to the fort as quickly as possible. After a while, Lemen took out journey cakes and they ate them, still watching the trail before them.

The waiting became unbearable, so Merrideth upped the speed. The sun rose quickly over them until it was in the west and lit up the white limestone bluffs.

And then in the distance was Fort Piggot!

It sat to the left of the trail, far enough away from the bluffs to be out of range of guns or arrows, just as the Piggot Papers had described. One of the documents said that the *Grand Riusseau* came down out of the bluffs just north of the fort. That also matched with what she'd just witnessed with James Lemen and Benjamin Ogle. They certainly hadn't crossed any streams getting there, so the creek had to be ahead on the other side of the fort as described.

Glenn and Eugene had been right. So why hadn't they uncovered any signs of the fort during the dig?

Fort Piggot was huge, the man-hours it must have taken to build it mind-boggling. But she hadn't expected it to have a cannon. Its barrel stuck out of a top floor window. Wouldn't Glenn and Eugene love to know that detail! As soon as she got the chance, she would pore over the Piggot Papers again to see if she could find any clues about where it had come from.

The entrance to the fort went through a proportionately large two-story blockhouse that sat in the middle of the front wall, facing the trail. A sentry stood guard at an upper window. From his high vantage point, he must have been able to see for miles in every direction. Obviously, Captain Piggot was serious about security. Merrideth un-paused, and immediately the sentry called out something she couldn't understand. Lemen answered in an equally unintelligible voice. Until Merrideth switched to virtual, it would be difficult to make out much of what they said.

Whatever Lemen said, it must have reassured the sentry. The double gate swung open and he and Benjamin Ogle went inside, Merrideth with them.

CHAPTER 18

A small town lay before them. Barns for livestock were just inside the gate on either side, and Merrideth caught sight of men working inside them. Beyond the barns, seventeen log cabins were crammed in with precious little space between them. In the common area of the enclosure, several children played at some game. They seemed unconcerned with the small size of their yard, but their parents probably got claustrophobic living in such close quarters. Merrideth saw now that the cabins' back walls were windowless and integrated into the stockade. It saved space and lumber, but probably made the cabins even darker than the Garretsons' had been.

While she'd been gawking at the inside of Fort Piggot, young men had come and taken the horses from Leman and Ogle, and now they walked across the common, greeting the children, and apparently meaning to go to one of the cabins on the other side. She paused the action while she decided which she wanted to do first.

She could follow Lemen and continue exploring the inside of the fort, gaining invaluable insight into what life there had been like. Or she could rewind until he was back outside and try to find a landmark that would help her figure out exactly where the fort sat. That seemed wiser, considering the vagaries of technology. If for some reason *Beautiful Houses* decided to quit working again, at least she'd be able to tell Glenn and Eugene where to find Fort Piggot.

Before she could begin rewinding, the cannon went off overhead, nearly causing her to drop her laptop. If she had been in virtual mode it would have surely deafened her. Lemen and Ogle put their hands to their ears and turned back toward the gate. People came pouring out of the cabins in alarm. The sentry called out, and two men lifted the gate's giant oak bar and pulled the doors inward. Several men and a few women came running in, their faces white with worry. The last through the gates was a half-grown boy who was shouting something Merrideth couldn't understand. The men started to close the gate, but a man came out of the blockhouse, waving for them to wait. The boy went to him and continued his emotional speech. The man patted his shoulder then hefted his musket and went to the gate. Two other similarly armed men seemed to appear out of nowhere at his side, ready to go out.

Merrideth paused the action, wishing like anything that she could transfer the lock onto the man with the musket. He had to be Captain Piggot. His aura of command was abundantly obvious. Wouldn't she like to get inside his head! But she couldn't take the lock off Lemen. It was the only reason she had been able to go along with him to Fort Piggot in the first place. If she tried to transfer it to Piggot, she'd be right back at the Garretsons' fort.

She saw that Lemen had also run forward, obviously intending to go with the men at the gate. It made sense. He still carried his gun and was suitably dressed for the cold. Benjamin Ogle was, too, and his eagerness to accompany Captain Piggot was obvious. But Lemen's frowning rejection of that idea was frozen on his face.

Fortunately, he couldn't forbid Merrideth. No telling what gruesome sights would be waiting for them—and her. But while she was outside, she could study the environs for clues to tell her exactly where the fort was. She un-paused Lemen's arrested race for the gate, and clicked *Virtual*.

James Lemen slipped through the gate just as it was shutting. Captain Piggot sent him a glance that conveyed gratitude, but then hurried on. He seemed to know exactly where he was going. The boy must have passed the word.

Captain Piggot led the three of them up the trail to the north.

They went silently in single file, each carrying his gun to the ready. When he saw that the others watched the bluffs, James trained his eyes over the settlers' fields to the left. The crops were all harvested, it being November. That helped visibility, as did the fact that the Cahokia court had granted the land in the French manner; the plots ran in narrow strips from the bluffs down to the river. Normally, none of the fields was so wide that a person couldn't see past it to what lay beyond. But dusk was nearly upon them, and already it was growing difficult to see well. However, he was confident Captain Piggot knew the terrain well.

James had come to Great Run specifically to talk to the captain, to test the political waters with him. It pleased him immensely that Piggot had made his position against slavery abundantly clear, and although James could not condone his adulterous living arrangement, he knew Piggot was otherwise a good and fair man. He intended to encourage him to seek a position on the judicial bench in Cahokia. Having such people in authority was an important part of the plan James and President Jefferson had privately mapped out for the future of the territory. In the two years James had been in the Illinois Country, he had used every opportunity given him to exhort the settlers against the evil practice of slavery. And, although it would be years before it could be implemented, he had already begun writing a state constitution that forbade slavery. In his saddlebags was a rough draft he had been laboring on for some time. He would show it to Captain Piggot when they got back to the fort.

If they made it back. He decided it behooved him to stop thinking about politics and start paying closer attention to his surroundings. After a few minutes, they came to the pontoon bridge the captain had built over the spring-fed creek that watered the fort. The grass and water reeds grew tall and thick there. James felt nervous, wondering if Indians were hiding there, but Captain Piggot led them on across to the other side.

James saw the blood just as a woman's voice called his name. It took a moment to realize it was the captain she called for, not him. Piggot lunged ahead into the blood-striped reeds, following a path that had been trampled through them during some mortal struggle.

When James caught up, he saw that the captain's woman, Frances Ballew, knelt at the side of a man who lay deathly still on a bloody bed of flattened reeds. He had numerous wounds hacked into his arms and chest, but most of the blood that had painted the reeds had come from his scalp, or rather his lack of one. The woman had tied a cloth around his bloody head. The fabric was nearly soaked through, its color and weave obscured by the blood, but he saw where she'd torn it from her blue skirt.

She looked up, relieved to see them. "He lives still, James. Hurry and get him back. I may be able to save him."

"Who lives, Frances?" Captain Piggot said. "I cannot tell."

"John Dempsey."

The two men who had come with them—James forgot their names—looked queasy, but took Dempsey by his arms and legs and carried him back down the trail. Frances Ballew walked alongside fussing with the bandage on his head. Captain Piggot went around them to the front, carrying his gun in firing position, and James took up the rear, doing the same. He had a strong desire to keep his own scalp intact and the blood inside his veins where it belonged, not only because that natural instinct was something every man was born with, but because President Jefferson had sent him to Illinois to stop the spread of slavery—to steer the course of history. And to do that, he had to stay alive in this violent place where even politicians had to be Indian fighters. So he kept his gun steady and his eyes alert.

The sun was nearly gone now, and already it was getting cool. Perhaps it would slow Dempsey's bleeding. That would be a good thing, but the dropping temperature had also caused a mist to rise up from the creek and the river beyond the field, making it all the more difficult to see. They walked carefully through the gloaming, tense and expecting to be attacked. A sound came from behind him, and he pivoted ready to shoot, realizing at the last moment that it was only a flock of turkeys calling to each other as they went to roost.

Captain Piggot wisely waited to call out to the sentry until they were close enough to make it to the gate before any Indians could get there before them, but not close enough to get shot in case they weren't recognized in the darkness.

The gates swung open, and the light from torches and cabin windows shown out to welcome them back. Benjamin was looking over the other men's heads, trying to see if he'd made it back alive. James tried to smile reassuringly, but he had already turned to look in horror at the bloody man they brought.

The crowd cleared to allow them in, and the gates were closed behind them. One woman pulled her little one's face into her skirt away from the sight. In the torch light James saw that blood still dripped from Dempsey's head, leaving a trail in the dust as they carried him to the door of the blockhouse where Captain Piggot and Frances Ballew lived.

A woman pushed her way through the crowd to Dempsey's side. "John, John."

"Let us get him inside, Joan, so I can tend to him," Frances said.

"Get away from my John, you hussy."

Frances' eyes went wide, and then she looked back at her patient. "I may be able to save him. If you let me."

Captain Piggot pulled Joan away and the men carried Dempsey into the cabin. He turned and spoke to a man nearby. "Take Mrs. Dempsey home, Nicholas. I'll send word when we know."

Benjamin was at his side, and James started to turn to him, but the captain put a hand out and said, "She'll need help, Lemen. I have to go talk to the sentries."

Swallowing the lump in his throat, James nodded his assent. As Captain Piggot hurried away, James turned to Benjamin. "Go on to the Huff's cabin. I'll be along later."

James stepped into the cabin expecting it to be a large living space. He knew the captain had three sons and Frances Ballew had two children. Together, they had several more. Wherever they slept, it was not here. The room was much too small, and most of the ordinary household equipment was missing, except that near the small fireplace was a chair and a pallet on the floor. The walls were covered in shelves upon which there were numerous bottles, baskets, and paper parcels much like a general store or infirmary might have.

While he was gawking, the men laid Dempsey down on a large plank table in the center of the room and hurried back to the door, ready to get out of there fast.

"We'll need more water, Philip," Frances said, nodding toward the buckets near the door. "Charles, help me get Mr. Dempsey's shirt off."

James remembered now that they were the Watts brothers. Philip sent a look to his brother and then took the buckets and left to get the water. Frances pulled one of Dempsey's arms out of his coat. Even before Charles finished removing his other arm, she took out a knife and slit the blood-soaked shirt beneath. Together they removed it.

Frances went to the shelves behind her and took down a paper packet and handed it to James. "Put a handful of this in the kettle."

Inside the packet was a pile of dry, crumbled gray-green leaves. He didn't recognize the herb, but a pleasant scent wafted in the air when he poured some into his hand and from it into the steaming water in the kettle. A torch lay ready on the stone apron in front of the fireplace. He held it to the flames until it lit and then took it over to the table where Dempsey lay.

Frances didn't waste time on words, but nodded her approval. With the torch light, James saw that the wounds in Dempsey's upper body were not severe, God be praised. Indeed, Frances didn't seem overly concerned with them. After a quick survey of the man's chest, she went to his head and began unwinding the bandage.

Philip came in with two buckets of water. Before the door shut, James saw that people still stood talking in low voices in the common.

"I brung the water like you said. But what's the use of any of this?" Philip said querulously. "He's going to die. They scalped him, didn't they?"

"He's right," Charles said. "Even if you patch him up enough so's he don't die tonight, how's he goin' to live without a scalp on his head?"

Frances Ballew looked up with the bloody bandage in her hands. "I've been reading Dr. Vance's tract. There's a procedure that…well, anyway, I think there's a way to give Mr. Dempsey back a scalp."

Philip sneered in blatant disdain. "That's crazy. I can't stay here no longer. I've got a wife and young'uns to see to."

With a last glance at Dempsey, the brothers left, not bothering with any of the common courtesies due a woman.

"Are you leaving, too, Mr. Lemen?"

"No, ma'am. I'll stay."

"It may work, you know. Dr. Vance's procedure. I saw a man in Carolina that survived because of it. He was scarred something fierce, and of course his hair did not grow back. But he was alive and well enough to work his fields. And I have the awl."

"Awl?"

"Dr. Vance says to drill holes through the skull every inch. You have to be careful not to go all the way through to the brain."

He must have shown his horror at the thought, because she quickly added, "You're wondering why I would do that. Hasn't the poor man suffered enough? The drilling causes proud flesh to grow. And then you drill through that, as many times as it takes for true skin to start forming. I know it sounds barbaric, but I saw that it works."

"You don't have to convince me, ma'am. Just tell me what to do, and I'll do it."

She grinned. "Aren't you the brave one. Rest assured, Mr. Lemen, we won't be doing any of that tonight. We've got to cleanse Mr. Dempsey's wounds and let him recover his strength before I put him through that."

Merrideth stopped the action, counting herself fortunate that she didn't have observe any of poor Mr. Dempsey's ordeal unless she wanted to, and she definitely did not want to. Then she set her laptop on the wall and stood to stretch. She did a little happy dance, to get her own blood moving, but also because of what she'd just learned about James Lemen.

It was true! Both were true: Thomas Jefferson, like Lincoln, opposed the spread of slavery into the territories, and the secret compact between Lemen and Jefferson was real, not a pleasant myth as she had previously believed. It was one of the little mysteries that got historians into arguments at parties, and she had just solved it. But it was maddening to know that she couldn't say one blasted word about the compact until, and unless, she got tangible proof.

But she would have to leave that challenge for another day, because finding the proof could take weeks of sifting through time. Which reminded her, what the heck was wrong with the clock on her computer?

She rubbed her temples and tried to think through the fog in her brain. She had followed James Lemen and Benjamin Ogle from a point just north of the Garretsons' all the way to Fort Piggot.

And then she had gone along with Lemen and Captain Piggot as they searched for the wounded man and then watched as Frances Ballew began treating him.

Altogether, she had spent most of a day and evening with Lemen, and the vast majority of that had run in real time. And yet, according to the clock on her computer, it was only two forty-five. She took out her phone and saw that the time on it matched. Only a little over two hours of her time had gone by.

There was no way around it. Something weird was happening to time.

Apparently, her hours were not equal to their hours, but why had she never noticed that before? The disparity must be small. For short time-surfing sessions it wouldn't be apparent unless she monitored her time closely, and she was always far too excited about what she was seeing to pay much attention to the clock.

But today she had time-surfed long enough that the discrepancy between her time and theirs accrued enough to become noticeable. As far as she could recall, today's marathon session was the longest she had ever time-surfed in one sitting. Before today, she had only been able to catch a few minutes here and there before it got too dark. And even back in the day with Abby and John there had always been interruptions, someone snooping around right when things were getting interesting.

So time was actually warping! She shook her head in amazement. It reminded her of a book she had recently read aloud to the girls—*The Phantom Toll Booth*. They had all thought the part about Milo's subtraction stew very funny. The more stew Milo ate, the hungrier he got. *Beautiful Houses* was acting in a similar fashion. The longer she time-surfed, the more time she had to do it. It meant that that every time she had fast-forwarded to save time she had actually been wasting it.

Except, of course, there was the boredom factor. She wouldn't be able to bring herself to watch every mundane minute of Lemen's or the Garretsons' lives as she continued her efforts to find Fort Piggot, even if it saved time over fast-forwarding.

She wished more than ever that she could tell Brett about her program and especially the time discrepancy it created. It would probably prove some theory he and other physicists worried over. But there was no way on earth Brett would want to keep it a secret, or even be able to. So she was on her own for the time being.

It was time to turn her thoughts away from time theory and back to the practical. She needed to examine the bluffs outside of Fort Piggot if she were to have any hope of finding its location. She sat back down and rewound to the point where James Lemen and Benjamin Ogle were almost to the fort. Then she paused them and zoomed out so she could see the bluffs to their right. It didn't help. Since Lemen wasn't looking at the bluffs, the angle was too acute for her to see much detail. But then she remembered the program's perspective tool. After a minute of refreshing her memory on how it worked, she manipulated the point of view until she was facing the bluffs, which was pretty amazing, since Lemen still faced north.

With the sun in the west, the bluffs were well lit. She zoomed in a little closer. If she could find and memorize any distinguishing features in the limestone she would be able to pinpoint them in her own bluffs now. Then it occurred to her that she didn't need to worry about remembering. Using the computer's screen shot feature, she captured an image of the section of the bluffs nearest to where Lemen stood. She labeled and saved that file, and then moved forward to the next section and did the same. She repeated the procedure five times until the program wouldn't let her go any farther from Lemen. But it didn't matter. The *Grand Ruisseau* Creek was only a little to the north of her last screen shot. Now, if she printed out the images of the bluffs, with a little luck she could track down the section of the bluffs James Piggot had seen when he opened the gates of his fort.

CHAPTER 19

Merrideth laid the six 8x10 prints in geographical order along her kitchen counter. She had ordered them from Walmart's one-hour photo lab as glossies for the sharpest clarity possible, but even so, the images weren't the greatest. And at first glance there wasn't enough detail to distinguish one section of the bluffs from the next. They were composed of sedimentary layers of limestone all pretty much the same whitish color. She took out the magnifying glass she had bought. After a few moments of poring over the photos, she began to see recognizable differences in shapes and colors. Maybe all those hours of doing jigsaw puzzles with the Old Dears were paying off.

In one photo an upper layer of stone projected over the main face of the bluff like a triangular roof. In another, the layers were ruffled like limestone icing oozing from a limestone layer cake. And in one, the bottom portion of the bluff was flattened, the usual horizontal striations missing.

Surely it wouldn't be too difficult to find one or more of those geological features.

Feeling like a public spectacle, Merrideth stood shivering on the narrow shoulder of Bluff Road, waiting for a group of motorcycles to go by so she could to cross to the other side. To the drivers it was a leisurely drive down a scenic route on a Sunday afternoon. From her point of view as a pedestrian, the traffic whizzed past in an alarming fashion. Perspective was everything.

She had driven back and forth along the stretch of Bluff Road in front of the dig site numerous times, rubber-necking to observe the rock formations south of Carr Creek. The drivers behind her had been annoyed at her slow speed. And she had been frustrated that she couldn't see the bluffs clearly enough to find the distinguishing details she was searching for. In the years since James Lemen had traveled the road, too many trees had grown up in the rich soil at the foot of the bluffs. Finally, she had pulled off and parked at the edge of Mr. Schneider's bean field where she and the other volunteers had spent so many fruitless hours digging and waited to get across the road for a closer look of the bluffs.

Eventually the traffic cleared, and she race-walked across, clutching the short stack of crucial 8x10 photos. She paused before going on to study the terrain. Just past the shoulder there was a shallow ditch, and just past that, the ground rose steeply to meet the limestone bluffs beyond. She hadn't counted on it being so…earthy. Nor had she expected a history professor's job to involve getting dirty or being exposed to the dangers of broken ankles, poison ivy, and snake bite. And birds. Glenn had said that swallows nested in the crevices of the bluffs and came swarming out on summer evenings to catch mosquitos. It sounded too much like that Alfred Hitchcock movie. Did swallows migrate south for the winter? If so, when? That made her think of the snakes again. Were they fully hibernating in early November, or did they come out on sunny Sunday afternoons to warm themselves on the rocks?

Putting those disturbing thoughts out of her head, she prepared to go forth and conquer. Then a horn honked behind her, and she nearly jumped out of her skin. When she turned, she saw that Brett had pulled onto the narrow shoulder and was leaning out of his passenger window. He did not look pleased to see her.

"It wouldn't have hurt for you to call me, you know." His voice was tinged with exasperation. A car zoomed past, drowning out the rest of whatever he was yelling at her about. He waved and then drove back onto the blacktop. She assumed he was leaving, having gotten whatever he was mad about off his chest, but he merely made a U-turn and parked next to her Subaru in Mr. Schneider's field. Then he was out of his car and jogging across the road to her. She remembered the 8x10s in her hand and reluctantly folded them and stuffed them into her coat pocket.

He was muttering something about stubborn women when he got to her side of the road. "So what's wrong with your car? The tires look okay."

"Of course they look okay. They're brand new. I take excellent care of my car."

"If you're not having car trouble, then what are you doing standing on the side of the road?"

"You're right. We shouldn't stand so close to the traffic. I'm going to go in there," she said pointing toward the trees, "and you hurry along to wherever you were going. Aunt Nelda's, I presume."

She climbed a couple of feet up the slope. Instantly she got her sneakers muddy. Then she slipped and one denim-covered knee landed in the mud, too. But it was worth it, because now that she was under the trees, she finally got her first good look at the bluffs. Tiny electronic beeps came to her, and she turned. Brett was still there. And he was still frowning, only now he held his phone to his ear.

"Aunt Nelda?"

He paused to listen to what she said, all the while glaring at Merrideth. "Sorry. Something's come up. I don't think I'm going to make it today, after all." After another pause, he said, "Love you, too," and put his phone in his pocket.

Merrideth came back down to where he stood and did some glaring of her own. "There is absolutely no need for you to cancel your plans out of some misguided notion that I need to be rescued. I am perfectly capable of going for a Sunday afternoon walk along the bluffs without some man to keep me company."

"Are you finished? Because here's the thing, I am not leaving you alone out in the…the wilderness. So deal with it."

"If you insist on accompanying me, then you have to go where I say."

"Just lead on, Sacajawea."

She rolled her eyes and started back up the slope, careful not to slip, so he wouldn't feel the necessity of helping her. Oak trees with their stubbornly clinging leaves shaded many parts of the bluffs, but in other places where the leaves were down, the limestone glowed, lit by the sun.

Beside her, Brett stopped and stared up at the bluffs. "Up close and personal, they're a lot more intricate than I realized."

He was right. There were crevices, cracks, indentations and other remarkable details. However, none of them within sight looked the least bit like the photos in her pocket, as far as she could remember. But that was probably because the scale was wrong. The photos had been taken from down on the trail, and she and Brett were standing much closer to the bluffs.

She'd like to take the photos out for another look, but how was she supposed to do that with Brett hanging over her shoulder?

"Okay," he said. "They're beautiful. Can we go home now?"

"*You*, Tonto, can go home anytime you like. I'm exploring."

"When I saw your car, I stopped to see if you needed help with a flat tire. I should have asked if you needed a lift back to the loony bin."

"Ha, ha. Come on. We'll have to go back down and walk along the side of the road a little farther."

"While avoiding being turned into roadkill by distracted motorists."

"Yes, that. Then we'll climb back up under the trees to examine the next stretch of bluffs."

"Right-o," he said with a posh British accent. "So, you're exploring the bluffs by yourself, in the middle of the winter because you're looking for—" He stopped and grabbed her hand. "You're looking for Fort Piggot."

She shook his hand off and continued down the slope. "I'm not likely to find it so close to the bluffs, now am I? The settlers would be sitting ducks to anyone shooting down at them. Come on. Yours is not to question why."

"But to do or die."

"Exactly."

The search area was relatively small, but even so, exploring was hard work for the non-pioneer, not that Brett seemed to notice. At least the exertion kept her warm. She sighed deeply. If her colleagues only knew what she endured for the sake of history.

Three hours later, the afternoon was growing old, and her patience was wearing thin. Brett, however, continued to follow her up and then down each section of the bluffs, without once complaining. Patience was an admirable quality, and she wished she had more of it.

And then she saw that the base of the bluffs they now stood in front of was not like that surrounding it. It was the first significant difference she had noticed all afternoon.

Brett heaved a disgusted sigh, apparently finally near the end of his patience. "If you would tell me what we're looking for, I might be able to spot it with my keen explorer eyes."

"So, Indiana Jones, notice anything different about that stretch of limestone?"

"It's black instead of the usual white." Without waiting for him, she took off up the slope. Brett reached her side only a moment later.

The black stone was flat, and instead of the usual horizontal layering there were vertical ridges reaching four or five feet high.

"What caused it to turn black?" he said.

"You're the man of science."

He rubbed away a patch of it. "It's some sort of mold or algae."

Beneath the mold the stone was the normal white color. And there were gouges.

"Oh! Look, Brett!" In her excitement, she slipped and sat down suddenly then scrambled up to rub away more of the mold. She took off her leather glove and ran her fingers over the scars.

Brett squinted at the scars in the limestone. "They're definitely man-made."

"Would you say they're the kind of gouges a stone cutter's chisel might make?"

He stared at her. "I would. I would also theorize that the limestone here blackened over time because the open wounds were a more hospitable climate for the mold to grow."

"We know Piggot and his men got slabs of limestone for the foundations of their cabins and the blockhouse from the bluffs. Getting them to the site would have been hard work, so *I* theorize that they procured the stone closest to hand."

"Like right in front of the fort," he said, grinning at her.

"Exactly."

They scrambled down the slope, crossed the road, and looked up at the bluffs.

"Now that I think of it, probably lots of people have harvested stone from the bluffs down through the years," Brett said. "You shouldn't get your hopes up."

Merrideth took the photos from her coat pocket, unfolded them, and clutched them to her chest. "Brett, I have something here that I think will confirm that I'm right. Unfortunately, I'm not at liberty to show them to you."

"Oh, come on! That's only going to make me be even more curious."

"I tried to get you to go home."

He shook his head wearily and turned away. "All right. But you're killing me."

She shuffled through the photos, hurrying in case Brett's curiosity got out of hand and he wrested them away from her.

It hadn't been noticeable when they had were so close to the bluffs, but now that they were down on the road, several details in the limestone matched one of the photos. The only major difference was that where now the base of the bluffs was black, in the photo it was white, whiter, in fact, than normal. Like it would be if someone had recently cut away the face of the stone.

She stuffed the photos back in her coat pocket. "You can turn around now."

"Well?"

"This is it. I'm sure of it."

A passing motorist honked. She caught his surprised look as he passed and realized she must have looked deranged, standing at the side of the road smiling up at the bluffs. They took a step back for safety sake, but she couldn't stop smiling.

Then she turned and looked to the west. A plowed field extended to a line of trees in the distance. It was empty except for a single large oak tree that farmers had been plowing around for a long time. On a treasure map there would have been an X with the words *Dig here* next to the tree.

"And there's where it was. Can't you just see it rising from the plain?"

"Not really. Since I have no idea what it looked like."

"Oh, I guess you don't."

"Congratulations, Dr. Randall. What a triumph it will be for you."

She grinned. "Thanks, Dr. Garrison. It will, won't it?"

"We'd better start hoofing it back to our cars before the light is gone."

"You're right." They started walking, keeping as far from the road as possible without falling into the ditch. The field and their two cars parked in it were not visible. They had explored their way farther south than she realized.

She stopped walking, and Brett turned to see why.

If she were the type to cry, she would have. "You'd better take back your congratulations, Brett. Some explorer I am. There's no creek."

"Creek?"

"Glenn and Eugene think that Carr Creek is the one the French called the *Grand Ruisseau*, the one that flowed just north of the fort."

"Then why were we looking so far away from it?"

"Because I thought that maybe they were wrong about Carr Creek. Maybe one of the other smaller creeks was really the *Grand Ruisseau*. But look around you. There's not even a drainage ditch in sight."

"But what about your evidence? You know, the evidence in your pocket that you won't let me see?"

She sat down on the road bank, her back to Brett—and to the blasted bluffs—and looked at the lone oak tree in the distance. It was just an ordinary tree, after all, and there was no treasure buried in the field. It must have just been wishful thinking that had her seeing details in the photos that matched the bluffs before them. Because that just couldn't be right. "It's like one of the Old Dears' jigsaw puzzles. You find a piece with just the right coloration and even the correct number of sticky-out thingies in the correct configuration, but when you go to put it in place, it doesn't fit. You find out later that it goes in a completely different location next to the tulips."

Brett laughed. "Sticky-out thingies?"

Merrideth looked up in alarm. "Did I say that out loud?"

"Yep. So who are the Old Dears? They sound like characters from Dickens."

"My grandmas. They were identical twins."

"How is it possible to have twin grandmas?"

"Don't be ridiculous. Of course you can't." Unless you came from the sort of family where they play banjos on their front porches. And even hers wasn't that dysfunctional.

"Okay, putting aside the Old Dears and sticky-out thingies, I'd be happy to peruse your evidence, if you like. I'm just saying."

"I told you I can't. Besides, it's pointless. There's no creek." Merrideth got up from the bank and brushed off the seat of her jeans. "I'm going home to nurse my wounds. I'll come back and try again next weekend. Just please don't tell anyone what a moron I've been."

Brett grabbed her coat sleeve to keep her from walking away.

"Think about it, Merri. Glenn based the fort's location on its position relative to Carr Creek *and* the bluffs. The bluffs are solid and unmoving. They haven't gone anywhere since this Piggot guy built his fort."

"Right." And not since James Lemen and Benjamin Ogle had traveled along the Kaskaskia Trail over 225 years before.

"But a creek is a transient thing," Brett said. "Events could have caused it to change course over the years. Think of the human activity down through the years. Roads and houses, whole subdivisions, have been built. And natural forces are always at work, too. After all, this is a Karst area, prone to sinkholes. And earthquakes aren't unheard of either."

Merrideth wanted to hop with excitement. "The New Madrid Earthquake! Of course, what was I thinking? Back in 1811, it caused the mighty Mississippi to change course, forming a new channel. And if it could do that, it could also change the course of the *Grand Ruisseau*. Maybe Carr Creek is right after all, only now it comes down out of the bluffs farther north than it once did."

"If that evidence you have there in your pocket suggests that the fort was built in front of this section of the bluffs, then I wouldn't worry too much about the creek."

She would tell Glenn and Eugene to bring the dowser to the field with the oak tree. And the field would yield its secrets, and at last they'd know exactly where Fort Piggot had been. "I can't tell you how happy this makes me."

He grinned. "You could try."

He surely understood the thrill she felt at finding Fort Piggot, so there was no need to tell him that. And the other emotions flooding her system had something to do with being with him, with sharing the discovery with him. And she *would* not tell him that. "Listen, about the other night," Merrideth said. "I'm sorry. I was rude to you. It's hard for me to trust people."

"I noticed that," Brett said wryly. And then he smiled broadly. "And yet you trusted me just now with your secret evidence."

"No, I trusted you with the knowledge that I *have* secret evidence."

"It's a step in the right direction," he said, grinning. "Now let's get out of here before some motorist hauls us both off to the loony bin."

CHAPTER 20

Merrideth arrived at McKendree on the Wednesday morning before Thanksgiving, wishing she knew how to whistle to express her cheerfulness. She felt virtuous for having walked, even though the morning was cold. And she was pleased that her new earmuffs had kept her warm the whole way. A hat or scarf would have meant a bad hair day. And the weather app on her phone displayed three snowflakes, indicating snow was in the forecast, which was always a cause for celebration in Merrideth's opinion.

Furthermore, she only had two classes to teach, and then the four-day weekend began. And, even though her mom was skipping out on Thanksgiving as usual, Abby had invited her to their house. She was even letting her bring the cranberry sauce, which showed a tremendous measure of trust on Abby's part. Merrideth wasn't exactly famous for her culinary skills, and Abby was a world-class cook. Not wanting to chance any blunders. Merrideth had asked Abby for her recipe. She was stopping after class to get the ingredients, so she could make it tonight.

The endorphin buzz from her walk continued all the way to her office, but ended when she unlocked her door and saw one of President Peterson's notecards with the college logo imprinted on the front lying on the floor. Even though it was still early, she immediately felt an irrational sense of guilt for not having arrived before he had. Would he think she was slacking because of the holiday?

She opened the note and saw that he'd written only two lines:

Please stop by my office when it's convenient. Peterson. It was concise to the point of rudeness. There were a million things she could read between the lines. Maybe students had complained about her distraction the past few weeks or the time it took her to return their papers. Maybe one of her fellow instructors had expressed a concern about her sleep-deprived zombie pallor. She herself had thought once or twice that her blood-shot eyes and dark shadows made her look like she had been boozing it up. Or worse, maybe Bill had started rumors about her and Brett that had gotten exaggerated into something sordid.

When it was *convenient*? There was no convenient time today. But she sure wasn't going to wait until Monday and let worry stew in her gut over the holiday weekend. She might as well go get it over with before classes started. She hung her coat on the antique coat tree Abby had bought her as an "office warming" gift. Turning, she saw Marla at the door, angrily wiping her eyes with a tissue

"So you got one too," Marla said. "Do I have mascara running down my face?"

"A little. Not too bad. You got a note from Peterson?"

Marla stepped inside and shut the door. "Yes, I just came from there. I felt like a twelve-year-old being sent to the principal's office."

"Why?"

"He heard about the argument with Bill Weisner."

"What argument? I didn't hear about it."

"That's because you don't spend much time in the lounge. You're wise not to. I know that, but I always end up there. Yesterday I got fed up with Bill and let him have it."

"Why, what did he do?"

"Just the usual stupid comments, but something snapped and there I was screaming at him. So Peterson calls me in to ask all concerned if I'm having personal problems and need to take time off. I swear he was dying to ask if I had PMS. Of course, Bill didn't get called on the carpet. Just me. This is precisely the kind of thing I warned you about."

"What stupid comments? All I've ever heard Bill talk about is weird physics mumbo jumbo."

"How could you miss it? He's always making sly digs about how superior Math and Science is to every other department. Well, yesterday he went too far. He said Humanities is the junior varsity department at McKendree. Kevin and Brett were right there and didn't say a word against him."

"Really?" Brett was so going to hear from her about that.

Marla pointed to the note from Peterson on her desk. "So what did *you* do?"

"I have no idea, but I guess I'll find out soon enough."

"Well, good luck."

Merrideth locked her door and began the long walk to the president's office. When she got there, Pamela, Peterson's executive assistant, was nowhere in sight, so maybe Merrideth would at least get points for being there before her.

His door was open, but Merrideth didn't know him well enough to just walk in. As usual, Lloyd Peterson was dressed dapperly in a three piece suit and bowtie. She'd heard one tenured member of the faculty tease him about being a walking caricature of a college president. Merrideth tapped on the door frame, and he looked up from the newspaper he was reading.

"Come in, come in, Dr. Randall."

"I came as soon as I saw your note."

"You needn't have rushed. Sit down. I've been wanting to talk to you about your performance. And then—"

"I've been getting more sleep lately. And I've nearly caught up on the freshman midterms." For crying out loud, she'd just interrupted the president of the college. She clamped her lips together and waited to hear what he would say.

"And then this was in yesterday's paper." He turned the newspaper around for her to see. It was the article about the Fort Piggot find. The reporter who interviewed her and the others had been vague about when the article would come out.

"Why didn't you tell me about your discovery, Dr. Randall. This is marvelous. How did you do it?"

Merrideth wheeled out the statement she'd come up with and perfected. "Mine was a small role. The bulk of the credit goes to Glenn Parton and Eugene Parks. Lots of people put in hours and hours of work. Even Brett...er...Dr. Garrison, helped a lot. He spent a Saturday morning at the dig."

"He was in here earlier and didn't say a word about his involvement. You're both too modest, Dr. Randall. I assure you this is going on the faculty hall of fame. And I hear good things about your classroom performance, too. One of your students put a most complimentary note about you in the Compliments and Comments box in the library. I won't mention any names, wink, wink, but rumor has it that it was Alyssa Holderman, certainly not an easy-to-please young lady."

"Thank you, President Peterson."

"Keep up the good work, Dr. Randall."

Merrideth left in a daze. Now she really felt like whistling. But then she remembered Brett, and the urge to whistle passed. She looked at her watch. There was still time to have a little talk with him before her first class.

The math and science department in Voigt Hall was quiet, and she wondered if some instructors were getting a head start on the holiday. She saw Bill Weisner busy at a desk in one office. On the wall behind him was one of those parody motivational posters. It showed a fast-food packet of French fries, and the caption read, *Not everyone grows up to be an astronaut.* She couldn't help but smile, but the poster surely wasn't encouraging to students who came asking for help with their math. Of course, that was probably a rare occurrence for Bill Weisner. She didn't stop to ask him directions to Brett's office, because she was pretty sure she wouldn't be able to prevent herself from choking him. Then she heard Brett's voice coming from another room down the short hall. She thought at first that he talking on the phone. But then a young female voice said, "Thanks, Professor Garrison. I think I've got it."

"Good," Brett said. "Is there anything else I can help you with?"

Merrideth halted her march down the hall and glanced at her watch. It had taken her longer than she thought to get to Voigt Hall and find the faculty offices. Now she had less than ten minutes before she would have to get back to her own turf and start her class. Hopefully, Brett's student would clear out soon.

The young voice turned wheedling. "If you have the time and don't mind, well, I'm having trouble with this one, too."

"Ah, yes, finding the slope of a quadratic function," Brett said.

"Right," she said doubtfully.

"This tangent line to a function f at a specific point is the graph of a linear function. That function is called the linear approximation to f at point z. Notice that it is a different function from f and is typically near f only when evaluated at a point x that is near to z."

The poor girl. Merrideth breathed a prayer of thanks that her days of suffering through all that were past. She had taken as little math as possible, and through a lot of hard work and a relentless determination not to let it mess up her grade point average, she had even aced the classes. It might have helped if she had gone to an instructor for help, but that had never occurred to her at the time.

Brett and his student were still talking away. This was going to take forever. She stuck her head in the room. Brett sat at a remarkably cluttered desk in an untidy office. A blond girl sat in a visitor's chair pulled up next to his. With her bombshell figure and her low-cut orange sweater she didn't give the appearance of being a serious student. Merrideth mentally scolded herself for stereotyping and wondered where such a catty thought had come from. It wasn't as if she were jealous of her. Brett and the girl were looking at a notebook covered in mathematical notation. From the hall, Brett's voice had sounded normal, but he sure didn't look normal. If she weren't mistaken, it was panic she saw on his face.

Maybe *panic* was too strong a word, but he clearly wasn't enjoying the encounter with his student. Merrideth smiled at the surprising realization. Then she had the unsettling thought that perhaps she'd been guilty of stereotyping Brett as well.

"Dr. Garrison? Could I talk to you for a moment?"

They looked up. The girl's face registered a touch of impatience. Brett looked relieved.

"Come in, Dr. Randall. We were just finishing."

The girl stood and gathered her notebook and purse. "Thanks, that was so helpful."

"Any time." He sounded sincere, but when she left he looked like a death-row inmate who'd just been granted a reprieve. He rose and came around the desk to Merrideth. "Thanks for rescuing me. I get nervous when one of the groupies corners me alone. I leave the door open, but still."

"So you do know about your fan club, then?"

"I'd have to be blind and deaf not to. I just ignore them, hoping they'll grow out of it."

"You're not tempted when they throw themselves at your feet?"

"Of course not!" He paused and then added, "I admit they're attractive. But I'm quite aware that despite their well-developed...assets, they're just young girls having an infatuation with their older teacher. It will pass. So what brings you here?"

She was pleased by his righteous indignation, and a little of her anger subsided. Not, however, all of it. "Just visiting from the Junior Varsity Department. I thought it was about time I came and paid homage at the Math and Science inner sanctum."

Brett let out a breath. "So you heard."

"I heard."

"You needn't look daggers at me. I didn't say it."

"But you thought it."

"I did not."

"Then why didn't you refute Bill?"

"What makes you think I didn't?"

"Uh, Marla. She said you didn't say a word."

"I did, too! Later. I went to her and explained that I don't think that."

"Oh, well then."

"Okay, I know I should have spoken up when it happened. But Marla was being obnoxious, telling everyone what to think, and well, it was hard to come to her defense. But if you must know, I blistered Bill's ears after she left. He's sending her flowers and an abject apology for being a jerk."

"Oh."

"He was just kidding, you know. He doesn't really think that Humanities is any less important than our department."

"What about you? What do you think?"

"I think that humanities classes make students well-rounded, useful members of society. I think that if Bill had been exposed to more humanities classes as an undergrad he wouldn't have turned out to be such a two-dimensional, left-brain-dominant, developmentally arrested, socially inept, sub-human idiot. I think without the humanities, civilization would come crashing to an end."

Merrideth sniffed. "Well, all right then."

Smiling, he walked her to the door. "Have a nice day, Merri."

Merrideth paused to let her students catch up with their note taking. Joe Diego still slumped in his chair, giving a good impression of being asleep. And Alyssa Holderman wore her usual bored half-smirking expression. But overall, Merrideth was pleased with the progress she'd made in the classroom. Most of her students seemed interested in what she had to say.

"As we have seen," Merrideth continued, "both the Articles of Confederation and the subsequent State Constitution of 1818 prohibited the ownership of slaves in Illinois. The fact that they did was not by chance. Brave men and women voiced their opinions loudly and often, steering the fledgling government to do the right thing. One of those was James Lemen, a Virginian from Harper's Ferry who came to the Illinois Country for just that purpose at the behest of Thomas Jefferson."

Alyssa Holderman's hand shot up. What would she complain about this time? "Yes, Ms. Holderman?"

"So you're saying the Compact was real and not some myth?"

"I'm impressed," Merrideth said, meaning it. "You've been reading." She tried to think how best to answer Alyssa's question. She knew for a fact that Jefferson had sent Lemen. She had heard him say so, or more accurately, think so. But she had not meant to let that slip since she did not have documentation to prove it. To tell her students to believe their teacher without any proof was irresponsible. The most important thing she could teach them was to base their opinions on fact, not rumor.

"Most historians think it's an unsubstantiated myth. I happen to believe it's true."

"I don't," Alyssa said. "Everyone knows Jefferson had slaves. He even slept with them. He's no American hero. Why didn't he free his slaves if he was so against slavery?"

Joe Diego in the back row straightened in his chair. "It wasn't that simple, Alyssa. He inherited the whole institution. He couldn't just—"

"Good point, Joe," Merrideth said, ridiculously pleased that he'd been listening. "I hope to be able to prove my position on Lemen one day, which would of course shed tremendous light on Jefferson's true attitude about slavery. But we'd better steer our discussion back to the topic. As I was saying, Lemen was a strong anti-slavery influence in the state."

Merrideth used her remote to lower the room lights and to project her first slide onto the screen behind her. "This is his home built in 1789. It was the first brick house in the American settlements, the second in Illinois. It's the only remaining sign of the village of New Design that he founded. It will be one of our stops on the History Club trip. Here's another." She clicked the remote and the next slide came up.

"The mansion you see here was built by a man named John Granger. It still stands in Equality, a couple of hours south of here and is amazingly well preserved, given that it was built in 1834. A lot of horrible things went on up on its third floor. But that's a story I'll save for History Club." Joe sat a little straighter, more heads popped up, more eyes opened a little wider.

"Suffice it to say, Granger built this house from the money he made off the backs of the slaves who worked the salt mine at the bottom of his hill. Salt was a very valuable commodity. At one time, the sale of salt from the Equality mine—"

Several student hands shot up. But before she could call on one, Joe said, "But that would have been illegal in a free state. How did he use slave labor without everyone knowing?"

"Oh, they did know. It was all done openly. Even though James Lemen and other lobbyists had been successful in making slavery illegal in Illinois, the law was quite handily circumvented. Because, as they say, where there's a will, there's a way. Actually, southern Illinois was in many ways indistinguishable from the slave states surrounding it. With salt being so important to the economy—accounting for as much as 65% of state revenue at one point—the Illinois legislature waived the anti-slavery law for Mr. Granger, that is, as long as he paid an annual fee into the state coffers."

"Figures," Joe said with a disgusted huff.

Exactly, Merrideth thought. "Furthermore, the slaves had to be registered in the state of Kentucky, where slavery was legal. And, in case you were thinking that at least slavery was limited to the salt mine, please understand that the free black population of Illinois was not much better off than those unfortunate souls laboring in the mine. For one thing, they were in constant danger of being kidnapped and sold to southern slave holders. John Granger ran a sideline business of it out of this house—a sort of Reverse Underground Railroad, if you will.

"We'll be discussing that next time. Please refer to your online syllabus for further reading. There are some pretty great links there, if I do say so myself. Pay special attention to the material on the Black Code, which, before you ask, will be on the final exam. And have a happy Thanksgiving, everyone."

She used the switch behind her to turn the room lights back up. Most of the students rushed out, seeming as eager as she was for the holiday break. But several, including Alyssa Holderman and Joe Diego, came up to her desk to ask if it was too late to get in on the History Club trip.

"No, not yet," Merrideth said. She tried to keep a properly cool expression on her face, even though inside she was doing cartwheels. She gave each of them the information sheet she'd created and encouraged them to register online. They took them and left, except for Dane Walters, who was dawdling, as he did lately, so he could talk her ear off about some obscure historical fact he'd just read.

She enjoyed talking with him, but today she just wanted to go home and make cranberry sauce. Maybe if she didn't make eye contact. She slid her notes into her briefcase and hurried to the classroom door just ahead of him. But outside the door, Brett was propping up the wall, so she gave up on escape.

He looked with interest at Dane and then grinned at her. Merrideth wondered if he knew his dimples showed when he did that. She ignored him and turned to Dane, who was frowning at Brett. "Did you have a question about the History Club trip?"

"No, I'm good, Professor Randall."

"Well then, see you next week."

"Sure, Professor Randall." Dane started down the hall and then turned back after a few steps. "Happy Thanksgiving, Professor Randall. You, too, Dr. Garrison."

When he was out of earshot, Brett laughed. "I see you've acquired a groupie of your own, lucky you. That boy is so crushing on you."

She laughed. "Don't be ridiculous. Dane just happens to love history."

"Trust me. I recognize the dazed look on his face. I often see it in my own mirror and it doesn't come from a love of history. And if you want to ward off the groupies, I suggest you try to look ugly. An impossible task, of course, verging on the Herculean level. But they do have those fake warts, complete with a black hair growing out of them at the Halloween costume shop. And Billy Bob teeth. I'd definitely get a set of those. It might work."

"You're making me blush."

"I wish you would. It would be so cute."

155

"It's no use flattering me, Brett. As I've said on occasions too numerous to count, I don't date faculty members."

"For your information, I wasn't leading up to a date. My pitifully wounded hide hasn't healed yet from the last time I asked you out. As to why I'm hanging around your door, I come bearing an invitation to Thanksgiving."

She started to speak, but he put up a hand to halt stop her. "Not from me. Aunt Nelda told me to, no, demanded that I invite you. I had nothing to do with the idea at all. She seems to think you don't have any family around, and well, you're invited to Thanksgiving."

"That is really sweet of her." Or very devious, Merrideth thought. "But please tell Nelda I have other plans."

"Do those plans involve eating a rubbery turkey dinner alone at a restaurant?"

"No, I have a family. Not a traditional family, but a family all the same."

"A new clue. I'm making progress. Baby steps. Baby steps."

Merrideth rolled her eyes. "Have a happy Thanksgiving, Professor Garrison."

He grinned. "Happy Thanksgiving, Merri."

CHAPTER 21

Merrideth rang Abby and John's doorbell. While she waited, she admired the Thanksgiving wreath on the door. It was a masterpiece of gourds, ears of dried corn, sheaves of wheat, and other symbols of bounty on the cornucopia theme. No doubt Abby had made it herself. Merrideth wished she'd inherited the creativity gene. The door opened and instead of being trampled by two excited girls as she had expected, John stepped out onto the porch and shut the door.

"Happy Thanksgiving, kiddo. Ah, good. You brought the cranberry sauce."

"Aren't you going to let me in?"

"I wanted to ask you something first." Putting his hands in his pockets against the cold, he turned and nodded toward the twin house next door. "Did you see the sign?"

"What sign?"

John walked down to the end of the porch and pointed. "That sign. It showed up there yesterday."

When Merrideth caught up to him she saw that a red, white, and blue *For Sale* sign was stuck in the Wilsons' front lawn. Advance Reality was the company her mother worked for, so Pat had to know that the house had gone on the market. And she had every opportunity to tell her so yesterday when Merrideth had seen her off on the seven-day cruise to Puerto Vallarta that Advance had awarded their number one seller. And yet she hadn't said a word. Typical. Of course, it wouldn't have occurred to her mother to consider how the sale of the Old Dears' house would make her feel, because that would require thinking of someone other than herself for more than a two-second stretch.

"You should buy it, Merri."

"I wish. You know I don't have that kind of money, John. And I'm swimming in college loans."

"But you have a good job and—"

"But no tenure."

"I could co-sign for you."

"You would do that?"

"Sure. Abby and I already talked about it. We hate the idea of the house going to anyone but you. The Old Dears would be so happy to know you owned it."

"I'd love to have it, but the commute time would put a strain on me. Together with the added debt..."

"So you're saying no?"

"I'm saying no, but very reluctantly. I hope it goes to someone who will take care of it better than the Wilsons did."

"Me, too. We have to see it every day, you know."

They stood looking at the house for a moment more. Then Merrideth said, "Okay, no more sad thoughts, John. It's Thanksgiving .Let me in. I'm hungry for turkey."

He opened the door for her, and the rich smells of Thanksgiving wafted out. After handing him the bowl of cranberry sauce she took off her coat and hung it in the hall closet. "Now, what can I do to help?"

"We have more help than we have room for in the kitchen. Dad's getting in Abby's way, waiting with knife in hand to carve the turkey the minute it comes out of the oven. Mom's finishing the relish tray. The only thing left to do is make the gravy, and that, kiddo, is my specialty. Abby said your assignment is to go hurry the girls along with their project so we can eat while the food's hot."

"Oh, good. I love projects."

The windows throughout the house were fogged up from all the cooking. The sunroom windows were as well, and there the girls had taken the opportunity to draw a series of stick figures of Pilgrims and Indians and other unrecognizable things in the steam. They looked up from their craft table and smiled in welcome.

"Aunt Mewwi!" Natalie said.

"Hi, Bug One and Bug Two. My, you're busy." Merrideth

kissed each girl's head and then looked over Lauren's shoulder at the conglomeration of construction paper, pipe cleaners, hot glue gun, scissors and the ubiquitous tubes of glitter paint littering the table. "What are you making?"

"Name tags," Lauren said. "So everyone will know where to sit."

Several tags made of somewhat rectangular pieces of orange construction paper were already finished, each with a wad of bent brown pipe cleaner hot-glued to it and the name of a guest written in glitter. *Aunt Merri* was spelled in hot pink.

Natalie pointed to the pipe cleaner figure on the tag labeled *Dad*. "It's a turkey," she explained helpfully. "'Cause that's what Dad likes the best. Mom's is a pumpkin."

Lauren put down the tag she had been working on and let out a satisfied huff of air. "There. All done."

"Here," Natalie said, handing Merrideth two of the tags. "These are for *your* mom and dad."

Lauren put a hand over her little sister's mouth. "Natalie! Mom said not to talk about them or it'll make Aunt Merri sad."

"That's all right, Lauren. I'm used to them not being around for Thanksgiving."

Lauren removed her hand from Natalie's mouth, leaving behind a glittery pink hand print.

Natalie put her hands on her hips and glared up at her big sister. Then she switched to studying Merrideth. "Do you got a mommy and a daddy?"

"I do, Bug, but Mom's not into holidays, and Dad lives too far away to come for Thanksgiving."

"Maybe you could mail his name tag to him."

"Good idea, Lauren." She could send it in a belated Thanksgiving card. But if it made it past the prison censors, who'd undoubtedly deem the turkey-shaped pipe cleaner much too dangerous to pass, her father would probably think a Thanksgiving card ironic. He never saw that he had anything to be grateful for. He might even think she was mocking him. "Come on Bug. Let's go amaze everyone with these masterpieces."

Everyone commented on the beauty of the girls' name tags, and their Grandpa Roberts declared that he couldn't have managed without his. Taking into consideration his Alzheimer's, Merrideth figured he might be serious about that. She was flattered that

Natalie put Merrideth's tag on one side of her own spot at the table and her mother's on the other. When John's dad said grace, Merrideth got choked up, thinking how grateful she was to be included in this little family. Afterward, Abby smiled a watery little smile and squeezed her hand. And when the sweet potatoes were passed, sweet Lauren, sensing Merrideth's emotion, insisted on dishing out an extra glob of melted marshmallow for her. But John was actually the most thoughtful. After a glance at her, he made a joke that turned the attention away from her.

The meal was delightful, as much for the conversation and laughter as for the food itself, although Abby's cooking was spectacular. John's mother had recovered from the pneumonia, but was still weak. And his father was a sparkling conversationalist, as long as the listener wasn't hung up on linear reasoning and strict factualness. But he had moments of piercing clarity. In one, he congratulated Merrideth on finding Fort Piggot, and the spotlight of attention was right back on her.

"Yes, what an amazing find," John said. "I want to get to the site sometime."

"There's nothing much to see yet," Merrideth said. "We won't start the dig until next fall."

"I know, but I'd like to see the scope of it. I keep thinking of how much work it must have been to build a fort that size. I wish I could see how they did it. Like how did they haul the slabs of limestone? Makes me wish we still had our *Beautiful Houses* program."

"I know. I miss it all the time," Abby said. "But we all decided it was too dangerous to use."

It confirmed that their opinion about using the program had not changed, and so unfortunately, she would have to continue keeping the secret from them. Merrideth looked down at her plate, certain John and Abby would read the guilt in her eyes if she looked at them.

"So, Merri," Abby said. "Tell us more about your part in the discovery. You were rather vague about that."

"Mine was a small role. The bulk of the credit goes to Glen Parton and Eugene Parks. Lots of people put in hours and hours of work. Even Brett spent a Saturday morning at the dig. And he helped in other ways, too."

"Brett?" John said with a sudden spike of interest. "Who's he?"

She should have known he would go into big brother mode. Merrideth put on casual smile. "Just one of my colleagues at the college. He teaches physics. You'd probably like him."

"Maybe I should meet him."

At the other end of the table, Abby's lips quirked up in amusement. "You can stand down, dear. Merri is twenty-six, not sixteen."

John frowned and wiped his mouth. "Sorry, Merri. Old habits."

Merrideth smiled. "That's okay, bro." She picked up the empty gravy boat and stood. "I'll go get the rest of your excellent gravy."

At least the mention of Brett had steered the conversation away from more questions about the precise nature of her role in the discovery. After the meal, everyone helped clear the table. Then the girls went off to play and their grandmother went upstairs to rest. John went with his dad to the living room to watch football. That left Abby and Merrideth to load the dishwasher and scrub the pots and pans.

They were hard at it when John stuck his head in the kitchen door. He opened his mouth to speak, but before he got anything out, Abby gave him a feral look and said, "John, do not ask me about dessert while I'm elbow deep in the pots and pans."

"Who, me?" He came in and kissed the back of his wife's neck.

Abby grinned. "I have soapy hands, and I'm not afraid to use them."

"Spare me, please," Merrideth said. "And why isn't he helping, I'd like to know?"

"He is a modern male 364 days of the year, but on Thanksgiving, he reverts back to Ward Cleaver."

"Okay," Merrideth said. "Then leave us to our women's work and go watch your silly football game."

"It is true that football is a required male activity for Thanksgiving afternoons. And football is in fact being broadcast in our living room, even as we speak. However, I am not obligated to actually watch the boring stuff."

Merrideth's cell vibrated in her pocket. She put down the pan she was drying and took out her phone. It was Brett.

She realized she was smiling and turned away from her friends' eagle eyes. "Hi. Happy Thanksgiving."

"You, too," Brett said. "Did you perform the annual ritual of stuffing yourself with stuffing?"

"Sure did. Wouldn't be right not to."

"Listen, I wouldn't call you while you're with your family, only Aunt Nelda here, is being mean to me and I need your help."

Merrideth laughed. "Really? Do you need me to come over, Brett?"

"I'd love it if you would, but that's not why I called."

"So what's up?"

"She says she has a surprise for me, but she won't tell me what it is. She says to ask you. So I'm asking."

"Put her on."

"Okay. Here she is. Make her tell me."

"Sorry. I let it slip," Nelda said. "Now's he's badgering me unmercifully. I told you he's like a second-grader."

"I'm sorry I didn't get back to you about the you-know-what. Guess you heard about Fort Piggot."

"Yes, I did. Sounds like you've been busy. It seems to me that now would be a good time to release the news about you-know-what."

Merrideth heard Brett in the background grousing loudly.

"If you can hold out just a little longer it would be good. There are a few more things I need to check on before the place is swarming with history buffs."

Nelda laughed. "Ha, he won't wear me down. I'll hold the fort, as it were."

Merrideth chuckled. "You do that. I'll let you know when you can tell him."

Merrideth was still smiling when she put her phone away and turned back to help Abby. She was getting the pie ready like a sensible person.

John, however, was standing there grinning at her like a chimpanzee. "Merri has a boyfriend. Merri has a boyfriend."

"Really, John? First you go all Mafia on me just hearing Brett's name, and now you're teasing me?"

John put his arm around her shoulders. "Hey, it's all part of the service."

Merrideth rolled her eyes. "Anyway, Brett's not my *boyfriend*. I don't date colleagues."

Abby grinned. "Sure, kiddo." Then she handed Merrideth a foil-covered paper plate. "Here. I made your pie to go."

Merrideth took it, because it was impossible to turn down

pumpkin pie. "Thanks. But I'm only leaving because I have something important to do before the snow gets here."

"It's not due until tomorrow, but whatever," John said.

"Oh, be quiet," Merrideth said and went to get her coat.

CHAPTER 22

Merrideth turned into Sundown Lane, hoping she wouldn't meet Brett leaving from Nelda's. It would be difficult to come up with a reason for being there. But she got the Subaru down into the woods and parked without anyone seeing her. Of course not. Normal people were tucked snugly into their homes, either already asleep or sneaking a midnight snack of leftover turkey, not driving around on back roads in the middle of the night.

It was the latest she'd ever been in the woods. Her adult brain knew that wolves had been gone from the Midwest for over a century and that coyotes were harmless to humans despite their unnerving howls. However, the part of her brain that still thought about monsters in closets was clamoring for her to leave there *tout de suite*. But she was determined to carry through with her obligation no matter how dark and scary the woods were. She had agreed to take on Nelda and Brett's family tree project, for which he was paying her good money, and instead she had spent all her time obsessing about Fort Piggot, selfishly putting her career ahead of her promise to them.

The woods wouldn't just be dark and scary, they would be cold, the coldest she'd experienced to date, although nothing compared to the low temperatures in the forecast. If they got the early and harsh winter some were predicting, tonight might be her last opportunity to time-surf there before spring Already, a few flakes of the snow John had said wouldn't come until tomorrow were landing on her windshield. But then it *was* almost tomorrow.

Not everyone had heroes in their family tree—brave pioneer leaders like Piggot and Lemen or fierce Indian fighters like William Whiteside and the Ogles with all their flaws. As Bill's stupid poster said, not everyone grows up to be an astronaut. But it would never do to let Odious Ogle have his hero without at least trying to find one or two for Nelda and Brett.

There was no stalling now. If she were going to do this, she'd have to get set up before snow covered everything. The prediction was for three inches. But first, she deserved a little treat for courage. She took out the paper plate of pumpkin pie Abby had sent, complete with plastic fork. Pumpkin pie was meant to be savored with family and friends, but she gulped it down in six bites.

And then she forced herself to get out of the security of her car. She snaked her orange extension cord down to the site, comforting herself with the knowledge that it would guide her back to her Subaru no matter how much snow fell while she was working. She plugged everything in and launched her program. When it was fully loaded, she saw that the date had skipped ahead to December 10, 1788, about a month from when she had last seen the Garretsons. It was as good a time to start from as any other. She settled into her Mylar cocoon and prepared to immerse herself in their world.

Panting, Isabelle paused to let her arms rest. Stirring wool was not her favorite chore. After only a moment she resumed stirring, because keeping the fabric moving evenly through the simmering lye water was essential, and she had no intention of letting all her hard work be wasted by laziness at this point in the long process. The fabric was coming along nicely. Only a little more boiling and the wool would be felted enough to keep out the worst cold and damp an Illinois winter could send their way. The walnuts had stained it a nice warm brown that would look good with Samuel's red hair.

The boy was still growing like a weed, and keeping him clothed took up a large portion of her time. But this fabric was for something special, his first grown-up Sunday suit. She couldn't wait to see his face on Christmas morning. It would take some doing to get it made without him realizing what it was. James Kyle would

165

also get good use of the suit when he was older. He was a sweet-natured boy who didn't seem to mind wearing his brother's outgrown clothes. But for Christmas she'd make something new just for him. Everyone down to little Mary would have something she had made with her own two hands.

It was unfortunate she couldn't be inside sewing the suit now, while the boys were busy stuffing sausages in the barn. Bless their hearts, they were working hard when she'd last looked in on them, even though everyone was tired from the butchering yesterday. Normally James would have been there to supervise the sausage from start to finish. But he'd left them after the pork was ground, because snow was coming and there was much to do before it got there. And since young Benjamin Ogle had showed up to visit Jane, James had commandeered his help in bringing in a hay stook from the hay field for the livestock.

Before he'd left, James had told his sons he had every confidence in their ability to handle the sausage-making by themselves. Samuel and James Kyle had swelled with pride at their father's words. Jane, too, was proud that her young man was being trusted to help her father with the hay, although she was disappointed that he'd been snatched right from under her nose. She stood on the wall perch watching for his return.

Isabelle wondered how the boys were doing. The hickory smoke scenting the air was awfully strong. When James got home, he'd make sure the fire in the smoke house was just right before they hung the sausages. That, he would not entirely trust to the boys.

"You had best hurry, Mother," Jane called from her observation post. "The snow will likely be here before nightfall."

Isabelle looked at the sky. "You're right, I think, Jane." She gave her wool one more stir and decided it was ready. Then she called Sarah, who came out of the cabin, slipping hurriedly into her cloak.

"Are the girls still embroidering?"

Sarah smiled. "They're almost finished. Bella is helping Mary with the French knots."

Smiling, Isabelle handed her daughter two wooden paddles and then took two more for herself. "Mind it doesn't drag in the dirt."

"I won't let it, Ma."

"I beg your pardon, Daughter. I know you won't. It's just habit to warn you."

Working together, they lifted the first section of steaming wool fabric out of the cauldron and moved it onto the log rack nearby. They dipped their paddles into the brown water again and again, until at last all the fabric was on the rack to drip dry. Hopefully, it would be dry enough to take inside before the snow got there. Then when it was fully dry, she could begin the part she liked best: turning the fabric into clothing for her family.

"We'll have to let the water cool before we can empty the cauldron," Isabelle said. "Go on inside out of this cold. I'll go see how Samuel and James Kyle are faring."

Before Isabelle reached the barn, distant shots rang out. Almost immediately Badger came out of the barn barking wildly and went to the gate, frantic to be let out. Jane shouted something, but Isabelle was running too hard to understand her.

Sarah came outside, the little girls behind her.

"Take them back inside, Sarah," Isabelle said. Without waiting to see if they obeyed, she looked up at Jane on her ledge. "What is it? Tell me what you see."

Jane's cheeks were white, not rosy from the cold as they'd been earlier. "The wagon's coming up from the hay field fast. The horses are spooked." Frowning fiercely, Jane turned back to look over the pickets. "There is scarcely any hay on the wagon, Ma."

"What about your father and Benjamin?" Isabelle said.

Jane didn't answer at first, just kept watching over the wall. After an eternity, she said, "Someone is slumped in the seat."

"O, God, be merciful!" Isabelle cried. Which one was it? Her husband or young Benjamin Ogle?

James Kyle and Samuel came running from the barn, their hands and clothes blood-tinged. Isabelle gasped and then remembered the sausage-making.

"Open the gate, James," Jane called.

"No! Not until I say," Samuel shouted and then scrambled up to stand next to his sister on the wall. "Your eyes are better than mine, Jane. Is it a trap?"

James Kyle stood at the gate, waiting for the command. Isabelle stood next to him, waiting to hear Jane's answer.

At last Jane said, "No, I don't see how." She continued to watch and then finally called, "It's Benjamin, Ma!" They came down the ladder, Jane stumbling in her haste to be there when the gate opened.

"Now, James!" Samuel shouted.

He swung the gate open, and the horses, the whites of their eyes showing in their terror, brought the rattling wagon into the stockade.

James wasn't in the wagon, and Benjamin was unconscious and unable to tell them where he was and what had happened. The right side of his shirt was soaked in blood. Jane hovered, crying as Samuel and James Kyle got Benjamin down from the wagon, carried him inside, and laid him gently on the table.

Isabelle pushed Jane out of her way. "Jane, honey, go get my medicine bag." She opened Benjamin's shirt and then had to stifle a gasp when she saw the wound. Blocking the view from Jane, she took the medicine bag from her and said, "Now go stoke the fire. We need to keep him warm. And I'll need the light."

Sarah corralled the little girls, who stood wide-eyed in the corner, then bent down and whispered something that had them turning away.

Isabelle pressed a cloth to Benjamin's wound, but still the blood seeped out of him. "Samuel, are you and James Kyle finished with the sausages?"

"Nearly, ma'am," Samuel said.

"Then you go back and finish. Then bring some for our supper. And some for us to make broth for Benjamin."

"James Kyle can finish," Samuel said. "I'm going out to look for Pa." He picked up his musket against the wall and checked to see that it was loaded. His hands were still bloody from the sausage.

At sixteen, he was nearly as tall as his father, and he was wearing the same mulish expression that James got when he was determined to do what he had decided needed doing. Ordinarily, Isabelle delighted in watching the way her sons were beginning to assert themselves as men. But she could not allow him that now.

"No, you are not, Samuel. You and James Kyle are going to get the sausage on to smoke. Mind that the fire is cool enough. And then you are going to take care of the horses and unload the hay. What there is left of it. And then you will both take your turn standing guard."

"But Pa is out there waiting for—"

"And so are the Kickapoo that did this, Samuel."

"I know!" He cursed hotly, first the Indians and then Sir Henry

Hamilton, too.

"Samuel! You will not use that kind of language in front of your sisters. Not in front of anyone."

He heaved a great sigh and swiped at his eyes with the sleeve of his coat. "I beg your pardon, Ma," he said more softly.

She spoke softly too, just for him to hear. "Your father would not want us to lose you, too, Samuel. I know this."

He grunted as if in pain, as if he had been the one shot in the shoulder. He put his musket down, then flung the door open and went outside. James Kyle followed after a worried glance at her. She girded herself against their distress and against thoughts of James. She would weep for him later. Meanwhile, she would see what she could do for Benjamin.

Isabelle lifted the cloth and saw that the bleeding had slowed, although his face was pale and his skin clammy to the touch. "Jane, come help me."

She came away from the fire, and Isabelle saw that she had already put the big pot on to boil. "Good. The sooner to make the broth."

Jane wiped her eyes with her sleeve. "Benjamin cannot die, Ma. I could not bear it if he did."

"I will do all I can, Jane. You know that I will. But if his wound turns putrid… then only God knows, Daughter." And if he lived, only God knew how he would be able to fully protect and provide for her daughter without the use of his right arm.

"Help me turn him."

With Jane's help she managed to get Benjamin turned enough for her to see that the ball had not gone all the way through his shoulder. They eased him back down. He groaned but did not awaken. Moving him had made the bleeding start again. She held the cloth to his shoulder until it slowed again and then cautiously used a finger to explore the wound. He groaned, and Jane touched his cheek to calm him. The musket ball was deep, wedged between the bones. He would bleed again before she was finished digging it out of him.

If Frances Ballew were here she would know what to do. Her hands were the most skilled of any of them, and Isabelle would welcome her help. But Frances was not likely to suddenly have a mind to leave Great Run and come for a visit, especially so late in the day, even if she were Isabelle's friend, which she was not.

Isabelle had not spoken out against Frances Ballew as some of the women did on every occasion possible. But neither had she spoken out against the women's rudeness to her. Nor had she gotten around to making the effort to befriend the woman. No, Frances Ballew would not come calling this day.

It was up to her to do what needed to be done. She took the knife from her medicine bag and looked at it in distaste. "Sarah, come help Jane hold Benjamin down." She looked into Jane's anguished eyes. "You will not cry, Jane. You will hold him down. And you will pray. Do you hear me?"

"Yes, ma'am."

Isabelle would pray for Benjamin, too. And for James—that he was not lying dead down in the hay field.

CHAPTER 23

Merrideth was jolted out of the eighteenth century and back into the twenty-first. She found herself lying at the bottom of the stone wall, miraculously still holding the laptop, and breathing like she'd been the one pulling the hay wagon. She had a vague recollection of standing and craning her head as if that would let her see what Jane was watching beyond the stockade.

Pausing the gruesome scene, Merrideth shuddered to think of Isabelle's knife—her unsterilized knife—digging into Benjamin Ogle's shoulder joint. So that was how he got the bum shoulder and why he hated the Indians so much. She thought of Brett's cell memory theory. Were the bigotry and hatefulness of Benjamin's descendent Walter Ogle because his cells carried a memory of this incident?

She took a breath of the crisp night air to blow the fog of the Garretsons' horror and anxiety out of her head. Then, with the aid of her flashlight, she rummaged in her backpack for aspirin and swallowed two with a swig of hot coffee. When she got home she'd look up Sir Henry Hamilton to find out who in the world he was and why Samuel blamed him for the attack. And hay. Didn't farmers bale hay in the summer? Why were the men down in the hayfield in December anyway? Not that the information was crucial to the job at hand, but it was curious all the same.

She drained her coffee cup and turned back to her laptop. If ever there were a reason to fast-forward, this was it. She ran ahead only a little. She didn't want to miss finding out what happened to James Garretson.

The thought of food made Isabelle a little sick, but she took a bite of sausage and chewed it, hoping it would stay down when she swallowed it. It did, but she knew that she couldn't keep down a second bite. She managed a smile for James Kyle, Sarah, and the little girls who sat picking at their own suppers. Samuel was on guard at the wall, and Jane still kneeled at Benjamin's pallet on the floor, dabbing the sweat from his forehead. Sarah had set a place at the table for her father, but it was empty. James had not come in to laugh away their fears.

Isabelle went to Jane and took her by the hand. "Come eat, sweeting. We will need our strength, the two of us."

Benjamin still slept. He had lost so much blood. In the end, Isabelle could only cauterize and bandage the wound, leaving the musket ball in his shoulder. The sounds of his groans still haunted her. Jane gave her beau one last look, then wiped at her eyes and came with her to the table.

They had barely begun to eat when Badger commenced barking, and Samuel called out from the watch post. Everyone rose at once, nearly upsetting the table. James Kyle was the first out the door, slamming the door closed behind him. Isabelle took her cape from the peg and donned it. Her hands had gone uncharacteristically clumsy and the latch would not open at first. But then she was outside, the wind buffeting her hood about her face.

Samuel was down from the perch and stood ready to lift the bar on the stockade gate. "James, mind the gate. Open it when I say."

"What is it?" Isabelle asked.

"It's Father."

"Are you sure?"

"I heard his whistle from yonder in the trees." Samuel opened the gate and went out, Badger following, and James Kyle barred it after him.

Isabelle climbed to the guard post and watched as Samuel ran to the edge of the clearing and disappeared in the shadows there. Then there were two silhouettes, stumbling together toward the gate.

Samuel whistled and James Kyle opened the gate for them. Then her James was there, supported by their son. His hat was gone and light from the cabin door reflected off his black hair and revealed that his face was pale. His buckskin trousers were caked with something dark, something that was probably blood. Badger whined and licked his fingers.

Crying out, Isabelle hurried to her husband and ran her hands over him to reassure herself he was really there and not an apparition. "How bad is it?"

"It is but a smallish wound, Wife, and I am truly sorry to have put that look on your face."

"My countenance will be much improved, husband, now that I have you home safe." She put his arm over her shoulder, and together with Samuel helped him into the cabin.

Merrideth paused the program and shook her head to clear it. The family's joy at James' return was almost as overwhelming to her senses as their despair had been before. She had no desire to watch Isabelle treat whatever horrible wound James had beneath his buckskins.

Again, Merrideth set the program to fast-forward. The images went by too fast to be disgusting. James was apparently not too severely wounded. The next morning Benjamin Ogle was awake, but looking terrible. Of course, not having Merrideth's advantage, poor Jane didn't know that he was going to survive. So she and the others wore worried looks as they bustled about caring for him and James along with doing their endless chores. It was exhausting to watch. Merrideth let several days go by on fast speed, hoping to find something heroic to share with Nelda and Brett.

She should probably stop fooling around and switch the lock from Isabelle to James. She could rewind his life back to Pennsylvania and meet the parents and family he had left behind there. That would be another generation to add to Nelda's tree, that is, if the lock held from that great a distance. If it did, and if, miracle of miracles, she could figure out a way to transfer the lock from him to his father, and then to his father's father, back to the first Garretson to immigrate to the Colonies, and then back to the European Garretsons, who knew how many generations she could find for Nelda and Brett?

But then Captain Joseph Ogle was at the Garretsons' cabin door, and Merrideth couldn't stand not to see what happened next. She would watch for just a minute or two longer, long enough to see his reaction to the latest Indian atrocity to be committed against the Ogle family, and then she would begin rewinding James Garretson's life. Merrideth changed the setting to virtual and prepared herself for his emotional explosion.

James Kyle held the door open and Captain Joseph Ogle ducked his head and came in, scanning the cabin, until he caught sight of Benjamin on the pallet in the corner. Isabelle got up from her spinning wheel to go greet him. She was grateful the girls were outside busy with their chores. They were frightened of Joseph's gruff ways. Heaven knew the man had had enough trials and tribulations in his life to turn ten men sour.

Across the room, James rose awkwardly from his bed and stood at attention. "Captain Ogle, sir," he said, saluting.

"We're not in the army anymore, James."

"No, sir, we are not, Captain Ogle. Sir."

Ogle shook his head, but returned James' salute. "Sit down, Sergeant Garretson, before you fall down."

"I think I had better, sir." James gingerly lowered himself onto his stool at the table.

"Thank you for sending word about Benjamin."

Benjamin stirred at the sound of his name. When he saw his father he also tried to stand. Ogle bent down and put his hands on his son's chest. "Stay down, boy."

Even the small effort had caused drops of perspiration to break out on Benjamin's forehead, and he trembled with obvious pain. "I don't have use of my arm, Pa."

Ogle turned from inspecting his son to look at Isabelle.

"I am so sorry," Isabelle said. "I couldn't get the musket ball out."

"No matter. It'll mend, boy. Now, tell me how many of the murderin' savages did you kill before they got you?"

Benjamin grimaced, although from pain or distress, Isabelle couldn't tell. "Them redskins are sneaky, Pa. You know that."

"You should have been on the lookout for that, Benjamin. But no matter, after you rest up a couple days, we'll get a posse and go clean out that nest of savages up north of Bellefontaine."

"Those are Osage, Captain Ogle," James said. "They've never caused any trouble. The ones that attacked us were Kickapoo."

"Doesn't make no never mind to me. There's no such thing as a good Indian."

Her husband looked as sick at the captain's attitude as she felt, but he did not comment. James Kyle looked outraged and started to say something, but a look from his father kept him quiet. Everyone knew the Ogles had suffered grievously at the hands of the Indians.

"Come, you should eat before you go," Isabelle said. Regardless of Captain Ogle's hateful words, he was a guest, and they got precious few.

On account of Benjamin being there, she had made extra corn pudding—much more, it turned out, than they needed. At the time she had imagined the scolding her mother would have given her, but now she was glad to have something to offer Captain Ogle. She brought the trenchers and the pot of honey and set them before the men at the table. Maybe the honey would sweeten his temperament.

"There's sassafras tea as well," she said.

"Thank you kindly, ma'am. For that and for tending my son."

James passed the trencher to the captain. "When you're ready to go, James Kyle can help you hoist Benjamin into the wagon."

Benjamin grinned weakly at his friend. "Oh, happy news."

James Kyle grinned back.

"I'm surprised you're not down in the hayfield helping your brother Samuel," Ogle said.

James Kyle's face paled and he turned away.

"What? Samuel's down in the hay?" James pushed himself up from the table and stood on trembling legs, staring at his son. "What do you know, James Kyle?"

"He went to gather the hay lost off the wagon. Mr. Reddick came by to offer his help, what with you being down and all."

James limped to the door and took his coat down from the peg. Isabelle went to help him get it on.

James Kyle handed his father his hat. "Don't worry, Pa."

"Don't worry? You saw what happened to me and Benjamin."

"But we need the hay, Pa."

"I know we do, son. I was planning to get it by and by."

"At least you had the sense to stay here, James Kyle," Isabelle said.

"Samuel wouldn't let me go," he mumbled angrily. He donned his own coat and helped his father out the door.

Captain Ogle turned toward Benjamin. "You'd best rest here, son, whilst we go see to the hay."

Isabelle put away the food that no one had eaten and went back to her spinning. It normally was soothing work, but now the whirring sound of the wheel filled her mind to overflowing with dread so that there was not room for hymns, much less her poetry. All she could manage was a disjointed and nearly wordless prayer. The verse in Romans came to her, and she latched onto it, whispering it over and over: "Likewise the Spirit also helpeth our infirmities: for we know not what we should pray for as we ought: but the Spirit itself maketh intercession for us with groanings which cannot be uttered."

After a while, Badger set to barking, and then the girls shouted. The gate hinges groaned, and then the sound of the wagon wheels and the horses' harness came to Isabelle. And still she sat spinning, the wheel whirring and her lips soundlessly moving as she recited the Scripture.

The cabin door flew open, banging against the wall and startling her. Captain Ogle staggered in carrying Samuel and put him on the table. The whirring sound grew louder, and Isabelle turned her eyes back to her work. In her startlement, she had made a nub in her thread. It was only a small imperfection, but it acted in her mother's stead to chastise her for her carelessness. When she looked back up, she saw that Captain Ogle was still in a bad temper. Maybe now he would eat some of her honey and be sweetened for it. In the corner young Benjamin Ogle cried out to his father, then struggled up from his pallet and stood leaning against the wall. Isabelle had nearly forgotten he was there.

Then James Kyle came in through the door, his fists covering his eyes. "I should have gone to help, Ma." He moaned it over and over. Isabelle wanted to go to him, but he would understand that she couldn't stop her wheel lest she made another mistake.

And then her husband was there, the girls behind him. He shut the door in their faces and stood there unmoving. His face was white and brittle. Then it seemed to dissolve, and he began weeping in huge gulps.

The shock of that made Isabelle blink in surprise. Samuel! Her husband and James Kyle were worried about Samuel. She slowed her spinning wheel until it stopped altogether. Curiously, the whirring sound continued on in her head, only it was the room and not her wheel that was spinning now.

She rose cautiously from her seat and went to the table where Samuel lay. She was surprised to see that he wasn't hurt after all. His clothes weren't even bloody, except for a small spot on his chest. She ran her hands down his arms and then his legs. Nothing seemed to be broken. "You're mistaken," she said, smiling encouragingly at her husband and James Kyle. The sight of Samuel's feet hanging off the table had her smiling even more. The boy's pants didn't cover his ankles. He'd be glad of his new suit at Christmas.

James didn't understand and still sobbed at James Kyle's side. She went to him and put her arms around him. "Hush, don't weep. Our Samuel will mend. We just need to let him sleep."

But then he gathered her into his own arms so tightly she could barely breathe. He said something in her ear, but the words wouldn't untangle themselves and flew away before she could decipher their meaning. She tried to pull away to go back to Samuel, but he wouldn't let her. He shook her, and she stopped her struggles. Then husband's words sorted themselves out and pierced her heart like arrows. A wail rose in her throat, threatening to strangle her.

She pulled away from his grip and lunged toward the table. Now she could see what before she had not allowed herself to. Samuel's thick red hair, so like her own, was gone. All that remained was a meaty wound. She thought of the hog they had butchered behind the barn. Her gorge rose, and she clamped her hand to her mouth until it settled back down.

"Send for Frances Ballew," she choked out. "She'll know what to do. Like she did for Mr. Dempsey. It will take time to heal, but Samuel's strong."

Her husband pulled her away from the table and shook her again. "He's gone, Isabelle. There's nothing for Frances Ballew to do. Nor anyone else."

"He didn't suffer, ma'am," Captain Ogle said. "Your boy was already shot dead when the heathens took his scalp."

Isabelle felt herself slipping out of his arms. She realized she was falling but couldn't seem to stop.

Merrideth barely managed to set the laptop aside and get to her knees in time to vomit out the pain and horror onto the ground. Isabelle had managed to choke hers back, proving herself made of sterner stuff than she. The retching stopped at last, and Merrideth fumbled in her backpack for her water bottle and a tissue. Pity for Isabelle, James, and the others overwhelmed her. So much violence and death! With the brief slice-of-life episodes she had seen, Merrideth had experienced only a fraction of what the pioneer families had suffered, and she was sick in her soul. What must they have felt?

Had they known before they left Pennsylvania how tenuous their lives would be? Had they thought that with the war over, the danger was past and there would be bright days ahead in the Illinois Country? Or had they known but even so considered the ownership of land a prize worth the risk?

It was snowing again, but only a little. Merrideth lay back and looked up at the white flakes coming out of the night sky from beyond the bare tree branches. She wished she could remember Nelda's poem. Something about more prayers than stars in the black sky. Her stomach pitched again and she willed herself not to vomit.

At last she sat up and risked a glance at the computer screen. When Isabelle fainted, Merrideth had lost her virtual lock on her, but still the sight of the family and the Ogles moving about the cabin was too horrible to watch. She stopped the action, and then rubbed her throbbing temples until the worst of the effects had lessened. Pushing aside her emotions, she analyzed what she had just experienced.

She had thought Nelda and Brett's ancestors not as brave as the Ogles and Whitesides, but anyone who persevered as they had was a hero in her book. She just hoped she could find the documentation to prove it.

She had gotten to see bits of their lives over the past weeks, but only God knew the hardships and bravery of the thousands of others she would never get to know. How did you measure their courage? What scale did you use? The Whitesides and Ogles had lost so many relatives. And Isabelle Garretson had seen her scalped boy laid out on her kitchen table. What horrible nightmares had that bloody scene caused for the little girls Bella and Mary?

Of all of them, she felt the most sympathy for James Kyle. He must have had a raging case of survivor's guilt, living with the fact that he had stayed safe in the stockade while his brother went to get the hay. How had he been able to forgive the Indians? It was one thing to forgive and forget, but for crying out loud, surely that didn't require that James had to hang out with them? And yet she had watched him ride into an Indian camp and sit around laughing and talking with them.

She realized she was thinking like a bigot and assuming James Kyle was one as well. Unlike the Ogles and Whitesides, he was being open-minded enough not to cast every tribe as his enemy, not to blame all Indians for the crimes of only a few. In that, he was admirable. Perhaps she had underestimated his depth of character.

It was after three o'clock in the morning. Some said it was the darkest hour of the day, the hour when a person's doubts and fears held sway over hope. It was no wonder that her thoughts were so bleak. She should pack up and go home. She would sleep the day away, and when she got up, she would cheer herself up by watching a good movie or baking a cake. Maybe both.

But she wasn't sleepy, and she couldn't pass up what might be the last opportunity she had to see what made James Kyle Garretson tick.

She took out her notebook and, holding it under the light from her flashlight, thumbed through the pages until she found the notes she'd taken to find her way back to the Indian village. The date was August 17, 1795.

She entered it and *Beautiful Houses* took her right where she

179

wanted to go. There was James Kyle Garretson on his horse, just entering the Indian village. She pulled the Mylar blanket closer and settled in to go virtual.

But then he made an expression that looked remarkably familiar. Merrideth paused his actions and squinted at her monitor. She laughed. If she didn't know better, she'd say it was a young Brett Garrison sitting on that horse. She zoomed in close, closer than she'd ever gone with him before and gasped. James Kyle Garretson had the same shock of glossy black hair, the same emerald eyes of the so-called Black Irish that Brett had. Even the jawline was the same. The physical similarities between the two men were astounding. She laughed again, imagining the debonair Brett Garrison in fringed deerskin.

More than ever she wished she could tell him about the program. Nelda, too. They'd get such a kick out of seeing James Kyle Garretson. But here she sat with no one to share it with. At last, she un-paused the action and watched to see what Brett's ancestor would do.

CHAPTER 24

James prayed with his eyes wide open. He asked God for safety, all the while scanning the woods on either side of the trail for danger. He couldn't see any of the Kickapoo, but he knew scouts were in there watching his approach. The first time he'd visited their camp a year ago, a dozen angry, young warriors had met him on the trail and escorted him to their chief. In truth, it had been more like they had herded him into camp. They had come out of the woods on both sides of the path and ridden their horses within inches of him in a show of aggression that had panicked his own horse and unnerved him. It was the first time he's seen the Kickapoo up close, although he had most certainly seen their handiwork. They hadn't been wearing war paint, but they were fierce enough all the same. He had thought sure he wouldn't make it out of their camp alive.

But God had kept him alive then and for three subsequent visits. Today, as always, in a show of trust and good will to the Indians, he kept his musket in its saddle holster, carrying only his Bible in his hands. He felt fairly sure that a tomahawk wouldn't come flying out of the woods and land in his back, and that he would arrive home with his hair still on his head. But other than that, there was no telling what would happen in the Kickapoo's camp.

Today, he made it all the way down the trail and into camp without an escort appearing. It was a mark of *their* growing trust, and he was pleased. Several men were scraping deer hides. They watched him dismount but didn't approach or speak to him. He knew that the majority of the people were at their northern summer encampment. This was only a small hunting camp, and most of them would be out in the woods, leaving a handful of men to guard their supplies and watch over the chief.

As usual, Chief Kewaunee was sitting outside his bark hut, smoking a pipe. He continued gazing off into the woods as James approached. He hadn't yet concluded whether the chief's eyesight was bad, or that he only pretended not to see him. He was old and frail and, James suspected, ill and in pain. As far as he could tell, the only thing the chief ever contributed to the hunting endeavor was to issue cranky complaints to whoever came close enough to hear him.

Ituah came out of the bark hut and gave James his usual suspicious look.

"Good day," James said.

Ituah spoke English fairly well, but he didn't waste any words on James, giving him only a quick nod of the head as a return greeting. Ituah was young, about his own age, and one of several of the old chief's grandsons that James had met during his visits. They translated when the need arose, and one of them was always in attendance, bringing the chief food and nasty-smelling medicinal herbal teas, and bearing the brunt of his ill-humor. No doubt they'd rather be out hunting deer, but they never showed anything but love and respect toward their grandfather.

At last Chief Kewaunee deigned to look up and acknowledge James' presence. He didn't smile. James had yet to see that expression on his face. But recognition showed in his eyes along with a slight, but definite glimmer of pleasure to see him. He spoke and gestured for James to be seated.

"He say is good you bring Good Book," Ituah said.

James sat down next to Chief Kewaunee and laid the Bible in his own lap. "I am always happy to bring the Good Book. Would you like me to read more of it today?"

Ituah translated his words, and the old man nodded his head wisely.

"He says you read more stories," Ituah said.

James opened the Bible to John chapter three, the passage he had chosen for the visit. And then he looked into Chief Kewaunee's eyes. He was a stubborn man who loved to argue. Unless he could be convinced of the truth of the Gospel there was little hope his people would be willing to accept it. "Open his eyes, Lord," James prayed silently. And then he read aloud:

There was a man of the Pharisees, named Nicodemus, a ruler of the Jews: The same came to Jesus by night, and said unto him, Rabbi, we know that thou art a teacher come from God: for no man can do these miracles that thou doest, except God be with him. Jesus answered and said unto him, Verily, verily, I say unto thee, Except a man be born again, he cannot see the kingdom of God. Nicodemus saith unto him, How can a man be born when he is old? Can he enter the second time into his mother's womb, and be born?

"Why do you waste Grandfather's time with foolish talk?" Ituah said.

James smiled. "The Gospel is foolish to them that do not believe."

Chief Kewaunee frowned and spoke querulously to Ituah, who rolled his eyes and answered. Hopefully, he was translating his words accurately. When he was finished Chief Kewaunee spoke again.

"My grandfather wants to know how Jesus answered this man," Ituah said. "What is meaning of words? He was telling riddle, yes?"

"Jesus meant that every man must be forgiven of his sins or he cannot reach heaven when he dies. We are all sinners, fallen short of God's glory. We must seek his forgiveness. And we must forgive one another or we won't be forgiven by God."

Ituah huffed his disdain at what he had said but translated for his grandfather. James smiled to himself. Ituah was right to be skeptical. The concept of forgiveness was an outlandish one.

When he had pondered what his grandson said, Chief Kewaunee spoke and Ituah translated, saying, "When we put our names alongside white men's on Treaty of Fallen Timbers, we put aside our war. We put away our weapons and lived in peace. But the white men came to the lodge on Shoals Creek and slaughtered our friends as they slept. I have forgiven the white man many things. Even the theft of our land. But this sin I cannot forgive. It is too great."

James inwardly cringed, wondering how much irreparable damage Captain Whiteside and Captain Ogle had done with that attack. The Indians had honored the treaty, and the whites had acted treacherously.

James looked at Ituah and said solemnly, "Tell your grandfather that it was a grave injustice done to your people. I know it is a big sin to forgive. But Jesus said we must always forgive those who have wronged us. He told Peter to forgive even seventy times seven times."

While Ituah translated, James tried to remember where the parable was. Yes, it was in the Gospel of Matthew. He thumbed through the chapters until he found it. He glanced at Ituah and then turned his gaze to Chief Kewaunee. The chief, looking more stubborn than ever, had put down his pipe and crossed his arms over his chest. "Truly, it is a hard saying," James said. "But listen, and I will tell you the story that Jesus told Peter to help him understand."

The kingdom of heaven is likened unto a certain king, who would take account of his servants. And when he had begun to reckon, one was brought unto him, who owed him ten thousand talents.

James looked up from the words and explained, "That means much money, much wampum." After Ituah translated, he continued:

But forasmuch as he had not to pay, his lord commanded him to be sold, and his wife, and children, and all that he had, and payment to be made. The servant therefore fell down, and worshipped him, saying, Lord, have patience with me, and I will pay thee all. Then the lord of that servant was moved with compassion, and loosed him, and forgave him the debt.

"This is generous man ," Ituah said. And when he translated, Chief Kewaunee nodded his head, also impressed with the story. James smiled and continued reading:

But the same servant went out, and found one of his fellow servants, which owed him an hundred pence: and he laid hands on him, and took him by the throat, saying, Pay me that thou owest. And his fellow servant fell down at his feet, and besought him, saying, Have patience with me, and I will pay thee all. And he would not: but went and cast him into prison, till he should pay the debt.

So when his fellow servants saw what was done, they were very sorry, and came and told unto their lord all that was done. Then his lord, after that he had called him, said unto him, O thou wicked servant, I forgave thee all that debt, because thou desiredst me. Shouldest not thou also have had compassion on thy fellow servant, even as I had pity on thee? And his lord was angry, and delivered him to the tormentors, till he should pay all that was due unto him. So likewise shall my heavenly Father do also unto you, if ye from your hearts forgive not everyone his brother their trespasses.

It was a lot to translate, but Ituah was an intelligent man, and James felt certain he would convey the meaning accurately, even if not word for word. Ituah spoke softly and with little emotion, but the more he said, the more riled up Chief Kewaunee became. At the end, he shouted and, eyes flashing, gestured for Ituah to help him stand. After a glare at James, the old man went into the bark hut. There came a sound of things being thrown about. Setting aside his Bible, James got to his feet and looked questioningly at Ituah, who only shrugged his shoulders in bewilderment.

Finally, Chief Kewaunee came doddering out of the hut. His face was suffused with red, conveying some strong emotion that looked like much more than simple anger. Now he was a "redskin" in truth. Chief Kewaunee spoke in a hard, brittle voice, spittle spraying from his mouth.

Ituah stood silently, his face a mask while his grandfather continued his angry tirade. The hope James had felt earlier shrank into a hard knot in his stomach. He didn't know how he had offended, but something he'd said had closed off the chief's heart to the Gospel.

"What does he say?" James said. "Tell me."

Some unnamed emotion crept onto Ituah's otherwise bland face, and at first it appeared that he wouldn't answer. At last he said, "Grandfather say first you forgive, then he will. He say if you know who he was, you would not come here with your Good Book stories and your smiles.

James had seen when Chief Kewaunee came out of the hut that he held something hidden behind his back. Now, after another angry comment, the old man brought it forth and flung it at James.

Instinctively, he put a hand out to catch it and then gasped in horror at what he held. Chief Kewaunee continued to shout, and Ituah continued to translate, but the English words had become as undecipherable to James as the Kickapoo language. It mattered not. He did not need Ituah's explanation to know that what he held in his hands was Samuel's scalp. The flesh had blackened and curled into a hard, leathery thing, but the hair was shiny clean and not horrifying at all. It had been seven years since he had last seen his brother, but the hair was instantly recognizable as Samuel's distinctive shade of fiery red. James struggled to contain his tears.

"My grandfather says I am to ask you now do you forgive seventy time seven times?"

Ithuah's words finally sank into his overloaded brain, and James looked up. The chief and his grandson wore complicated, but nearly identical expressions that looked like a concoction of hatred and satisfaction, but also regret, guilt, and shame.

James sniffed hard to clear his throat of unshed tears. "Do you think I would come here with the Gospel if I had not forgiven you for killing my brother?"

"But you did not know that it was Grandfather who—" Ituah said.

"I knew," James said quietly. "I've always known." He held up the red-haired scalp of his brother. "I saw this hanging from his saddle the first time I came to your camp."

Ituah's eyes widened and spoke sharply to his grandfather. James didn't know if he was angry or shocked by what he'd just told him.

Chief Kewaunee turned his face away. Then he started to fall, but Ituah eased him gently down to his seat in front of the hut. The old man looked up and held out an age-spotted hand to him. James was amazed to see that tears were welling in his eyes. The chief spoke, but it was so softly that he felt sure Ituah would not be able to understand.

But when he had finished speaking, Ituah said, "He wants you to tell him more about this Jesus."

James sat down close to the chief. At first he didn't know what to do with his brother's pitiful remains. He most assuredly would not give it back to the old man. No, it must be buried with proper respect. He would do it later when he left camp. He laid his brother's scalp beside him on the mat.

Chief Kewaunee still held out his hand to him. James shook it firmly, and then he opened his Bible.

Merrideth stopped the scene and set the laptop beside her on the ruins. Weeks ago when she'd first seen James Kyle Garretson go to the Indian camp, the scene had left a bad taste in her mouth, knowing as she did the United States' shameful history of forcing Native Americans to convert to Christianity.

But James Kyle had been nothing but kind and respectful to them. And the magnitude of his forgiveness was nothing short of astonishing. Yes, she had her hero to give to Nelda and Brett.

Merrideth drew the Mylar blanket closer and thought about the parable James had read. She could never be as good at forgiving as James Kyle had been. That was crazy. But perhaps she should try a little harder to forgive her parents. Although they hadn't done anything as egregious as Chief Kewaunee had, they were still in the wrong, especially her father. They should ask for her forgiveness, and then she would think about it.

But that was for another day. It was almost six o'clock, and she was colder than she could remember ever being in her entire life. But before she left, was there anything else she should see before closing down her laptop and the Garrison/Garretson case?

The scalp. James Kyle was going to bury his brother's scalp, presumably wherever the rest of his remains were. And Brett and Nelda would want to know where that was. Or even if they didn't, she wanted to know.

Merrideth took the laptop into her lap and set the program to fast-forward. The scene with the chief and his grandson quickly slid past, and soon James Kyle was riding out of camp. He came out of the woods onto Kaskaskia Trail and headed south. Would he take the scalp to the blockhouse and show it to his parents and sisters before he buried it? No, he would not. He passed their home and kept riding. After a while, he turned his horse into a path that went up through the bluffs to the high ground. She slowed to almost real time so she could get a better sense of how long it took him to get to where he was going.

After a while, James Kyle turned down yet another winding path that, as far as she could tell, headed west back toward the bluffs. He came to a small, peaceful cemetery. The grass had been cut, no easy matter back then, and eight or ten wooden crosses marked graves. He got down from his horse and went to stand at one that was surely his brother Samuel's. She didn't wait to see him bury the scalp.

Merrideth closed down the laptop and began gathering her equipment. All the while, she wondered if the cemetery still existed. Had those wooden markers rotted away, leaving no indication of the bodies that had been laid to rest there? Or had they been replaced with more permanent grave stones? The long, cold night had ended, and dawn had arrived some time ago. It was light enough. She might as well go find the answer to her question before she went home to her bed.

CHAPTER 25

By car, the cemetery wasn't far away at all, but if she hadn't watched James Garretson's ride there, she would never have found it. The bridle path he had taken was now a winding country road up to the top of the bluffs. And where he had turned, there were other roads. She made a note of their names so she could find her way back with Brett and Nelda. Finally, she arrived at a sign that said *Eagle Cliff-Miles Cemetery. Open Dawn to Dusk.*

The sky was gray with the impending snow, but dawn was long past, and yet there was still a chain across the road, preventing her from entering. Maybe the caretaker was enjoying sleeping in on Thanksgiving weekend, like sane people did. She pulled up in front of the chain so she was off the road and turned off the car. There were no gravestones visible from where she sat. She could easily step over the chain and go take a closer look, but then if the caretaker showed up she'd be in hot water. So she ate a granola bar and drank the last of the coffee in her thermos while she waited for him to show up.

At seven o'clock, she gave up on him and entered the cemetery. The air was heavy with moisture, giving the cold temperature the extra power to sneak past her past coat and into her flesh. Hands in pockets, she started down the gravel lane. It was still a small cemetery, although there were lots more markers than when James Kyle Garretson had visited his brother's grave. But things looked so different that she couldn't decide where Samuel's grave should be.

Naturally, the only markers now were made of granite or sandstone, not wood, but they were all old, very old, and tilted every which way. The inscriptions on the first stones she came to were too worn to read. Others were broken, bits and pieces of them piled next to trees out of the way of lawn mowers. Her hope of finding Samuel's grave diminished. And then she saw that there were large gaps between graves where stones were completely missing, which lowered her hopes even further.

There was a sign that gave the history of the Miles Mausoleum, which was apparently the cemetery's claim to fame. It was not what she'd come looking for, but nevertheless she felt compelled to go see it. The sign had said that visitors could go inside by walking down a path to the front of it. But when Merrideth reached the mausoleum she forgot all about that.

She found herself standing on the brim of the bluffs high over the American Bottom. It stretched for miles in both directions, and Bluff Road, once known as the Kaskaskia Trail, was a narrow ribbon curling through it. In the distance was the Mississippi River. It must have been amazing to look down and see the forts dotting the trail like beads on a string. The eye would have been drawn to Piggot's fort because of its size. But James and Isabelle Garretson's small fort would have been visible, too.

Now, the land was bare of even crops. The farmers' fields had been harvested, but most not yet plowed. The variations of color and texture of the crop stubble made a pretty patchwork quilt of earth tones. The wind whipped Merrideth's hood back, and a snowflake landed on her face, and then another. The snow had arrived. She drew her hood a little closer and pulled the zipper on her coat a little higher. Then she turned back to search for the Garretsons' stones.

After fifteen minutes of stooping and squinting at inscriptions she found a name she recognized: Shadrach Bond. The Monroe County Historical Society had put a small sign near his grave, explaining that he was the uncle of the first governor of Illinois and that his first wife Rachel Gott Bond was the first to be buried in the cemetery in 1806.

Of course they were wrong about that last part. As soon as Merrideth saw the 1806 date, she knew that she wouldn't find Samuel Garretson's gravestone. It was either missing or too worn to read, a casualty of the weather or vandals. But she knew that he had been buried there in 1788. And she suspected that his father had died not long after the church service in 1795. Undoubtedly they would have buried him near Samuel. And certainly when James Kyle had stopped to visit his brother's grave that same year, there were already quite a few graves.

Merrideth sighed. It was something she would probably never be able to clear up for the historical society. She turned away to continue her search, and the name on the next stone leapt out at her: Isabelle Kyle Garretson Bond. So Isabelle had remarried after James died.

She assumed his stone would be close by, but it wasn't. It took her another five minutes to find it near the edge of the bluffs. The name *James Thomas Garretson* was clear enough, but his death date was unreadable. And next to it was a small, misshapen stone jutting from the ground. Could it be Samuel's? There was a fragment of a phrase, but even taking her gloves off to trace the words, she couldn't make out what it said. Perhaps it had once said something like, "Samuel Garretson, born in Pennsylvania. Killed by Indians December 10, 1788 in the Illinois Country."

The snow was coming harder now, and she was too cold and too drained of energy to look for any of the other Garretsons. But she decided to text Brett while she still had a few brain cells awake enough to do it. On second thought, he had said to call, hadn't he? Of course, once she did, he'd have her number, too. But, wouldn't it be fun for him to hear his phone ring at dawn on a holiday morning?

Smiling at the thought, she punched in the phone number he'd given her and heard it ring in her ear.

He mumbled something undecipherable in a sleep-clogged voice.

"Good morning, Professor Garrison," she said in her cheeriest voice. "I'm ready to tell you the secret now. We can go somewhere for dinner, and I'll tell you all about it."

"Really?" He sounded measurably more awake.

"Yes. Give your Aunt Nelda a call and set something up for Saturday."

"What?" He sounded like he was being strangled. "Aunt Nelda. Dinner date. They don't go in the same sentence."

"It's not a date, Brett. It's strictly a business dinner. You know, for my new sideline genealogy business."

"Right. Not a date. I'll take it. I mean you. I'll take you to whatever kind of dinner you like."

"Good. Just text me the details. Don't call. I'll be asleep."

"Can *I* go back to sleep now?"

"Yes. I'll see you Saturday," she said with a laugh, but he'd already hung up.

CHAPTER 26

"During the Revolutionary War, Lord Henry Hamilton, the British commander at Fort Detroit, employed Indians to punish the colonial rebels and discourage them from settling on the frontier. Hamilton earned the nickname 'The Hair Buyer' because he paid Indians for each scalp they delivered. He used a sliding scale with children at one end and military age men on the other."

Brett leaned back in his chair and studied Merrideth. "That was a fascinating bit of history."

"Are you being sarcastic?"

"No! I mean it. That's the sort of detail you should include in your lectures."

"Oh. Well, thanks." Merrideth pulled her hand away from the bread basket the waitress had set on the table in front of her. In her excitement, she had nearly taken a roll. She passed the basket to Brett. "Here, take this temptation away, will you?"

Brett frowned. "What have you got to worry about, skinny Minny?"

"Hmmph," Merrideth said. "You obviously didn't know me as a child."

"I'm sure you were a lovely child," Aunt Nelda said. "But pass it to me, Brett. I have no will power at all."

"Surely you do," Merrideth said. "You come from a long line of strong and brave ancestors. They literally held the fort."

"Ah, yes," Brett said peevishly. "The secret fort."

"Sorry I couldn't tell you, honey," Nelda said. "But you know

193

you have a big mouth." She leaned in toward Merrideth and spoke confidentially. "Brett told Amanda Linnett about the surprise birthday party her mom and I were planning for her."

"Let the record state that I was in second grade at the time," he said.

Merrideth turned to Nelda. "That's your basis for saying Brett can't keep a secret?"

"Well, his blabber mouth spoiled everything—the balloon artist, the pony rides, the face painting and—"

"I've gotten better at keeping secrets since. So if I cross my heart and hope to die, can I go take a look at the fort? On second thought, will Odious shoot me?"

Merrideth smiled. "I suppose we could chance it, Nelda. He hasn't told anyone my nickname. As far as I know." And he hadn't breathed a word about her secret evidence either.

"All right then, Brett," Nelda said. "Only you'll have to wait until the snow is gone."

Brett sniffed. "That's all right. I am a patient man. It's one of my many virtues. Along with being discreet."

Nelda laughed. "Then I shall I tell you our other secret."

"What?" Brett said.

"We may not have to worry about Walter Ogle shooting you, or anyone else," Nelda said. "You see, he put half of his bottom acres on the market. It includes the land that once belonged to our family, and the fort, of course. I'm buying it back."

"One day, we hope there will be a plaque to mark the spot for tourists," Merrideth said. "If the state can find the funds for it."

"I have decided I'm not waiting around for the state, Merrideth," Nelda said. "I'll design a sign and put it there myself. And a nice bark path, too."

Brett laughed. "We'll be known as the poet and professor farmers."

"I like the sound of that." Eyes bright, Nelda rubbed her hands together in anticipation. "Okay, Merrideth, tell us what you found out about the Garrisons."

"Let me apologize right off that I didn't have the opportunity to take your line back to Europe as I had hoped, Nelda. But I will. I promise."

Nelda laughed. "You were a little busy, I suppose, what with teaching classes and discovering Fort Piggot."

"True, but I apologize all the same." The snow would probably not last long, but the cold would be with them until spring. The thought of sitting in the woods one more minute made her shiver. So she would probably continue the search the old-fashioned way.

"Anyway, I was able to go back far enough to discover that the Garrisons, that is, the Garretsons, were one of the earliest families in Monroe County. To be specific, one of the first five families." She flipped through her notebook to the right page. "I found a comment in an obscure account about the pioneers that said James Garretson was an upright, honest citizen, but he always refused to hold a public office. And I quote, 'He was a brave man and an excellent soldier and did his part to protect the settlements from the attacks of Indians.'"

"A soldier?" Brett said.

Merrideth grinned. "Yep. And heroic. He fought in the Revolutionary War under Colonel George Rogers Clark during the campaign that secured the Illinois Country for America. So you can apply for DAR membership, Nelda, if you're into that sort of thing."

Nelda snorted inelegantly.

Merrideth took the genealogy charts she'd prepared out of her bag and handed each a copy. "James Garretson was your seventh great grandfather, Nelda. He married Isabelle Kyle and they had six children. As you can see, you're descended from their son James Kyle Garretson. The oldest deed on record for Monroe county is actually a land sale between James Kyle Garrison and Benjamin Ogle, dated 1798. They became best friends when they first met in the Illinois Country."

Brett's expression grew concerned. "Really. Any relation to Odious?"

"Yes. And to you, as well."

"No. Please don't tell me that."

She laughed. "Just kidding. But you are related by marriage. Benjamin Ogle married James' sister Jane Garretson."

"And now you and Odious Ogle are neighbors," Brett said to Nelda with a pained smile. "How sweet."

Nelda laughed at his expression and then went back to studying the genealogy chart. "It looks like the other brother died young."

"Yes, Samuel was only sixteen when he died in 1788." Merrideth looked at her plate for a moment until she was sure her face was under control. Then she told them about the Indian attacks and Samuel's death. "One thing was certain about the forts. None of the Americans would have survived without them."

She had eventually found the Garretson incident in several old history books, although a lot of what was written was factually inaccurate. Governor John Reynolds' history, for example, stated that it was the senior James Garretson's *brother* Samuel, not his *son* Samuel, who had been scalped. Fortunately, Merrideth had found family records on a genealogy website to verify what she knew to be true.

But much of what she had experienced was unsubstantiated in the history books, and she couldn't very well tell Brett and Nelda that she knew it because she had been there. She would face the same dilemma when it came time to use what she had learned in her college history classes. For example, she had not found any documentation to explain the extreme hatred the Ogles and Whitesides had for the Indians. The atrocities they spoke of at the church service were not in any of the history books she had been able to find. So, she could not tell them any of that. And especially she could not tell Brett that he was the spitting image of James Kyle Garretson. It was maddening.

But she told them what she could. When she was finished she set her napkin on the table. "If you like, I can take you to the cemetery where the Garretsons are buried."

"I'd like that," Nelda said.

"Why didn't we know any of this, Aunt Nelda?" Brett asked indignantly.

"It only takes the failure of one generation to pass on the family history to their children," she said. "I do hope you'll take a little more interest now."

"How's this for interesting?" Merrideth said. "James Kyle Garretson was a Baptist minister. In 1818 he was appointed overseer for the poor. And get this: He was a missionary to the Kickapoo Indians."

"Why do you sound so surprised by that?" Nelda said.

"It was the Kickapoo who scalped his brother Samuel, and yet, amazingly, he forgave them. He used to read the Bible to Chief…" She stopped herself in time and changed the course of her conversation. "Anyway, James Garretson's reaction was in huge contrast to that of his friend Benjamin Ogle, who was shot in the same attack. Ogle carried a musket ball in his shoulder until the day he died. It must have been painful."

"I take it he wasn't so forgiving?" Brett said.

"That's an understatement. Several years later, Benjamin Ogle got revenge for the attack when he and some other settlers murdered sixty sleeping Potawatomi Indians—men, women, and children. Notice I said *Potawatomi*? They weren't even the same tribe. Even more barbaric, Ogle scalped several of them. He was positively gleeful about it. And this was after a peace treaty had been signed."

"I'm not sure I'd be able to forgive them if they scalped my brother," Brett said. "If I had one."

"It would be impossible," Merrideth said.

"Of course it would be," Nelda said. "By ourselves it is quite impossible to forgive as James Garretson did. I know I never would have been able to forgive Walter Ogle if God hadn't given me the grace to do so."

Merrideth and Brett turned to stare at her. "What did he do?" Brett demanded. "Tell me and I'll go squash him like the cockroach he is."

"You'll do nothing of the kind," Nelda said.

"Oh, all right," Brett said. "But you have to tell me. You can't just bring up something like that and not finish the story."

Nelda delicately blotted her mouth with her napkin and then put it back in her lap. "It was what he said about Lucas. I was home alone when I got the word that he had been killed in action. Alone, except for Walter Ogle. He was there at the house wanting to inform my parents about some perceived harm done to his property when the army officers arrived with the news. I suppose they thought Walter would be a comfort to me, but they soon figured out the sort of man Walter is. They chased him off and stayed with me until Mother and Father got home." Nelda smiled as if her story was finished, complete with a happy ending.

Brett put one of his hands over hers. "Oh, no you don't," he said gently. "Go on and tell us the rest."

Nelda stared sightlessly across the restaurant, obviously remembering that day. "I recall he smiled. Walter Ogle smiled and said didn't I see that it was a mercy from God that Lucas had died before I could marry him? That now I wouldn't foolishly mix my blood with that of a black man's. Only he used the *N* word."

Brett blinked. "Lucas Gideon was black?"

"Didn't I ever tell you that?"

"No, Aunt Nelda. I'm sure I'd remember."

"That's absolutely disgusting," Merrideth said.

Nelda's eyes widened and Merrideth hurried to explain. "I mean Walter Ogle is disgusting. He really is Odious Ogle."

Nelda smiled sadly. "The thing is, I'm sure Walter meant it kindly, which in a way, made it even more horrible. He was sweet on me. I'd realized that long before that day. I think he thought I'd marry him once that Lucas was conveniently out of the way."

"I just realized I told you a lie, Aunt Nelda," Brett said. "I am going to go over there and—"

"No you aren't, Brett. I forgave Walter a long time ago. As well I should, you too. Ephesians 3:8 and all that."

Brett heaved a disgusted sigh. "Thanks a lot, Aunt Nelda."

"What do you mean?" Merrideth said.

"She's reminding me that I'm just as odious as Odious is."

Nelda smiled widely. "That's right, Brett. I've taught you well."

"How can you say that?" Merrideth said hotly. "He certainly is not odious."

"Well, thank you," Brett said, grinning.

Merrideth felt her face heat. She wanted to say that Brett was one of the nicest men she had ever met. But she kept her mouth shut, because if she went around saying things like that, there would be no way to keep their relationship at the friendship level. And she wasn't sure yet if even being friends with him was safe.

Nelda smiled. "We're all rather odious, you know, Merrideth. The verse I referred to says, 'For all have sinned and come short of the glory of God.'"

Merrideth frowned at the thought. "I agree that we all make mistakes. Call it *sin*, if you like. But you and I aren't racial bigots like Walter Ogle, and we certainly don't go around putting people's heads on pikes like the Indians did in Virginia."

"I'm astounded by all that you uncovered, Merrideth," Nelda said.

Merrideth nearly choked. There she went again, saying more than she should. Hopefully, they wouldn't ask for substantiation. "It's all a matter of finding the right Google search terms," she said weakly and then turned to Brett, anxious to change the subject. "Is Walter proof for your theory, do you think? An example of cell memory at work?"

"Not my theory," Brett said. "But, interesting all the same."

Merrideth saw that Nelda was wondering what on earth they were talking about. "It's a theory that people are who they are because they inherit memories from their parents and all their ancestors, actually. Not consciously, of course, but they have an impact on the person, even in terms of health."

"So you're weighing in on the side of Nature in the old Nature versus Nurture debate?" Nelda said. "You're saying our boy Brett here quotes Bible verses and Walter Ogle spews racial slurs because they are products of their inherited DNA?"

"Maybe," Merrideth said.

"I lean more toward Nurture," Brett said. "I am who I am, in part, because Aunt Nelda taught me that Bible verse—and lots of others."

"Yes, it's obvious what a positive influence she has been," Merrideth said. "Just like James Kyle Garretson came from a nurturing family. His parents taught him to forgive, and he lived that out in a big way. Joseph Ogle learned to hate the Indians back in Virginia and he taught his son Benjamin to hate them, too. The family's hatred is understandable, of course. They suffered so much and lost so many family members to raiding Indians. I could tell you stories, but they aren't appropriate for the dinner table."

"Like you said before, 'The sins of the father,'" Brett said.

"Right," Merrideth said. "But the Garretsons also suffered, and James didn't turn out like his friend Benjamin Ogle. It proves both Nature and Nurture play a part."

"Brett, you quoted that part about the sins of the fathers," Nelda said. "But don't forget the corollary passage: 'Know therefore that the Lord thy God keepeth covenant and mercy with them that love him and keep his commandments to a thousand generations.'"

Merrideth found herself saying the last part along with her. "I'm surprised I still remember that verse after all this time."

"It's not normally one people memorize," Nelda said.

"Two old friends used to quote it. I guess it stuck in my head."

"What does that verse mean, Aunt Nelda? In the context of the Nurture versus Nature debate?"

"It means that, as Merrideth says, it is both Nature and Nurture. And it is neither. Yes, we are influenced for good or evil by our parents and those around us. But even if we could manage to grow up in a vacuum, we've all inherited a sinful nature."

"What a dismal thought for those who didn't happen to grow up in a *Leave It to Beaver* home," Merrideth said. "Guess they're just out of luck."

"It is dismal, isn't it?" Nelda's smile was kind as always. There was also a touch of sadness in her eyes, and Merrideth had the sudden and irrational thought that she could see inside her, that she knew the sort of family Merrideth had grown up in.

"Even more dismal when you consider that we each bear the responsibility for our sins, no matter our past, no matter how we were raised," Nelda said. "It would be hopeless, except that God can break through the cycle of sin and make a person a part of *his* family. The verse is saying God promises believers, makes a solemn covenant with them, that he will bless their children and their children's children, to a thousand generations. Despite my failings toward Brett, and trust me, they were many, God has blessed him with faith to believe too."

Merrideth wondered where that left her. Was she cursed because of the sins of her father or blessed for a thousand generations because she was a Christian? At least she'd always assumed she was. After all, she went to church fairly regularly and had ever since Abby had first taken her when she was eleven. She always put something in the offering plate. Granted, some weeks it wasn't much. She certainly didn't lie or steal, and she tried to be kind to others. Nelda and Brett made being a Christian sound like something more, but Merrideth couldn't put her finger on what was different about their religion.

She snapped out of her reverie and saw that Nelda was digging in her purse. "I almost forgot. I wrote a poem in honor of our Garretson ancestors, Brett. It came to me as soon as Merrideth called with the news. Would you like to hear it?"

"I'd love to, Aunt Nelda."

"He does love poetry, Nelda," Merrideth said.

Brett nudged her foot under the table. She smiled innocently. Nelda read:

According to This Map

Down the back
Road we went
Down the heart
Of what could
Not be touched
Only followed
Into the eclipse

Where those who
Came before us
Knew it was only
Matter that was
Heavy, their
Hearts however

Were light with
The power to
Forgive here down
The back unearthly
Silver radiance
At the turn
In the grave

Stones heavy as
The prayers falling
From our lips
Then rising just
Slow enough for
Us to follow

At the same
Pace – steady
In our hearts
In our light
God-given
Horizon

"That's lovely," Merrideth said. "You should put it on the sign for the fort."

Merrideth pictured Isabelle Garretson sitting at her wheel, spinning wool into thread and words into poetry, and wished so much that she could tell Nelda about her. Isabelle had been ahead of her time with a verse form that was eerily modern. It was too bad she would never have the joy of seeing her poems in print, but wouldn't she have loved knowing that her talent lived on in her descendent Nelda? Perhaps Merrideth could revisit Isabelle in the spring. She could transcribe some of her poems and then send them to Nelda, anonymously, of course.

"Thank you," Nelda said. "And thanks again, Merrideth, for doing our genealogy. You did such a great job on it."

"Yes, Merrideth, congratulations on your first consulting job." Brett lifted his iced tea in a toast. "Here's to many more."

"I hope so." Merrideth reached into her bag and drew out a small stack of the business cards she had designed for herself. It had taken a while to come up with just the right look. She had finally decided on "Merrideth Randall, Family Tree Consultant" with a logo of a stylized apple tree, much like the one the Old Dears had once had hanging on their dining room wall. Wouldn't they cackle with delight if they could see her business cards? She smiled, thinking of it, and handed one to Nelda and then to Brett.

"What do you think?"

Brett smiled warmly. "Now you're talking, Merri. These are great."

"I love your logo," Nelda said. "The clients are going to pour in."

"Speaking of which, Brett, I guess I never told you my consulting fee."

"You're to send the invoice to me, Merrideth," Nelda said. "Whatever your fee, it's money well spent."

Surprised, Merrideth directed her eyes toward Brett, wondering what had happened to his offer to pay.

His expression was one of wounded indignation. "Don't look at me that way. I'm not being a cheapskate. She won't let me pay."

"Hey, I didn't say anything," Merrideth said.

From the look on Nelda's face, Merrideth had the distinct feeling that this was a part of her match-making agenda. She probably thought that making herself Merrideth's employer instead of Brett would remove an awkward impediment to a romance.

Even to Merrideth's generation, there was just something unsavory about a man paying the woman he was dating. And the thought of taking money from him had bothered her a little all along, even though they were definitely not dating. She wondered if Brett had told her they were. But no matter. Nelda's decision worked equally well in Merrideth's own counter-agenda of keeping herself disentangled from Brett. She wanted to laugh at the irony.

Smiling, Nelda put her napkin down and rose from her chair. "Well, I'll leave you two young people to discuss physics and philosophy. Or philanthropy and physiology. Or whatever else is on your minds."

Nelda said the last part with a wink at Brett, who didn't seem to see it. He only chuckled and said, "You're a poet and you know it, Aunt Nelda," as he helped her put on her coat. "I'm sure you want to get back to your jewelry-making. Or is there a different project du jour?"

"I just finished several pieces of jewelry that turned out especially nice, if I do say so myself—in silver, as Merrideth prefers. Bring her by so she can pick out which one she wants."

"Thanks, Nelda," Merrideth said. "Brett's far too busy to drive me out there, but I could always drop by one day. I would love to own an authentic N/A Garrison creation."

"Any time, Merrideth." Nelda's smile grew brighter. "But call first if you're not coming with Brett. Duke, you know. I'm sure he will let you approach the door, once he gets to know you better—eventually."

In spite of her annoyance at Nelda' not-so-subtle attempts to put her and Brett together, Merrideth couldn't help laughing to herself at the strategy. It was brilliant, and it might have worked, too, if she and Duke hadn't already become buddies down in the woods. When she was gone, Brett sat back down across from Merrideth. "So how much are you charging her?"

"Never mind, nosy. After all, you're not the one paying." She took her credit card out her wallet and placed it on the table. "And you're not paying for dinner either."

Brett sighed dramatically. "Because that would be a date."

"That's right. Friends go Dutch."

"So you admit we're at least friends, then?"

"Sure. I guess."

"Then can I at least walk you to your car, friend?"

Merrideth pictured it clearly. As they left the restaurant, the light from the windows would be reflecting off the fluffy snow coming down, and Brett would do all those pointless things men did in the movies as if women were helpless ninnies. They were pointless gestures, perhaps, but definitely romantic, even to a woman who prided herself on her independence. Yes, he would walk close by her side, putting a possessive hand in the small of her back to guide her, and where the sidewalk was slick, he would put an arm around her to keep her from falling. And when they reached her car, he would stop her from getting in. Then he would lean in and—

"Well, can I?" Her romantic co-star was frowning at her.

"I don't think so," Merrideth said. "Not a good idea. In fact, it's a superbly bad idea."

She expected his frown to grow, but it slipped away, and instead, he looked almost happy, tender even. Merrideth found it terrifying, much more disturbing than his cranky look. He put a hand out as if he would touch her but then withdrew it and put it on the table. "What Aunt Nelda should have said was that it was my parents, not she, who failed me. She did a fine job of raising me, so don't pay any attention to what she said about that."

"I can see that. But why are you telling me this?"

"I wouldn't even bring it up, but I feel the need to confess a flaw of mine."

"Which one?"

"Very funny. It's nosiness, just as you said."

"Really? I hadn't noticed."

"Would you let me apologize? When I was at your apartment... well, I saw the letter on the couch and I couldn't help but read the return address. Sorry, I shouldn't have looked. It's just that my eyes are always drawn to numbers."

Heat rose up her neck and spread like wildfire onto her face. Please, God, let him not be referring to *that* letter, she thought. "What letter?" she asked cautiously.

"The one from Bradley Randall, #1254387, Route 53 Joliet, IL 60403."

She felt sick that he had seen it, but all she could do was stare at him in amazement. "You remember that. From a glance weeks ago."

"Three weeks ago." He looked at his watch. "Almost exactly.

It's weird, right? Anyway, I just wanted to say sorry for being nosy." All the laughter had left his eyes, and he looked more serious than she'd ever seen him. "Even though I'm about to be nosy again." He studied her face for a moment, and she braced herself for what he would say next. "Because I'd like to know who Bradley Randall is."

"Then you're going to be so disappointed, aren't you?"

"Don't feel like you have to tell me about him, if he's a cousin or brother. That is, unless you want to."

"That's magnanimous of you, Brett. Because I have no intention of doing so."

"But if he's a husband, then I sort of need to know that."

"You do, do you?" Right when she thought their relationship had reached a pleasant and safe balance he had to go ruin it by talking about husbands. But then it occurred to her that even if he meant to go on as a friend only, he would—and should—be concerned about her having a husband off stage somewhere. So she let out a huff and said, "Well, then don't worry."

"Don't worry about what, exactly?" he asked cautiously.

"That an angry psychopath with prison tattoos is going to come after you for poaching his woman."

"Yes! I knew it!" Brett said. "Oh, sorry. It's just…"

"Okay, I'm leaving now."

Merrideth stood and gathered her tote bag and purse. Brett also rose from his chair and smiled at her. At that moment, her brain finished sorting through the ridiculous conversation they had just had and pointed out that the most important and pertinent fact uncovered was that Brett had known her secret all this time, and yet he had pursued her anyway, as if she were actually… normal, and not some toxic misfit, after all. Relief flooded her system, putting out the remaining little flames of annoyance and confusion.

"Everyone has family secrets, Merri."

She blinked in surprise. Perfect Brett Garrison had a family secret? But then a disturbing thought popped into her head. "You told Nelda, didn't you? You just couldn't keep it a secret and you went and told her. That's why she looked at me like—"

"Of course I didn't tell her."

"You didn't?"

"Nor anyone else." He was back to the tender look.

"I've misjudged you, Brett Garrison. On several counts."

"Does this mean you'll let me walk you to your car? We could swap family stories."

"Oh, no. You're much too dangerous for that, more than I even realized."

"Do you remember what I said earlier, Merri?"

"You said lots of things, Professor."

"I said that I am a patient man." His smile turned downright devilish. "And I wasn't kidding."

Merrideth rolled her eyes. "Goodbye, Brett."

The End

A NOTE FROM THE AUTHOR

As I say in the disclaimer at the front of this book, this is a fictional work. All of the contemporary characters and events are products of my imagination. I want to emphasize that Walter "Odious" Ogle has absolutely no connection to any members of the very real Ogle family who used to live in Monroe county (and maybe still do.) And if any of my characters bear any resemblance to the actual faculty, staff, and students of McKendree College (now McKendree University) it is purely by coincidence.

The setting—the bluffs, the American Bottom, the towns of Waterloo and Columbia, the cemetery—are all real places that I am quite fond of. And historians really do continue to search for the location of Fort Piggot. But I have fictionalized all of this to one degree or another. For example, unlike Professor Randall, the real-live experts are fairly certain where the various blockhouse forts, including the Garretson's, were situated. And don't go looking for Sundown Lane or chisel marks in the bluffs, because you won't find them.

As for the characters from the 1780s, they were very real inhabitants of the Illinois Country (with the exception of Chief Kewaunee and his grandson Ituah). However, while it is true that James Garretson, junior, was a Baptist minister, I made up that part about him taking the Gospel to the Indians. (Who knows, maybe he did.) And his middle name was not actually Kyle. I borrowed that from his brother Samuel so I could distinguish him from James Garretson, senior. Other than that, the actions and attitudes of the brave pioneers are based on what I read in the books listed in my bibliography.

Of course, you can only cram so much authentic history into a novel, and so I posted the following articles on my website in hopes of giving readers a little fuller understanding of the pioneers' lives in the Illinois Country:

Why in the world were the Garretsons in their hayfield in December anyway? See cool photos of Romanian farmers putting up hay the way the Garretsons and other pioneers did.

When Histories Collide. The history books don't always have it right. (You did realize that, right?) Not only are there inconsistencies about the spelling of their name, Garretson vs. Garrison, but also about who actually died that day in the hayfield. I tell why I wrote the story as I did and also reveal another tragedy the Garretsons suffered, which I didn't include it in *Once Again*, because I figured you wouldn't believe a family could go through so much. Life really is stranger than fiction.

The American Bottom. It's much superior to anyone else's bottom, and I have the photos to prove it. Find out more about the Kaskaskia Trail, the forts, George Rogers Clark, the Eagle Cliff-Miles Cemetery, the mound builder civilization, and how the rich soil of the American Bottom was formed.

The Indians of the Illinois Country. Read more about the tribes present and the political pressures that led them to attack the settlers. There is also a cool photo of a replica of a typical blockhouse fort with stockade.

The First Five in Monroe County. Here you'll find more about the earliest American settlers in the Illinois Country, including the Garretsons.

Illinois: the Western Frontier. I explain more about George Rogers Clark's campaign that won the Illinois Country for America during the Revolutionary War, thus leading to the First Five coming to Monroe County.

FOR FURTHER READING

Arrowheads to Aerojets January 1, 1967. Historical Book Committe of Monroe Historial Society. Helen Ragland Klein (Editor)

Annals of the West by James Handasyd Perkins and James R. Albach. (1852)

Captains of the Wilderness. Carl R. Baldwin. (1986)

The Combined History of Randolph, Monroe, and Perry Counties (1883)

The Pioneer History of Illinois by Illinois governor John Reynolds. (1887)

The History of the Lemen Family of Illinois and Virginia by Frank B. Lemen (1898)

Echoes Of Their Voices: A Saga Of The Pioneers Who Pushed The Frontier Westward To the Mississippi by Carl R. Baldwin

ABOUT THE AUTHOR

Deborah Heal, the author of the Time and Again "history mystery" trilogy, which has been described as "Back to the Future meets virtual reality with a dash of Seventh Heaven thrown in," was born not far from the setting of her novel *Every Hill and Mountain* and grew up just down the road from the settings of *Time and Again* and *Unclaimed Legacy*.

Today she lives with her husband in Monroe County, Illinois, not far from the setting of *Once Again*. She enjoys reading, gardening, and learning about regional history. She has three grown children, five grandchildren, and two canine buddies Digger and Scout, a.k.a. Dr. Bob in Unclaimed Legacy.

LET'S KEEP IN TOUCH

I'd love to hear what you think of *Once Again*. If you enjoyed it, please write a review for it and post it wherever you can, especially on Amazon and Goodreads . Or if you're not a member, you could post your review in the comment section of any of the articles on my website.

And sign up to get my newsletter **V.I.P. Perks** (in the right sidebar of my website). You'll get updates on new books in the series and insider information about contests, giveaways, and when my books are scheduled to be free or reduced.

I'd really appreciate it if you'd "like," "follow," or otherwise connect with me.

My Website: www.deborahheal.com

Facebook: http://www.facebook.com/DeborahHeal

Twitter: www.twitter.com/DeborahHeal

Goodreads: www.goodreads.com

BOOK 2 COMING JANUARY 2015

ONLY ONE WAY HOME
AN INSPIRATIONAL NOVEL OF HISTORY, MYSTERY & ROMANCE

Professor Randall gets another interesting genealogy consulting job, this time in the small southern Illinois town of Golconda on the Ohio River. She expects to have to research the old fashioned way, at the courthouse, but thankfully, she discovers that her client's Fraley ancestors once hung out in the town's ancient Ferry House Inn, and that means *Beautiful Houses*, her amazing time-rewinding software, will work after all.

She gets a first-hand view of the life of one intriguing ancestor, Matthias Fraley and a cold December day in 1838, when the first of the Cherokee arrive on the Golconda Ferry bound for the Oklahoma Country along the Trail of Tears. When Matthias sees a young pregnant widow named White Dove being herded down Main Street while the townsfolk only watch, or even cheer, he goes above and beyond to help her and her family survive the cold and hunger, changing his life forever in the process.

READ THE ORIGINAL TRILOGY THAT STARTED IT ALL!

Meet Merrideth's friends Abby and John as they first discover *Beautiful Houses*. And see Merrideth Randall at her pre-teen bratty worst.

All three novels are available as **Audiobooks**, as well as **Kindle, Nook**, and **paperback.** You can read descriptions of ***Time and Again, Unclaimed Legacy,*** and ***Every Hill and Mountain*** on my website. Save money by picking up the Kindle boxed 3-book set on Amazon.